Princess Olga

UNCOVERING MY HEADSTRONG MOTHER'S VENEZUELAN CONNECTION

DOUGLAS C. SMYTH

IMAGINATION FURY ARTS | ALBANY, NY

Princess Olga © 2017 by Douglas C. Smyth
IBSN 978-1-944190-08-8 (HC)
IBSN 978-1-944190-04-0 (PB)
IBSN 978-1-944190-07-1 (EB)

Printed in the United States of America
Book and cover design by Ray Curenton

Publisher's Cataloging-in-Publication data

Names: Smyth, Douglas C., author.
Title: Princess Olga : uncovering my headstrong mother's Venezuelan connection / Douglas C. Smyth.
Description: Albany, NY: Imagination Fury Arts, 2017.
Identifiers: ISBN 9781944190040 (pbk.) | 9781944190088 (Hardcover) | 9781944190071 (ebook) | LCCN 2017942436
Subjects: LCSH Biographical fiction, Venezuelan. | Emigration and immigration—Fiction. | Venezuela—Fiction. | Trinidad and Tobago—Fiction. | Family—Fiction. | BISAC FICTION / Biographical. | FICTION / General.
Classification: PS3619 .M6983 P75 2017 | DDC 813.6—dc23

First Edition

First Impression

Imagination Fury Arts
P.O. Box 66265
Albany, NY 12206
imaginationfuryarts.com

Introduction

In 2010, Olga, at age 97, began to dream of her childhood. It was a different world in the Trinidad of 1924. It was a British Crown Colony: Britons ran it, African and (East) Indian descendants made up the bulk of the labor force, including servants. Venezuelan exiles made up a small professional minority, but except for the nuns in school and the servants, they were Olga's society.

Venezuela, where Olga's family is from, was governed by a dictatorship. Juan Vicente Gómez ruled it, either as Presidente, or as strongman, head of the military, from 1908 to 1935. His trusted second in command, Generale Velasco, was Olga's uncle by marriage. Olga's father and all but one of his brothers worked for Velasco during Gómez's regime in various government roles, including her father's youngest brother, Benjamin, who was Consul-General in Trinidad. Her father worked far away, in the goldfields of the Amazon, so Uncle Benjamin figured in Olga's mother's life in his stead.

In 1928 (four years after Olga's family's sudden departure from Trinidad) there was an uprising in Caracas, but there was occasional resistance to Gómez throughout Venezuela (and especially among its exiles), because Gómez was the first Venezuelan ruler to prevent local caudillos from rising. He had created the first truly national army, manned almost exclusively by his fellow "Andinos," people from the mountainous states of Merida and Táchira. In 1935 Gómez died of natural causes. When Gómez was dying, Velasco piled all his treasures into a gunboat, delayed news of Gómez's death for a day, and took off for Costa Rica. Olga's father, not forewarned, fled Venezuela later, abandoning his estates, no longer able to support the family.

When Olga visited her Velasco cousins in Venezuela in 1930, oil was just beginning to change it, promoted by Gómez. It had at that time the largest proven oil reserves in the world.

Olga's mother's family was from the Venezuelan islands. There was a clear cultural divide between Andean and island people (patriarchal vs. matriarchal). Islanders were also darker, and since she had married an Andino, this may have contributed to Olga's mother's sensitivity about skin color. Olga instinctively rejected cultivated whiteness, and became quite brown, once she was in the U.S. Generally, even today, Venezuelans who look more like their Amerindian ancestors, like the late populist President Chávez, were, and still are, looked down upon by their lighter-skinned countrymen, who often claim to be pure Spanish: most are not.

Olga's mother, Ana Antonia, lived in Trinidad on the gold coins her distant Andino husband sent her monthly from Amazonas state, enabling her to live the life of her class. Her family in Margarita and Coche were business people, engaged in trade, especially in pearls. Her brother-in-law, Benjamin, held real power as Gómez's representative, hobnobbing with the upper crust on the island, including British officeholders. Ana Antonia bought houses and a cacao plantation.

There was a casual racism among Venezuelans (and Britons) in 1924. To Olga it was unconscious; she was always more concerned about class.

Olga covertly began to resist her uncle, when it became clear that his efforts to stymie rebellion against the Gómez regime would cramp her freedom. Her distinct leftward tilt in American politics was consistent with her childhood rebellion in Trinidad.

This story is how it happened: her evolution from conservative class protector to an 11-year-old, one-girl anti-regime saboteur. It was therefore natural, once in America, to become a Communist sympathizer, political liberal and education radical. Olga's dreaming reveals how a pampered princess of the Caribbean, became the Olga who was not only a saboteur, but the first Pan American Scholar at Mount Holyoke, an innovative educator, founder of a small school, teacher of migrant workers' children, and, at one point, the only member of the Democratic Committee in her adopted, conservative rural town.

Prologue

Everyone knew Olga was a princess, even if one of her own devising. She was 101 and 10 months old when she died, on December 4th, 2014.

There is a photo, art quality, that Julian took of Olga in 1933. She is nude, her back turned to the camera, her face in silhouette. You can see her finely sculpted eyebrows, the perfect nose, her hair cut radically short, especially in back; you can see that she had a perfect, if voluptuous, figure. She is not white in that black and white photograph; her skin has a tone to it that could only come from a warmer color. The photo is half life-size: framed, behind glass. Julian took it the year before they were married; she was 20. It hung in her bedroom even 40 years after Julian died.

When Olga was six months old, her mother uprooted the family from the tiny island of Coché, near the larger island of Margarita, Venezuela. Ana Antonia had a five-year old son, her babe in arms and a third on the way, and she was traveling to Trinidad to live without her husband. His "business" took him to the gold fields in Amazonas state; she wanted no part of it. She had told him: she wouldn't raise her children "in the jungle."

"I was named by a Russian princess," Olga told the story many times. "I charmed her, when I was just a baby, and she said, to my mother, "Why, you must name her after *me!*" A Russian princess—she must have been in her forties, daughter of the previous Tsar, sister to the present one—was a big deal in those days; it was 1913, a year before WWI, four years before the Russian Revolution.

Princess Olga had a retinue of servants. They were on ship, on their way to Trinidad.

Olga must have been named something before this, but she arrived in Trinidad as Olga Quintero. The naming had taken place on-board ship.

Princess Olga; one succeeded the other; the first was Russian, the second Venezuelan. A story can shape a life.

I never got a straight account about what happened after, in Trinidad. Olga's mother and her children were living high, wide, and handsome: her mother had two houses, a retinue of servants, a cacao plantation and one of the first automobiles on the island, and they left it all—hurriedly—to come to New York. They lived in Harlem for a year, and then moved to Jackson Heights. Olga's mother worked in a hat factory with her sister, who had come to live with them. It's clear that they must have left Trinidad in a hurry. My uncle sued for payment for the houses, and the cacao plantation, 40 years later: the family got a small settlement.

So, herein lies the first mystery: according to my uncle, their family came to New York because Olga was so brilliant—and she was—but why so suddenly? There may be another explanation, which also makes clear why they suddenly gave up so much. It may also explain Olga. It was the time in her life when she first believed in her power, like her role model: Princess Olga.

The cake is in front of her, on the table, the table where—97 it says on the cake! "I'm ninety seven? Oh my god!"

Olga turns to see her son, grayish-haired, and her daughter, or something—in-law? They smile at her.

The bluff-faced man is where he usually is. Oh, she's back here.

Olga closes her eyes, to get back to where she was, where she really is: the garden at Belmont Circle, in Port of Spain. She was eleven. No, is eleven.

She opens her eyes: her gray-haired son and daughter—whatever—are still there.

She gives them a blinding smile (she's so good at that), "Oh, I'm so glad you've come!"

They are insisting, yes, congratulating, well she did like adulation, but—she's 97?

She closes her eyes—

She slipped back into the garden. Palms clattered overhead in the late afternoon breeze. She sighed: she was eleven again.

Mama had gone out all dressed up, and wearing her *cochanos*, her necklace of polished gold nuggets, sent to her by Olga's father, Heriberto, Mama's long-absent husband. Olga had gone with her on a few carriage rides, but she wasn't interested in going again; they were boring, and you had to get all dressed up. She hated getting all dressed up, especially the stockings and sun veil.

When Mama came back, Olga sensed something extraordinary had happened. Her mother was radiant, even beautiful, and distracted, caressing the sideboard with trailing fingers, looking at nothing. Then she turned to Olga, and her whole face changed.

"Olga. Olgita." The smile she turned on Olga didn't feel quite real. "Sit down with me. It is very important." Her Spanish was suddenly formal.

Olga wondered what she had done wrong. Well, she knew she'd been running around with her little brother earlier, and her stockings were torn, her dress dirty. And yet, her mother wasn't glaring at her the way she did when she was about to scold her. There was something a little strange about the way her mother was looking at her. Olga didn't understand it.

"Now, Olga, you told me about that girl who shouted at you...."

Oh, that. Olga had completely forgotten about it, but now she could see Amalia's open mouth as she shouted: "Everyone who works for El Presidente is a murderer...." She had pointed right at her! She felt frozen, unable to open her mouth; her classmates stood, amazed. She remembered the nun, Sister Mary, shaking her head, saying, "We cannot have this! We cannot have this!"

"...and I'm very sorry that one of your schoolmates was so rude, so," she searched for the right word, "so wrong! Murderers, she said? It is very unfortunate, and at such a good school, too. Um, do you know her name?"

Olga shrugged. "I don't know her; she's in one of the upper classes, Mama, but they call her Amalia."

"Amalia. Does she have a family name?"

Olga thought about that for a moment. The taller Sister, Sister Rosa, had come out and grabbed Amalia by the wrist and—"The Sister called her Miss..." Olga shook her head, "...something; she grabbed her and told her to stop."

"Well, I'm glad the Sister did the right thing, but," her mother leaned forward, fixing her with her dark eyes, "it is very important. You must find out her family name, Little One! Will you promise me? We, uh, I need to know. You will find out and tell me, now, won't you?"

We? Olga wondered at that 'we', but she nodded. "I'll find out, Mama. I think Wednesday is Mass, so they call roll for the whole school."

"That's a good girl." Her mother smiled at her, then noticed her torn stockings. Instead of scolding her, she said, mildly, "Go clean up. Put on a nice dress. We're having your uncle Benjamin for dinner."

Dinner! Not "supper" with Miriam.

"Okay, Mama!"

Olga almost skipped down the corridor to her room, where Miriam was waiting for her with a clean dress. She didn't pay much attention when Miriam started going on about "You stockings! You dirty face!"

"Your," corrected Olga, but she was thinking about something else entirely: why does Mama say Amalia's family name is important? And who is 'we'?

Uncle Benjamin!

As Olga thought this, she remembered how her mother had said his name, softly, the Spanish way of course, but almost as if she were kissing it. And she had looked so happy when she came back from her carriage ride.

Olga had read about love in the King Arthur stories, in *Chansons de Geste* and most recently she'd been reading *Le Rouge et le Noir* for school. It only began to dawn on her, as she put on her dress and washed her face in the sink next to the kitchen, that the women must have looked like her mother did at that moment: the men had worn their colors, or their silks, or had climbed palace walls to rescue them. Was it like that with Mama and Uncle Benjamin?

As she walked down the walkway from the bathroom, past her bedroom, her brothers' rooms and the sitting room, she thought, but what was this other thing, about Amalia? Why did Mama, or—it was Uncle Benjamin—why did he want to know her family name? She's just a girl in her school.

Her family.

Why did he want to know?

Her mother's voice: "There are dangerous people, Olga, people who want to take, take everything we have! They have revolution in Russia, and those people, they've killed the Tsar, and probably poor Princess Olga, the one I named you for! There are dangerous people here, too! People who hate El Presidente!"

Mama had also told her, over and over: "El Presidente Gomez is a great man, and El Generale Velasco, is so generous, our patron. They are fighting for the good of the nation." Together, they brought all Venezuelans together, she told Olga, many times over; it was their family story, and the story told by other families they were friendly with. Before El Presidente, there was always fighting between the warlords over controlling different parts of the country, but the Andinos had brought everyone together—even her family of the islands and Olga's father's family from high up in the mountains, in La Grita, in El Táchira.

"Yes," she had told Olga, "Your father and your uncle, that's where they come from. Someday, maybe we'll go visit their family, up in those mountains. Would you like that?"

Olga wondered, momentarily, how much bigger mountains were than the hills she'd seen when they went up once to Matelot on the north coast. Those were big! And the jungle was so wild!

Her family name. Her family, but why would 'we' want to know about his family?

It was Uncle Benjamin.

He works for El Presidente. That's why. Was he worried about Communists? Could Amalia's family be...." Olga shook her head. Amalia wasn't very nice, whoever she was, but she didn't look like a Communist. Her uniform was new, not shabby and threadbare, like some of the others.

She would tell Mama Amalia's name, if she heard it at school tomorrow. But what would happen if her father really were a Communist?

Then, he would deserve whatever happened—if those Communists, or rebels, or whatever they were—Reds?—wanted to take everything away. That wasn't fair. Mama bought this house, and all the nice things in it.

Olga looked ahead at the lighted dining room, and smoothed down her dress. It was a pretty room, even from the corridor. It had windows and shutters looking out on the garden, and its lights streamed out over the garden path and sliced the palm trunks into light and dark shadow.

She could hear Uncle Benjamin saying something to her mother before she opened the door, so she paused and listened, curious about what he would say to Mama when she wasn't there.

"...don't worry your beautiful little head about him. I think I know who he is. What I want to know is: who was behind it. My men will find out, oh, don't you worry!"

"I hope..." Mama's voice sounded little, and so scared! Olga didn't like hearing her mother talk like that—so she opened the door.

"Here I am, Mama. Hello, Uncle Benjamin."

Her uncle sat at the head of the table facing the door; her mother was sitting next to him, looking out towards the street.

"Oh!" For just an instant, her mother looked startled. Then her face composed itself, as she looked her up and down; she smiled. "You look very nice, Olga. Thank you." Her Spanish was formal.

Uncle Benjamin rose, and held out his hand. "Olga! My favorite niece! You are really very pretty, I can see that now, especially in that lovely dress." His English was very cultured; he sounded almost like the British planters, but nicer.

Olga preened. What was it they said in novels? "Thank you, kind sir."

Benjamin laughed, and turned to her mother. "She's going to be a beauty, Ana, and I can see she's already a handful. Just like you!" His Spanish was different from Mama's; they said it was how her father spoke, too, but she didn't remember.

Olga turned, confused for just an instant. Her mother was a handful? What did he mean?

"Oh, she's a handful, all right, aren't you, Olgita?"

"And you are, too?"

"Heh!" Benjamin half-sighed, half snorted. "She's also quick!"

Mama nodded. They were both looking at her, both smiling, so Olga struck a pose, one she'd seen on a movie poster.

Uncle Benjamin laughed, but her mother frowned: "Olga! Where did you see something like that?"

Her uncle looked back at her mother, and shook his head. He was smiling as if, as if— "I've seen them everywhere, Ana! It's for the latest films. Almost all of them have this one or that one posing like that—you know Louise Brooks, Mary Pickford.... I'm sure there are ones even on the way to her school, isn't that right, Olga?"

Olga tried to curtsey, saying, "Quite right, good Sir." She wasn't sure she had gotten the curtsey right, but he didn't seem to mind.

Her mother smiled at her, looking relieved, but worry, worry about whatever it was, still showed in the creases and shadows around her eyes. "Come here, Olga. Sit next to your uncle, please." She looked towards the door. "I do hope," she said, in her girl to girl voice, "your brothers will come soon."

Olga sat, at right angles to her uncle, facing her mother. She didn't really like this seat, even though she could look out into the garden; it was dark out, anyway. She could only see a little of the bottoms of the tree trunks in the dining room light. "Darkness falls like thunder...on...the bay at Mandalay." She couldn't remember why she had had to learn that Kipling poem. It was dark all of a sudden every night, in Trinidad.

"I don't know where Henry is, and I don't ever know where Julio is."

"Well, I did tell them to get ready. Oh, here they are!"

Henry rushed in, carrying his small fire engine in his left hand. The dirt on his face had been smeared away with a splash of water, and his wild, black hair was combed. His short pants were still dusty, but his shirt was clean; it hadn't been the last time Olga had seen him; Rebecca must have made him wear a clean one.

Henry smiled at his uncle, who said, "Hi, Nephew! Henry's such a good English name." Henry bent to his fire engine and looked embarrassed.

Olga knew that Henry didn't quite know what to say or do— boys were so stupid!

He grinned, said, "Hi," and went to sit next to his mother, eyes still fixed on his fire truck.

Julio ambled in behind Henry, looking tired, or mean. She hated him. He sneered at her. She hated that he was light-skinned, blond, and tall, and she wasn't, but most of all, she hated him because he thought he knew everything and she was too young to "understand," but he was so stupid.

He slouched into the dining room, rolling his shoulders as if he was a big man. He had on white trousers; he didn't quite manage to smile at their uncle.

"Julio! You're becoming a young man! We really have to talk about your career. What are you studying in school?"

Olga was pretty sure he didn't study anything; he was even stupider than Henry.

"Ah," Julio shrugged, "you know...Spanish, um, books, um, science, stuff..." he shrugged, as if to pretend he wasn't quite as stupid as Olga knew he was.

"And girls?"

Julio smirked, his eyes flashed, but so did his cheeks, pale until then. "I, er...oh, yeah, I mean...."

Benjamin threw back his head and laughed. "I can see what really interests you. And why not?" He shook his head. "You look just like your father when he was your age."

Mama directed Julio to sit at the opposite end of the table, so he was nearer to Olga, who wasn't happy about that, but neither was Henry, since he was even closer. Julio's eyes went flat and sullen, as he looked from her to Henry and back again. "Thank you, Ambassador."

"No, no, just Consul," murmured Benjamin.

Olga turned, her back to her mother and uncle and stuck out her tongue at Julio, far enough that only he could see it.

Julio glared at her, but turned to Henry instead; she could hear him whisper, "Negrito, negrito, negrito...."

At that moment, Dominic, their East Indian butler, came in backwards through the doors, bearing a bottle of wine all shrouded in a crisp white linen napkin.

Olga wondered what the napkin was for.

A moment later, she found out: After Dominic lifted the seal on the top and pulled out the cork, with a pop, he wiped the lip of the bottle with it, after pouring a little bit of wine into her uncle's glass.

Uncle Benjamin held the glass up high, to catch the light of the overhead chandelier, and examined its color, the color of bougainvillea. Then he sniffed it and rolled it around in the glass, saying, "This is how they taste wine: first the color, then the bouquet, then," he took a sip and Olga could see him savoring it. Finally, he nodded to Dominic, who then poured a full glass for her mother, and filled up his glass, as well.

"Give to them un poco," said her mother to Dominic, gesturing towards her three children. "Es bueno con pabellon, no?" she asked Uncle Benjamin.

Oh, thought Olga, pabellon, a real treat!

Dominic placed wine glasses by each of their places, then, with a flourish, poured a little in each. Olga looked up at him and held up her fingers about an inch apart. A curve of a smile teased at the edges of his mouth, as he glanced back at her mother, then he nodded and poured her more.

He didn't give Julio any more, or Henry. They didn't even notice. Boys were dumb.

"Dominic, bring camarones con pimenton, now, please."

Oh! Shrimp, too? She had only had it once before, that she could remember, but it wasn't a dish she'd forget.

Dominic brought out little dishes with pink shrimp in a circle on the outside, the sautéed pepper and oil on the inside, and two platters with tiny pieces of bread, one for each end of the table.

"Oh, thank you, Mama!" said Henry, as he chewed the first shrimp on an oil-soaked piece of bread.

Olga grinned to see Henry and his food. He was more interested in food than even his fire truck.

It was good.

"It was on sale in the market, when I was going by," said Mama, smiling at their uncle, as if they shared some secret. "So, Benjamin's driver bought some for me."

Olga sipped some wine and considered this: she was going by the market in her uncle's carriage, then. With her uncle? Why not in her carriage?

Olga sipped some more wine; it wasn't sweet, but she liked it, and her head felt pleasantly light. Was that what grownups felt?

Her two brothers were sopping up bread and shrimp almost as fast as they could cram them into their mouths, so Olga took a couple of pieces of bread before it was all gone.

Her uncle's carriage was larger; it was the Consul's, with a great seal or insignia on it. Maybe they had more room in it?

Julio had whispered to her the other day that their mother was doing "nasty things" with "the Consul, our uncle, I bet." What nasty things? She had looked so happy when she came home, before the worry now creasing her brow: no, more than happy, beautiful, almost shining—what was that word she'd seen in the English dictionary? Luminous.

Why would something nasty make her mother shine so?

Maybe she'd do something nasty someday, too. What did Julio know!

Next came the pabellon; it was so tender, flakes of beef came off when she touched it with her fork.

Henry had a sheen of oil all over his chin.

Julio was pretending he didn't like it, sneering at his plate. What was wrong with him? It was how he was most of the time. Then she noticed: he was eating even more than Henry.

Olga glanced over at her mother and uncle; their heads were together, and he looked slyly amused. She looked up at him as if there was no one else in the room.

Olga didn't like that. "Mama! Mama!"

Her mother looked around. "What, Olga?"

"Can I have some more wine, please?"

"Olga! Tu tienes coste—taste?—sola; demasiado—"

"Let her have some more," Uncle Benjamin whispered to her— only Olga could hear him; she was nearest to him.

Her mother glared at him. Quickly in Spanish: "I don't know what to do with her! And then you encourage her."

Olga couldn't tell what her uncle did next: his face was turned towards her mother's, but she sighed, and said, "Oh, muy bien!" Her face suddenly softened, almost as if Olga's eyes had gotten a little blurry.

Dominic was pouring her more than half a glass of wine, when they heard Blaine calling him from outside. Dominic finished pouring, and then excused himself.

Uncle Benjamin asked, "Who is it?"

Her mother shrugged. "No se. Is Blaine. Gardener."

Once, not long ago, Dominic had lost his merino, or undershirt, and Blaine had held an all-night investigation—it was like a trial: he questioned all the servants, and all the serving people who came to the house. Each time he questioned someone, he'd tell them to tell the truth for "Jesusmaryandjoseph sake." He did something with a twirling stick, and everyone just told him whatever they knew.

Olga had watched for a while, but they hadn't found out until late at night that it was a beggar who came by every week. Blaine had said it was "very serious" if someone had your merino, but he didn't explain why.

Was it something like that?

Dominic came back in. He looked more than serious, as if someone had told him something terrible.

"'Scuse me, Señora, it Blaine. He say, one of you people found, in ten foot of water."

Mama looked frightened. Uncle Benjamin scanned Dominic's face as if he was looking for the answer to a question he hadn't asked yet. "My good man! What do you mean by 'one of you people?'"

"From you country, Señor. He found in ten foot of water, in his carriage. Blaine say he hear—door was locked."

"Did he mention the man's name?"

"Señor Hernandez, he say."

"And he's dead?" Something funny happened to her uncle's face, as if it didn't know whether to grin or grimace; it stayed halfway in between.

"Don't live down in ten foot of water for long, Sir. He dead!"

"Yes, of course." Her uncle turned to her mother. Olga couldn't see his face, but she was close enough to hear him say, very softly, in Spanish, "You don't need to worry, now," before turning back to Dominic: "Why this is terrible! As his Consul, I am supposed to protect him! I shall have to represent the nation at his funeral."

Olga wasn't sure, but she thought she saw just the slightest trace of an upward curve at the corner of her uncle's mouth. Why was he smiling?

Olga didn't understand.

She still didn't understand, later, when she went down the corridor to get ready for bed.

A man had drowned: her uncle had said, "You don't need to worry, now," to her mother; he had looked like he was pleased, and then acted concerned and said all the things an important man was supposed to say. It didn't make sense.

Olga opened her eyes. Her gray-haired son and her daughter, no, daughter in—something like that, they were patting her on the shoulder, kissing her on the cheek: she didn't mind, much.

"Well, I hope you enjoy the rest of your birthday," her son was saying.

Birthday? Oh. Yes. "Thank you so much for coming." An old nun's voice echoed in her ear.

A man drowned? Uncle Benjamin knew about it? And her mother...her face—scared.

Olga's eyes were closing. The old English nun was drilling them: "Thank you so much for coming. So nice to see you. I hope you will come again."

2

"It's time for breakfast, Olga!"

She opened her eyes. The care person. "All right, if you really insist. But I want breakfast here."

The care person shook her head. "C'mon, Olga. I'll help you if you need to go to the bathroom first."

How did she know? "I was just going to tell you; I have to go, first." She smirked at the care person. The care person laughed.

The bathroom. Olga knew what she had to do, and she did it, hardly noticing, trying not to hear the care person saying, "Let me check you; you don't want sores down there."

The long slog, pushing her walker, down the hallway to the table in the Common Room. Plates on the table, bowls, steam rising from them.

Breakfast, she thought, and realized: she was hungry.

And then, she could go back to where—where she really was.

Breakfast. Soggy stuff in a bowl, but she can't remember what it is, and then remembers: oatmeal. Next to it is...yellow, formless...scrambled egg? Toast. Coffee. She nibbles some egg, then raises a quivering spoonful of oatmeal, opens her mouth; it slides in; drinks her coffee, nibbles at the edge of the piece of toast...her uncle and her mother—was that when it started?

Her eyes close.

The stars are large and bright, above the dancing blackness of the palm trees high above her. She loves the night.

Olga liked to stay up after she was supposed to go to bed. Miriam would see her to bed, after saying her prayers. Her prayers: Olga always mumbled them, because they didn't mean anything to her: prayers were silly. Once Miriam went down the corridor to the servants' quarters, Olga would get up, put on a sweater—Trinidad nights were chilly—and she'd go out to the garden.

One of the best things about her bedroom was that it had a door that opened directly onto the garden, in addition to the one that opened on the corridor. Her brothers' bedrooms had garden doors, too, but they never used them, so that made it even better; neither of them spent much time in the garden, either; it was hers.

One step and she was in a night wonder-scape of dancing palm trees and fluttering giant leaves high above her, and the Jackfruit tree with its pendulous fruit, swaying and trembling down by the street. Light from the moon, when it was out some nights, contrasted with the waving tree shadows, and was shot through with the yellow light from windows in the house. Tonight there was no moon.

When she had looked out the window from the lighted dining room, she could only see where the light fell; the slash of light revealed the bottom few feet of palm trunks; everything else was invisible in the blackness. Olga knew from long experience: if she was in the darkness, no one inside could see her, although she could see them, clearly. That alone gave her a feeling of power: invisibility, and, and...other powers. She also just loved to go outside at night for the light and shadow, and for the night sounds, like those loud crickets, and the night calls of birds and a few far off howler monkeys that had somehow found their way here from the mainland.

It wasn't unusual for Olga to go out into the garden in her nightgown. It wasn't out of the ordinary for her to retreat to the darkness. But this was no ordinary night: her uncle was still here. She could hear his deep man's voice, still, in the sitting room next to the dining room; it overlooked the garden as well. Its open window streamed yellow light out into the garden.

From where she was, by her bedroom, Olga couldn't hear what he was saying, and she couldn't see them. She went closer, being careful to stay in the darkness, and not to trip on any of the plant-ings, or the benches along the walkways.

There! She could see them; see both of them, because they were so close together, sitting close on the love seat.

Olga had seen people sit close like that, but only married peo-ple. She'd seen men and women get close like that when they were dancing at parties, too, but she knew it wasn't the way people usu-ally sat together. When women hugged each other, only their tops touched, not the rest of them.

So, what did it mean that Mama was sitting so close to Uncle Benjamin?

"But Benjamin, I don't understand." Mama's voice.

Olga was amazed. From the tree stump where she had come to sit, she could even hear her mother breathe!

"What part don't you understand?" Uncle Benjamin's voice. "He wasn't Hernandez; he worked for us, but Hernandez thought he worked for him."

"But why did this Hernandez man drown? I don't understand."

Olga could feel her mother's anxiety—about the man who had drowned? It was confusing. He wasn't the man who—did what?

Olga heard Uncle Benjamin's dry chuckle: "Sometimes some-one just drowns—or hangs himself, or shoots himself—and it's better we just don't ask questions."

Olga could hear the grin in his voice.

Mama sighed loudly. "I hope it wasn't just because that man saw me—"

Uncle Benjamin was shaking his head: "Of course not, Ana. What a foolish idea!" His voice sounded so nice, soothing: "It had nothing to do with you. Now, my dear Ana, Ana, my love, we really shouldn't talk about this anymore, you know. We get so little time together...."

There was a long silence, but Olga could see her mother gazing into his eyes. Then, she sighed, "Oh, Benjamin!"

She said his name like that again, like it was music, or she was caressing it with her lips.

Then the breeze shifted, and it was harder to hear what they were saying. They weren't saying as much, and then what they did say was buried in each other's hair. Then they weren't saying anything, except sounds and first her mother, and then her uncle dropped out of sight.

Olga liked hearing the sounds her mother made. She didn't know what they meant. They weren't sitting together anymore. Olga couldn't see them, except for her uncle's head, occasionally, but she could hear them, so they must be on the floor.

She knew she shouldn't creep closer; she'd be in the light, unless she could duck behind trees, but she had to see what they were doing. Julio had said they did "nasty things;" she wanted to know what that was.

Carefully, slowly—Olga knew quick movement could catch someone's eye—she stepped forward, always keeping a tree trunk between her and the sitting room's light.

Ooh! Lucky she was going so slowly! Her foot brushed up against a potted plant; she had just missed knocking it over; the side of her foot sliding along it, before she pulled back.

Now. From behind a palm trunk almost next to the window, she could look down into the room: Mama was on the floor. Her dress was up, her legs bare and spread wide. Her uncle's pants were down—she could see his bare behind! And he was in between her mother's legs!

Olga couldn't look away.

It looked like they were moving together, from the middle, like a wave, or one of those new dances. Mama was still making those sounds. Her uncle was breathing hard, then harder; they were moving together faster, Mama began to gasp, "ahhhh, ohhhh!" Somehow, Olga knew her uncle wasn't hurting her. Then he sighed.

Slowly, they stopped moving, and lay there together, he on top of her.

Wasn't he too heavy?

Olga sensed that in another moment, her uncle would look around. So, slowly she began to back away, then slowly, behind the next tree, she turned around and tiptoed back to her bedroom, always in the shadow of the night.

Was that "nasty things?"

It looked like fun. Maybe someday, when she was grown up—

Olga was so fixated on what she had just seen, that she forgot what her uncle had said.

As she silently opened her bedroom door and slipped inside, her uncle's voice sounded inside her head: What does that mean: 'sometimes people just drown and you shouldn't ask questions?' Why? And why did Mama think this other man—he looked at her?— had something to do with the drowned man?

It took her a long time to get to sleep. She kept on seeing her mother and uncle, or rather those bare parts of them, moving together, and then she wondered about Uncle Benjamin: why had he acted so, as if he was pretending being sorry that the man had drowned?

That night, Olga didn't sleep well; she dreamed.

She was falling, so gently, so effortlessly, and then slowly, she knew: she was underwater; she could see the sunlight shining on the surface of the water, far above her. A fish as large as she was swam by her, as if she were a rock to avoid. It didn't seem at all strange that she could breathe, just like the fish.

It was a strange world, but a wonderful one. The things from above the water didn't belong here. But she did, and yet it was like looking at things through a blue-green glass with ripples in it. She didn't feel the water, either. She liked the way the plants waved at her, and everything pulsed, almost like her mother and uncle, the way they were moving—

"Olga! It's time for coffee and cookies. I'll help you up.... That's it."

She heaved herself up, wondering, do I have to? Can't I stay? The dream—was it a dream? She had dreamed of breathing underwater before, especially when that man drowned nearby.

Drowned?

She sat down at the table, after maneuvering herself as close as she could, and then collapsed on the angled out chair. She knew the aide would have to shove it in with her on it, but she couldn't walk and sit.

She ate a cookie, savored its sweetness—she always ate everything— sipped from the cup of coffee. Here again. TV at the head of the table, that blunt-headed old man at the table's end, the weak-faced man across from her—

She closed her eyes, wishing she could go back to the dream....

Julio sneered at her and whispered "Negrita," and "nasty things," but she couldn't tell if he was in the water, or somewhere else. She hated Julio.

That was when something even stranger happened.

One moment, she was standing on the dock, looking out at the city's harbor, the next she heard a loud screeching! It was coming towards her. She jumped aside, and a carriage, pulled by what looked like a demon horse, was rushing towards her, rushing towards the end of the dock, arcing into the horizon, then plummeting into the water!

Then, she was underneath, in the water as this strange, huge fish plunged towards her. No, it was the horse thrashing madly, and the carriage sinking, pulling them down.

There was a face glued to the inside of the carriage window, its mouth wide open, stuck to the glass, its eyes staring, horrified, terrified.

Olga wanted to pull the door open and tell him it was okay, but there was something wrong.

He couldn't breathe!

The dream woke Olga. She almost never got up at night, but when she did, it was only because she had to go.

She didn't need to go though, not for quite a while.

She couldn't get the face out of her mind; its mouth against the glass, its horrified eyes like marbles, or frozen stones.

Then, she was looking up, her lips were stuck to the glass. Her eyes strained to see through the clouded carriage window. She was going to die, she couldn't breathe; she was drowning!

That woke her up completely! She couldn't get back to sleep.

The dream made her angry. That she couldn't go back to sleep made her angrier, still.

Why did that man drown?

"He deserved it. He was a rebel," Uncle Benjamin's voice.

Was her uncle there? Olga opened her eyes. She was in her own bedroom; no one was there.

But it comforted her to know that someone thought he deserved it: her mother was so softhearted.

Olga sat up and the world tilted crazily; it wasn't so dark!

What could he have done to deserve dying like that? Maybe he was one of those revolutionaries, or a spy. A revolutionary, like the Bolsheviks; they wanted to take everything away from us. Or a criminal.

Maybe he was a traitor. Someone who wanted to shoot El Presidente.

It didn't make sense. When she remembered how her mother had looked, just that afternoon: glowing, beautiful, how could that be "nasty" or, or why had someone drowned?

Sunrise. Time to get up.

3

The sun rose, and Olga didn't feel tired. Those were just silly dreams, and she always felt good when it was time to get up.

She tolerated Miriam as she brushed her hair and told her she should wear her better uniform. Olga insisted that she could dress herself and didn't need help.

Miriam squinted at her.

"Just go away, and I'll tell you when I'm dressed, and maybe I will wear that uniform."

"Well, Miss highty-mighty! You should, for Mass."

"But I'm not going to get dressed at all, until you leave." She almost stamped her foot, but she knew she was too old for that.

Miriam scowled at her, and Olga knew what she was thinking: what is she trying to get away with?

Olga just stood there and stared back. Finally, with a "humph," Miriam retreated.

Olga put on the good uniform, not the more threadbare one—she actually had about five others, but some were too small and others were dirty. She did not pull on a garter belt or stockings; she hated wearing them.

When she called to Miriam that she was dressed, she was already on her way to the kitchen for her hot chocolate.

Today her chocolate was hot and thick, and the bun was soft and warm under its shiny crust.

Miriam didn't stop her and tell her she had to wear stockings. Maybe she didn't notice, or maybe she pretended not to. Olga didn't really care which it was. What mattered was: she didn't have to wear stockings today!

It was going to be a good day.

Shem was waiting for her when she had finished her chocolate. He was the yard boy who walked her to school. Before him, Dominic had walked with her. Dominic was really good-looking and Shem wasn't, but she was glad Dominic had gotten too high and mighty—he was their "butler—" to walk her to school. He was so serious, and had hurried her; always afraid she'd be late to school.

Shem didn't seem to know much about time, or care much about it, which was okay with Olga, who liked to stop and look at things, and liked to talk with her friends on the way. She knew they left every morning with plenty of time, anyway.

So, today was a good day, too, because Magdalena stopped and waited for her, and they talked in front, while her yard boy and Shem followed behind; she could hear them talking, in low voices.

Olga wondered momentarily what boys talked about, but Magdalena was asking: "Who's that jazzy boy with the teeny mustache; I saw him with your brother?"

"Hah! You think I'd even look at anybody with Julio? You're not getting interested in 'boys,' like those silly upper class girls, are you?"

Magdalena smiled weakly. "Oh, no, uh, just, just wondered if you knew who he was, but 'course I'm not interested: boys are silly."

Olga smiled, gratified; she had prevailed. It was true she didn't know the boy's name: she never paid attention to Julio; he was mean, and even stupider than Henry.

Not long before they got to school, Antoinetta joined them, so it was even more of a good day, even though today they had Mass.

Oh. Mass.

For the first time, Olga wondered what would happen if she found out Amalia's last name, and told Mama. Would her father drown, too? She wasn't even sure why she thought that. Her uncle had said people drown sometimes, and it's "better not to ask questions." Would something happen to Amalia's father?

She didn't ever see her own father, well, not since she was six. Uncle Benjamin did look like and sound like him, Miriam told her, but different, too.

What if she found out and didn't tell?

"El Presidente is a great and good man," she could hear Mama tell her. Maybe someone whose daughter is so nasty is also a traitor, someone who wants to shoot El Presidente. So, she should tell. It was for the good of her country.

Her country, but she had never seen it. Mama had told her about it, and her uncle, too, but she had never been there. Maybe she would someday.

A vision of the two of them on the floor, Uncle Benjamin's bare behind writhing in time to Mama's bare middle....

Olga shook the pictures from her head; she was glad she'd learned to do that. A little shake usually did it. Then she wondered what Magdalena and Antoinetta were talking about: she hadn't been paying attention. She wouldn't dare tell them what she had just been thinking!

As time came for the roll call, when all the girls were assembled in the meeting room, and the hard-faced nun from Breton had shushed them, Olga had a moment of indecision, but then, as the names were called out, she paid attention.

"...Elizavieta de Gonzalez...

"...Rosita de Juarez...

"Amalia, uh," the old nun faltered over the name, "de Suarez."

A girl in the back row—the one whose wide-open mouth she had pictured since that moment of accusation—stood up and said "présente."

So, now she knew.

It was a good day. And when she went home, she would tell

Mama. That girl really was mean. Seeing her reminded Olga of how mean. She didn't care what happened to her father! If something did, then it'd serve them both right!

Mama took her aside, as soon as she got home. It was that important!

Olga told her. Mama didn't smile; she thanked her formally, saying, "This is for the good of the nation. You must understand that, Little One. You have done something important."

Olga preened, but only to herself, not in front of her mother: for the good of the nation. Something important.

Olga smiled, as she drifted back into sleep in her chair, in the common room. She could hear, faintly, the voice of one of the other residents, but she didn't pay attention. For the good of the nation.... What was? Nation? Oh, Venezuela. Why did Mama say 'importante?'

Olga opened one eye. The care lady was kneeling at her chair. "C'mon, Olga. Time for dinner."

Dinner already?

The chair began to rise and tilt with a whirring noise. Olga sighed. She would have to be here, for a while. With supreme effort, she rose from the upholstered chair and hobbled towards the chair at the table; then she used her walker and the chair arm to ease herself down.

Doris was already there, of course. At the near end of table, there was the bluff-faced man. His name was Norm. He was already sitting there, too. Eating.

Olga contemplated the plate of food, then picked up the glass of milk. She drank it, then picked at a piece of potato, scooped up some peas with a trembling fork, and then lay back, closed her eyes.

Olga saw again, still dreaming, those parts she'd seen—bare bottoms and bare middles, expanses of bare skin—undulating together; she knew that the one on top was a man, and the one on the bottom was a woman, but it wasn't until she awakened, in her bedroom, the moon silvering the garden outside, that she realized: Mama on the bottom, her uncle on top.

When she went back to sleep, she could see that girl's mouth, again, shouting at her, but she couldn't make out the words; they sounded all harsh and jagged.

Then she heard the words.

"You're all murderers! Your family works for Gomez; you work for Gomez. He's a murderer, so you must be..."

Olga didn't stand there in shock, with her mouth open. No, she shouted back, "You're the murderers! I defend our homeland, Venezuela!"

Even as she dreamt this she thought: that sounds so fake! I've never even seen Venezuela!

Something niggled at the edges—she had been there? Confusing! How could she remember, when it was so many years later?

She awoke to the sunrise gilding the palm trunks outside her window.

Venezuela. It was hard for her to imagine: mountains, they said, all around Caracas, and mountains in el Táchira so high there was snow on them, and Amazonas: endless rainforest. That's where her father was. Was he digging for gold?

Venezuela was not where she wanted to go. She had been reading about New York; they had "skyscrapers" there. She didn't want to stay in tiny, old Trinidad; she wanted to see the world. She wondered if she'd like winter, a real winter, one with snow and ice.

But they weren't going anywhere. Mama had a beautiful house, and a big carriage and....

Olga slid out of bed and pulled on her uniform—the more worn one for today. She wasn't even tired.

Miriam wasn't there to insure she was wearing stockings—

Miriam knocked, saying, "Time to get up, sleepy—oh!" She looked shocked to see Olga almost dressed. "But you put on stockings, Miss! You mama say you have to wear—"

"Okay, okay!" Olga pulled on her stockings—Miriam had laid them out for her. She made a face at Miriam, but the older woman just shook her head.

"Don't you make face at me, Miss! You mama say—"

"It's 'your'," corrected Olga, "and I know, I know, I know, about the damn stockings! But she's wrong—and so are you!"

Olga sipped her hot chocolate a few minutes later, her forehead still furrowed in a frown, and nibbled at the sticky bun. The hot chocolate wasn't hot, and the bun was too soft, a little mealy.

But it was still going to be a good day. Shem was waiting for her, and the sun shone; a soft breeze lifted the palm leaves above her, and she didn't even feel hot in her stupid stockings and sun veil. She'd take off the veil when they were around the corner, and put it in her book bag.

But it wasn't a good day: they were too late, and Magdalena and Antoinetta hadn't waited on the way. They were waiting for her outside the school gate. The Sister rang the bell just as Olga and Shem arrived, so all she could do was greet them gaily before they went into school together.

Olga glanced back at Shem as she went in the gate. He was squinting at one of the older girls. He grinned at her, his white teeth gleaming in his black face, then he shoved his hands in the pockets of his dusty shorts, and started strolling towards home.

Olga opened one eye. She was in her chair, her feet up, covered by a blue and white crocheted blanket. Outside, it was a blinding white. Snow. Olga closed her eyes. What had happened that day at school?

It must have been days or weeks later: Olga was starting for school with a triumphant grin. Miriam had, as usual, insisted on "you sun veil," but hadn't noticed that she wasn't wearing stockings. And the hot chocolate had been so hot, she'd had to wait for a minute before sipping at it.

It was going to be another good day, especially since they were early enough that she could see other girls with their black escorts ahead of them.

But then, as they rounded the corner from her street to their first turn, she saw a whole group of girls ahead of her, about half-way up the block; they were all staring at something in the yard closest to them, and Olga wondered what it was.

"Do you see what they're staring at, Shem?"

Shem's eyes went wide. "I see somethin'. Don' like what I see!"

Now Olga could see it, too. One of the girls ahead of them was pointing at it, her arm shaking.

A man, hanging from a tree!

"Is, is he alive?"

"Ain't no one live like that, with neck broke like that," muttered Shem. The whites of his eyes were huge.

"Who is it?" she asked Blanquita, when she came up to her. Her friend looked pale, a little green around the mouth.

Olga turned to look at the hanging man: his eyes were bulging out, and his tongue hung limp, his face was mottled, blue, black, red, white. He was a white man, or rather, he had been a white man. He didn't look as if he'd ever been alive, though; he just looked dead. She didn't wonder why he was hanging there, not really. She wondered what it must have felt like when the rope jerked.

Blanquita was shaking her head, but one of the other, older girls said, "It's Señor Francisco Suarez." Then the older girl rounded on Olga. "You sure you don't know something about this?"

Her? Why should she know—"I don't even know who Señor Suarez is—was!"

"Señor Suarez," said another girl, looking at her meaningfully, "was Amalia's father."

Oh! The one who—Olga shook her head; she was careful to control her face. She did know something! She'd never tell!

It was a blur until Olga got to school; she didn't know if anyone was walking with her, or if they'd all waited until she went on ahead. Inwardly, she sighed with relief when she passed through the school gates: school was a refuge. No one stared at her in class, and of course, she shone: she was brilliant, as usual. She'd heard the nuns talk about her, not realizing she was just around the corner. She'd heard the word 'brilliant' more than once.

Even so, it was not a good day.

After school, she looked for Magdalena, or Antoinetta; they were just about to set off together, but they both shook their heads when she said, "C'mon. Let's go home—juntos."

"We, uhh, we're going the other way: to Elizavieta's house," said Magdalena. She looked and sounded scared.

Scared? Of her? Because of that hanging man? But she didn't— She couldn't say anything, except a muted, "Oh."

She hadn't been invited. Elizavieta lived just down the street from the school. "Um, see you tomorrow, then."

Shem walked with her, but that was his job.

A very bad day.

"Hi, Olga! How are you today?"

Olga opened her eyes. It was her son. What was his name? Oh, Douglas. "As good as can be expected." There.

She still glimpsed the other girls turning away from her, having to walk home with Shem—

The gray-haired—oh, her son—grinned at her. "No better than that?"

He wanted more? Olga sighed. "I'm okay. What can you expect for—how old am I?"

"Ninety-seven."

"That's pretty old!"

Her eyes closed. She was in her bedroom, the one in Belmont Circle—

"Where do you go, uh, when you're not here?"

Her son's voice. She opened her eyes and looked at him, looked at her bed, at the pictures on the wall: one was of her husband—so long ago! The face looking at her looked so much like Julian. For a moment, she was confused.

"Where do you go?" he insisted.

Oh. Her son. Where did she go? She shrugged. She didn't want to tell him: "St Maarten...Venezuela...."

"Ever go to Trinidad?"

She looked at him: how did he know? "Occasionally."

He nodded, thoughtfully. "Did you know I did some research on El Generale Velasco?"

El Generale. Something about him jiggled at the edges of her ragged memory, but it was too much effort, remembering.

Her eyes were closing again, as he was saying, "...not just Gomez's *right hand man, our family's patron. He was known for a particular kind of torture...."*

Olga's eyes snapped open. She looked at her son, but she didn't hear anything more. Not until he was saying, "Well, I guess you want to take a nap, don't you, so I'll say goodbye, now."

She nodded. "Goodbye."

Now, she could get back to—

Her bedroom in Belmont Circle. It was dark. She had come in from the garden, but she didn't know if she could sleep. That image, of the man, hanging there—

She knew she was sleeping, but he was still there. His eyes were still bugged out, almost as if they were about to pop out of their sockets: he was staring at her!

She tried to stamp her foot at him, but he just kept staring, as if, as if it was her fault! And she didn't have anything to stamp her foot on: she was still in bed! It wasn't fair!

He was blue, black, paper-white, green—ugh!

Then, it wasn't him, at all. She was underwater, but the water was thick, like a black cloud you couldn't see through. Then a man was floating, his mouth wide, his eyes all white in his head, floating past her in the thick, almost black water. Far, far above her she could just make out the yellow shine of sunlight, on the top of a little wavelet.

The water turned him around, until he was facing her, his arms out-flung. Horribly, he slowly rotated until his arm pointed towards her, and then, slowly, so slowly, his hand closed, except for one finger: he was pointing at her! He was blue, black, paper-white, green—the same as the hanging man!

No, she tried to say, no, I didn't do it; I don't know anything about you; I don't know who you are—

"Hernandez." Her uncle's voice.

"Velasco." Her son's voice.

Oh, it was so confusing! She had to—

She fought to the surface, gasping for air—and lay, her eyes wide open, in the darkness. She could hear the bird sounds outside, and she could just make out the garden door to her bedroom.

She gasped, sighed with relief. She was home.

But it didn't feel safe.

Not safe? She opened her eyes and looked out at the winter landscape outside her window. Snow. Not Trinidad. Safe. Maybe she really should go to St Maarten. Safer there. Again, she closed her eyes.

She was looking out towards the yellow-white of the sand beach; through the manchineal trees; it was where she and Julian—

Julian came around the corner. His hair wasn't red anymore; it was the color of beach sand, and dust. He was puffing hard, rolling a large water tank in front of him; he was headed towards the back of the house—something bad was going to happen! Couldn't she stop him?

It had happened, already; she could feel it.

He staggered back around the house: exhausted, his face drained, pale, despite the deep tan. He'd mowed all the lawns at home, in the heat, before they'd left, and then, after all those hours on the plane, and the wait in crowded San Juan, they'd taken another plane and then the taxi ride. When they arrived, they found the water tank had been left in the wrong place. It was so heavy she couldn't even budge it; he'd moved it all the way to the back of the house, where the cistern pipe came out.

"Too strong for his own good," someone said in her head.

"Oh, Julian!" She wanted to hold him, but he was so tired he didn't even hear her.

"I'm getting a daiquiri," he mumbled, "...got a splitting headache."

"I'll get it for you." She never waited on him—and he never

asked her to. She wouldn't know how to make a daiquiri; didn't have the slightest idea, but that didn't register; she was just concerned for Julian.

He frowned, shook his head and waved his arm, rejecting. "I know how to make it—the way I like it."

Olga opened her eyes. Even the snow outside was better than the thing she could feel was coming—in St Maarten! Not safe.

She closed her eyes again, hoping to go somewhere else, even though she heard the care person calling for her at the door.

"Olga? Time for dinner."

Resignedly, Olga opened her eyes. Dinner; she did want dinner.

In another five minutes, she was on her way to the dining room table, step by agonizing step: there was nothing else in the world at that moment but the next step forward. Then the cockatoo screeched out in the hall.

A why floated above her as she trundled along; why wasn't it safe—in St Maarten? She had a vague memory of a disaster: it had happened to Julian. There. But she was too tired to think of it any further. She just wanted to go to bed. Dinner already!

Finally, in bed! She must have had dinner, but she didn't remember.

She didn't have to get up until morning. She glimpsed the photo of Julian, natty in a checked sports jacket and tie, she next to him, his arm around her; they were both smiling. She didn't want to go back where she'd been—St Maarten—no. She'd witnessed what happened there once; that was enough, even if she didn't remember the details: she knew it was bad. Poor Julian!

She closed her eyes tight and wished for Trinidad.

The parrot screamed. She looked around her. It wasn't the white cockatoo in the cage outside the common room. She was young again!

It was red and green, a parrot, and it was shrieking at her from the palm tree just overhead. Morning. The parrot had awakened her; it often did.

What had she been dreaming? Olga shook her head. It was sunny, warm enough not to wear stockings—well, it always was—Olga wondered what it would be like if there were seasons, like the ones she read about in English novels, and American ones, too. Was it really cold in the winter?

It might be interesting. New York. She'd heard Señora Velasquez say she was taking her two beautiful daughters to New York.

Señora Velasquez had been talking to her mother, when Olga heard her, telling Mama why. "It's all the worst sort, here, Ana; they're drawn like flies to Maria, and Marta," she sighed, "she sticks to them like bees to honey, ay caramba! So, we're going. I'm taking them to New York. They're pretty, aren't they? In New York, I'm sure they'll find better. At least that. Maybe they can act, or model: who knows!"

There were some things Olga didn't understand: who were the 'worst sort', and what did it mean: 'sticks to them like bees to honey?' Why was that so bad?

Olga remembered her mother's radiance: Was that the same thing? Bees to honey?

The exciting thing was: they were going to New York!

Why couldn't she go, too?

Slowly, Olga dressed herself, fending off Miriam, who still wanted to dress her, even though she was eleven, almost twelve. She even fooled her again, by telling her to go away and then marching out to the sink without telling her. She wasn't wearing stockings, and she wasn't going to.

Olga stuck out her chin at the day. Magdalena and Antoinetta, and all her other friends, were afraid of her. That was no fun. They wouldn't walk or talk with her; they avoided her, all because of Amalia. She couldn't tell them anything, but that just made it worse. Besides, Amalia had been mean. Olga stared at the mirror, trying to make her face express the determination that was already clenching her hands into fists.

The Nuns said she was brilliant. So, she'd go talk with them, instead. So there!

It was a long and lonely walk, with only Shem beside her; he didn't talk much, and she didn't try to think of anything to talk about with him. They just walked. She looked at the houses, instead, and at the plantings of bougainvillea, the thick clumps of bamboo screening some houses, the palm trees with their clusters of fruit so high up, the citrus trees, with star-white blossoms and orange or yellow fruit, jackfruit trees like theirs with their large, funny, pendulous, dusty green fruit hanging so randomly. She also scanned the houses: almost none of them were as nice as theirs.

After she arrived at school, Olga ignored the whispers she heard around her; they sounded like falling leaves as she pushed through the throng of girls. Just inside the entrance, she found who she was looking for: "Bon jour, Soeur Rose Marie! Could I help you before class?" Sister Rose Marie, her History teacher, was the nicest of the Sisters. She was the one Olga had overheard saying she was brilliant.

"Why, merci, Olga! That would be marvelous. You could help carry these books with me. I'm taking them to the classroom."

History was Olga's first class of the day.

"I'll clean the blackboard, too," offered Olga, when she put down the heavy books. "My silly classmates think it's more important to gossip out in the yard."

The Sister, who was very tall and thin, with a red, English face, turned around to gape at her. Then, she shook her head. "No, no, Olga, they are afraid, maybe of you, because of those horrible deaths; the deaths are so fresh. It's silly, I know, but they're overwrought. Some of them may think that because his daughter, Amalia shouted at you...."

"Because she shouted at me?" Olga pretended not to understand.

The Sister smiled at her. It was a grace-giving smile, almost like the ones the Sisters wore when the priest gave benediction. "It doesn't make sense, I know, but they will get over it, I'm sure."

But Olga knew: it did make sense. She shrugged that knowledge away. "I'll just ignore them." She wasn't so sure they'd 'get over it,' but she'd act as if they would. In the meantime, "Maybe, the board needs a damp rag?"

Sister Rose Marie smiled down at her and shook her head. "It's clean enough for now, Olga; it's like the Soul after Confession, but not as white as the driven snow, as it is after Baptism—or Final Absolution." The Sister grinned. She must have been making one of those 'Sister jokes.'

Olga wondered what driven snow looked like.

"Thank you, Olga. We're finished for now. It's just about time for Sister Chalfont to ring the bell, so you might as well take your seat, and get out your books. You have been most helpful."

Sister Chalfont. So, that was her name, the old nun who rang the bell. She didn't teach, so Olga had never heard her name before. If she hung around the nuns for a little while, she might learn things. Useful things.

Olga had read the assignment for the day; she had actually read ahead through the next chapter. She liked reading about the bloody English kings. Of all the other girls, only Antoinetta might have done that. That made Olga all the more determined to be the first to answer any questions the Sister asked.

"Olga? Time to come to the table now. It's lunchtime." The care person's voice.

Olga opened one eye. The common room. The blunt-faced old man—she couldn't remember his name, but it didn't matter—was sitting at his place at the end of the table. Doris was sitting in her place, next to Olga's empty chair. Doris's pile of books had been shoved out of the way.

Food? Olga opened both eyes. Her chair was rising in back, lowering in front. She grabbed the chair arms and laboriously pushed herself upright, then grabbed the walker.

Food.

Olga drank the last of her coffee, then closed her eyes. Where was she?

She opened her eyes: still at the table, in the common room. Norm—was that his name—was saying something. She laughed, even though she really couldn't hear whatever it was he was saying. But she didn't want to be here. She searched around behind her for her walker. As she tried to get up from the chair, she could feel a helping hand. She looked up. It was the young girl, the one with little children. She was grateful for her firm arm as, haltingly, she made her way to the corridor.

"You want to rest in your room?"

Olga nodded. "Yes."

It was such a long trip! At the end of it, she sank gratefully onto her bed, hardly even noticing the sun glancing off the window ledge, and far off, the sun reflecting off the creek's slowly flowing water. She did see a little green out there, but she was too tired to think about what it meant. She closed her eyes.

Her uncle's coachman was ushering her to her uncle's towering carriage: the one with the coat of arms on the door. Uncle Benjamin, dressed beautifully, as usual, greeted her at the step, and gave her a hand up.

Olga looked back. Girls, her classmates, including Magdalena and Antoinetta, were staring. Some of the younger ones were wide-eyed.

Why was she going home in her uncle's carriage?

She waved at them. A few raised their arms, tentatively waving back: mostly the younger girls.

As the coach pulled away, Olga turned to her uncle, who was saying something; she hadn't been paying attention, "...so, we thought you could use a bit of an outing. We're going down to the port first. There's a store there where they have the best candy." He was smiling down at her.

Didn't he understand? She knew this was bad. If they thought she had something to do with Amalia's father before, this made it worse! Much worse.

She smiled at her uncle, and pretended to pay attention as he went on about how pretty she was, and how he really should get her some pretty dresses.

"Unfortunately, there are no dress shops here that are at all worthwhile; the English have no sense of style, you know. The Syrian shopkeepers have no idea, either, apparently. I'm sending away for some things. I hope your mother's measurements are correct."

So, that's why Mama handed Miriam a tape measure a few days before; she had told her, "Here. Hacerlo, do para Olga. Escribio. Write."

Olga shrugged. "I don't know. Guess that's what Miriam was doing with the tape measure a few days ago. She wrote something down." She really wasn't much interested in dresses. Uncle Benjamin seemed to think she was.

Maybe he thought she should be interested in dresses. She

glanced over at him. He was looking thoughtfully out the window. Maybe Mama told him about how she was always ruining her stockings and her dresses. She grinned to think of that. But why should she be interested in dresses? Were boys so interested in—in pants and shirts?

Maybe, when she was pretty, when she had a "shape," then she'd be interested. Maybe. Only a little. She didn't have any shape, yet. Some of the older girls in school had too much! There was one—Olga didn't know her name, the girl was in the higher grades—she and Magdalena had nicknamed her "Top-Heavy."

She remembered giggling together and that made her regret what she'd lost. They were afraid of her now. Would her friends ever get over it?

Olga looked out the window on the other side, and saw a tall ship, out in the harbor. She must have come in something bigger than that, but of course, she didn't remember—except her mother's story about the Russian Princess Olga.

"Where's your—it's a consulate, isn't it?"

Uncle Benjamin smiled at her, but he looked a little surprised: "We'll pass it on the way to the shop, but you are a funny girl! More interested in my offices, than in dresses? My brother, Miguel-Angel's daughter, Nené, that's all she talks about—except jewelry. All the cousins, all the girls—except you—were in Caracas, I can't remember why, and that's all they talked about, too! But you are very pretty, you know, and for a woman that's even more important than for a man being handsome." The corner of his lip curled and he brushed at his moustache. He turned to face her; his smile was, well, it reminded her unpleasantly of her older brother, Julio. "Especially," he added, "in the diplomatic corps."

He was handsome, she guessed. And he probably was interested in pants and shirts—and jackets; he always dressed very well; she realized that, looking at him.

"I don't want to be in the diplomatic corps," Olga said. "But I don't want to be stuck at home like my mother, either."

Her uncle laughed. "Ana Antonia's not stuck at home! Heriberto sends her enough gold for her to do what she wants." He cocked his head at her. "Maybe that's what makes you different, too: she's a Margariteña; some of her sisters didn't even bother to get married. One of them runs the family's pearl fisheries. Maybe that's why she wants to go into business! And, why you're interested in other things than dresses." He was very handsome, she thought, as he smiled at her.

"What's the crest on the outside of the coach? It's not Venezuela, is it?"

"Oh, hoh! You really are interested in other things. You're right; it's not the Venezuelan crest of arms. It's a duke's; I forget which, of Spain, of course. When Bolivar won our independence, the new government claimed the coach; it had been used by the Duke, when he represented the Spanish Crown, here on Trinidad."

Olga brushed the velvet seat with her hand. "It's very old then."

"Well, yes." He grinned at her. "Quick, can you tell me when Venezuela won her independence?"

"Of course! July 7, 1811, was when we declared our independence, when the Declaration was ratified by our congress."

"Very good!" Olga could see he was impressed. After all, they didn't teach Venezuelan history here in her school. "I think," he said, "it was about 1812 when this coach became Venezuelan property. It's definitely a piece of history. I may replace it with a motor car, however."

"A motor car!" Now, Olga was impressed. "I've only seen them in pictures."

Houses, with wide roofs, passed by. The horse was trotting fast.

"Ah, that's the Consulate." He pointed to a large, rambling bungalow with sweeping roofs, surrounded by towering royal palms. "Where I spend a lot of my time, unfortunately." He grinned at her, and she could feel its effect. "I'd much rather be talking with you—or your mother.

"Now, the candy shop should be just a few blocks further down. I think.

"Martin!" He rapped on the front window of the coach with a cane. "That candy shop?"

"Yes, Sir!" Martin had a very deep voice, one that almost boomed, the kind Olga expected to come from a black man his size.

Only a minute later, suddenly, they came to a stop. The coach creaked. Her uncle opened the door, jumped out, and then reached in to help her out. She could have jumped out, too. But it was nice being treated like this, having her handsome uncle hand her down from the high carriage.

Like most shops in Trinidad, this one was open to the sea breezes. The shop had the most amazing display of sweets Olga had ever seen: from little boxes that said 'chocolat' in gold letters, to a dizzying array of bon bons, toffees, licorice sticks and lollipops of all kinds, sizes and colors.

At first, Olga just couldn't decide. They all looked so tempting. Then she thought to herself: I should get something to last, at least for a little while. And something I wouldn't have to share with Henry. That's when she saw a huge lollipop the color of raw sugar; it was caramel, one of her favorite flavors, and it could last her until suppertime, at least. "I want that one."

"And my dear Niece shall have it," said her uncle, handing it to her ceremoniously. A dark-faced man with a hooked nose emerged from the shadows in the back as soon as Uncle Benjamin picked up the lollipop. He was the Syrian shopkeeper. Her uncle paid him.

"Oh, thank you, Uncle Benjamin!"

Olga nursed the large disk of caramel all afternoon, once they got home. As she was beginning to savor it, however, she heard her uncle explain to her mother, "I thought, after what she saw today—you know: it was right on the street, on the way to school—"

"Oh!" Mama sounded dismayed.

"...that she needed a treat—Oh, and the girls at her school needed a reminder, too. Seeing me—well, you know." A single chuckle escaped from the side of his mouth.

A reminder? Olga wasn't sure what he was talking about. She stole a glance at him, over the top of her sucker: he looked pleased with himself.

Something about him made her vaguely uncomfortable. She got up, while they were still talking, and went out into the garden: they wouldn't notice. All she knew was: now her friends would be even more frightened of her. She wished he hadn't given her that ride. The lollipop, well, it was good, at least.

She wondered: were they having dinner together again, or would Mama and Uncle Benjamin have dinner alone? She was sure of one thing: he was staying at their house for the evening. She had a vision again of their bare skin—bottom, middle—undulating together—Olga couldn't help grinning at the memory; it didn't look nasty like Julio said. Maybe it's just what grownups did.

The bright green of the garden faded, as did her uncle's voice. Instead, a woman's voice was insistently saying something. Resigned, Olga opened one eye. The care person—Pam—was saying, "C'mon, Olga. Time for dinner. I'll help you up."

She pushed herself up to a sitting position and looked out the window: it was a northern scene: a rushing creek, the trees still bare, a little green on the ground. Had she been somewhere else a minute before? Intense green? Life was confusing.

Food. It didn't matter what it was; she wanted to eat. She hobbled forward with her walker, the care person ahead of her.

With some maneuvering, with a helpful hand supporting her elbow, she let herself down in her chair. The care person pushed it in from behind. There was a plate with a little cup of something, a cup of milk, some slices of bread, those orange stick things, some fork-size pieces of—she tasted one:

meat. She had two more pieces, then picked up one of the orange sticks and chewed it; it was a carrot, of course! She drank some milk, then ate a piece of bread. She decided she'd try the stuff in the cup. Tentatively, she tasted: she knew it was something familiar, but she couldn't remember the word. It would be good with bread.

After eating a little of this, a little of that, Olga closed her eyes.

She was looking out from under pine boughs. The seacoast was rocky and wild, when Julian emerged from around the corner, his red hair sticking out at crazy angles, carrying a bucket of, of quahogs, he called them?

The sky was getting all orangey-red down the coast, west, yes, west; this was Downeast, and Julian's eyes were shining when he looked at her.

Olga opened her eyes and dipped some bread in the sauce. She savored it as she chewed. Like an old horse, she thought randomly, remembering how they looked when they were chewing at their oats. A very old horse.

Meracooneegan Farm; that's where it was! Huge old barn, looking out to sea. Maine? She wished she could go back there, but when she closed her eyes, she had no idea where she'd be next—so many parts of her life—was it her life? She'd open her eyes and be somewhere else, somewhere she'd been before, in the midst of something....

Miriam put her plate down before her; it was fried chicken, still steaming, some manioc in a white mass, and a cooked green. Olga picked at the chicken and wondered: were they doing it now?

What were they really doing? What did it feel like? Mama had looked so happy.

She had told Mama Amalia's name, and Amalia's father had hung himself—or someone strung him up. Her uncle had acted strangely about the drowned man, too. After this one, he had taken her for a ride in his carriage, and had bought her the lollipop. She looked at it: it was a kind of payment. But it was sweet. She had laid it down beside her plate.

She considered it now.

You couldn't stop sucking on a lollipop. If someone left one on the ground, it would be covered with big black ants, flies and bees swarming around it in a cloud. It would only take minutes.

She'd had enough of it, though.

"Hey, what's that?" Henry was pointing at the lollipop.

"It's a lollipop. Uncle Benjamin gave it to me."

"That's not fair! I want one, too!"

"You can't have one. And I'm throwing it away!"

Henry jumped up from his seat and was waving his fists at her. "You make me so mad, I'm, I'm going to scream!"

Olga laughed, stabbed the lollipop into the middle of what was left of the manioc and got up; she started towards the garden. When she turned back to look, Henry was standing, looking down at her plate, his nose wrinkled; he looked confused, not quite sure whether to scream, to cry, or to take the discarded lollipop.

She didn't care. She just hoped he wouldn't follow her out into the garden.

It was dark out here. The lights from the sitting room and Mama's bedroom shone like rays on the trunks of the nearby trees.

Mama's voice, asking in Spanish, "...did he hang himself?" The 'por que' hung in the air—until her uncle laughed once.

"That's the story! Let's just leave it at that."

"But, Benjamin—"

"No, no. It's better we don't talk about it. Just think of it this way," Olga could hear the beguiling charm of his smile, "someone was plotting against the state, but he's no longer around to make trouble."

"He was?"

"Oh, yes! We knew there was someone; we heard it from a number of sources, and there were shipments of arms we intercepted, too. It was a lucky break when your lovely daughter—So, well, just let's say, he hung himself," Olga could hear the hardly suppressed chuckle, "and we don't ask any more questions. Esta bien?"

Mama sighed. "Bien."

"And we need to keep our eyes open."

"Olga?" Miriam was calling her. She'd have to go in. As she made her way through the dark garden, she heard her mother saying, "...it isn't something I really want to do, mi Caro, but if you say—"

Her uncle was making mollifying noises: "Of course it's hard, but for the good of the nation...."

Maybe he really did hang himself. She couldn't picture Uncle Benjamin stringing him up on that tree. He was so...so well dressed.

Olga shook her head. She wouldn't think about it any more. Besides, revolutionaries would take all this away if they had their nasty revolution. She climbed the step to her room. Miriam was waiting for her.

Olga woke with her jaw clamped tight. She looked out the window at the northern creek, now in spate, but saw only that it was late in the afternoon. She could hear Pam calling her. She tried to smile graciously at Pam coming into the room, as—as the nuns had taught her—was that long ago? That's when she realized her jaw was clamped so tight it was aching. Was it from what had just happened? She could still hear the persuasive tone of her uncle's voice—she opened her mouth, wiggled her jaw, then smiled at Pam. "Sorry." For the good of the nation? Where had she heard that before?

"Are you ready to go to the bathroom?"

"Estoy lista." Olga, slowly, swung her legs out of the bed, pulling herself up with the bar halfway down its length.

The blunt-faced man looked at her and smiled as he shuffled past. Olga smiled back. She always did attract the men.

6

The tall man with the shapeless pink face and limp brownish hair loomed over Doris. A vacant smile dangled across his lips, as he reached for her shoulder.

"Get away from me!" Doris shrieked. Olga could hear the fear, but she was too tired to know what to do about it. She stayed lying down in her recliner chair, her feet up.

It really wasn't fair: did she have to take care of people here, too? And, and she couldn't!

The girl, the one with children, was turning the tall man around, saying, "Now, Lou, you can't do that. I'll take you to your chair. You can sit down next to your wife. Would you like that?"

He made a noise that sounded agreeable. His vacant smile became more focused; he was looking at the woman across the room from Olga. She, craggy and thin, with a long nose and chin and a mane of straight white hair, was leaning forward, fluttering her hand at him, puckering her lips.

Olga closed her eyes. She just didn't want to be here.

When she opened them, she was wiping a blackboard down with a damp rag. "Is that how it should be cleaned, Sister Rosa?"

"Why, thank you, Olga! That's wonderful. I don't think we have anything more to do now, so you still have time to visit with your friends, until Sister Chalfont rings the bell."

"I don't have any friends. Not any more, Sister Rosa. They're all afraid of me!"

Sister Rosa smiled; it was the expression she and Magdalena had jointly labeled the Beatitude. Magdalena and she had laughed and laughed afterwards. It made her angry to think: those times were gone; her friends weren't friends anymore.

"Poor Olga! But your friends will come back. Just give them a few days."

Olga felt like stamping her foot, but she didn't. You didn't do that to the Nuns. Maybe her friends would come back, but it sure didn't feel like it!

Olga looked out at the common room from—it was her chair. The man with the shapeless face was sleeping in his; the woman with the sharp face was also sleeping, in the chair next to his. There was just a hint of green outside the large window, or glass door—whatever it was.

She was comfortable, but something felt unresolved, as if she still didn't know the answer to something: she wasn't sure what. She closed her eyes again.

She was holding up her hand; Sister Rosa nodded to her. She began, "Dans Le Rouge et Le Noir c'est l'hypocrisie de...."

Out of the corner of her eye she glimpsed Antoinetta squinting with concentration, then nodding, as she went on, explaining how Julien Sorel was driven to shoot Madame Renal, in church, by the falseness of everyone around him.

"Même Mathilde, Olga?"

Olga remembered the scene where Mathilde kisses the lips of Julien's severed head and answered: "Peut-être, peut-être que non," smiling over at Antoinetta.

Antoinetta grinned at her, and raised her hand. She had read it, too.

After class, Antoinetta murmured to her as they left the room, "They were all awful people, weren't they?"

Olga wrinkled her nose. "Not any of them were very nice." She shrugged. "Guess that's why it's a good story."

"Wonder what it'd be like to kiss a dead man's lips!" Antoinetta made a face.

"Ugh!" They both laughed.

Friends again. She could see Magdalena hovering in the background.

Maybe things weren't so bad, after all.

Things were even better when one of the older girls, who said her name was Maria de Gonzales, came up to her after her Algebra class and asked her: "Is the Consul really your uncle? Is that why he picked you up? He's the most important man on the island!"

She was almost admiring. Olga felt powerful and important, especially when she stopped herself from saying something about Uncle Benjamin and her mother. It made her realize: she knew things. Powerful things.

Then, she wondered, who was that girl who had questioned her about Amalia's father? Maybe her uncle should know about her.

Maybe she'd find out—at the next Mass, on Wednesday.

Olga awoke with a smile. She didn't know why—something about friends—where? She didn't know where she was, until she glimpsed the window and the trees outside; she could see just the barest hint of green on the trees nearest to the window. When she raised her head, she saw a glint of rushing water. She still didn't know why she had awakened. After a minute or two, hearing nothing, she decided there was no reason to stay awake, so she closed her eyes again.

"You see this?" Olga held up her prize; Antoinetta and Magdalena gawped at it. They had just come out of the gate from school at the end of the day. Olga had pulled it out of her bag once their backs were to the gate. She was pretty sure the Sister, behind them at the gate couldn't see it. They were waiting for their yard boys to arrive.

It was a book she'd picked up off the floor in the classroom, behind the Sister's desk, when she'd helped her clean up after class.

There was a picture of a woman with long blonde hair, her hands fumbling with her dress, which was already halfway open down to her middle, or at least it looked that way. A man, tall and dark, was holding her around the waist—Olga couldn't see where his other hand was. He was leering down at her and she was gazing up at him as if—Olga didn't know what! Large red letters slashed across the cover: *Love Your Enemy!*

"Oh, my God!" said Magdalena; she looked both shocked and fascinated, her eyes shining. "You better put that away before the Sister sees it!"

Olga's grin felt so wide, but she couldn't help it. "I found it behind her desk, underneath, hidden, when I was cleaning up. So, I bet it's the Sister's!"

"Ooh, Olga!" Antoinetta almost squealed.

Magdalena's face had stilled from her first excitement, then, it paled. "You gonna threaten them, too?" Her voice was dead-pan.

Olga frowned at her, and stood, legs apart, facing her, arms akimbo, angry suddenly. "I didn't threaten anyone! And I didn't have anything to do with that man getting hanged, either. But," she couldn't help grinning to think of it, "I've got something on a Sister, and I'm finding out other things, too."

For a long moment, Magdalena looked at her without saying anything. Then slowly she nodded, her face beginning to lighten, respectful, still a little wary. "You gonna tell us, when you find out... things?"

"Of course! You're my friends."

They were all still giggling about the book when they parted ways on their way home.

That had been a triumph. And older girls had treated her as if she was somebody; well, she was.

So, now, as reward for her good fortune, Olga was going to read the book. She sprawled on a bench next to her room, the book in her hand.

She was about to open it at the first page, when she heard something in the back of the garden. She knew Blaine hung his hammock up there sometimes in the afternoon, when he was taking a siesta, but the noise sounded more distant, as if it was in the jungly yard behind them.

"Who there!" Blaine's voice. He sounded alarmed. "This here Quintero's garden! You don' have no right—"

Olga heard the footsteps; they were going away. Then she heard Blaine muttering on his way to the very back, and heard stone fall on stone.

Olga was about to get up and investigate, when she saw Blaine, through the trees. He was doing something strange with his hands.

She wanted to see what he was doing. She got up, and as soundlessly as she could, she made her way to the back of the yard, staying in the shade, hiding behind the trunks of trees.

She could hear him mumbling something. He'd go a few steps along the back fence, then stop, do this thing with his hands, all the while mumbling something, then move on another couple of steps before repeating whatever it was.

She peered out at him from behind a tree, and finally saw: he was marking a circle with his left index finger, then forming a cross with a finger of each hand. As he did this, she heard him mutter, "Protect them in Jesusmaryandjoseph name."

He had said the same names, in the same way, when he was divining who had taken Dominic's merino. It was his spell.

Protect them? Protect her and Mama? Who from?

Blaine turned the corner and began to go down the side of the yard, doing the same thing. Olga kept the tree trunks between her and him, but she followed after.

He went along the drive; when he went behind the house, she couldn't follow without him seeing her, so she waited; then he re-emerged where the garden overlooked the roadway.

Olga watched him from behind the largest palm trees, until he turned the corner from the road and started up the other side, all the time doing the same thing: the circle with his finger, then the cross with two fingers, and the muttered incantation. She could hear him each time, but she was too far away to hear the words distinctly the way she had in the back of the yard. Still, she was pretty sure he was saying the same thing.

After seeing him turn the third corner, she finally was certain about what he was doing: he was making a sacred fence "to protect them." Was it to keep people out? Bad people.

Maybe that man in the yard in back? Revolutionaries?

This was even more exciting than that book! She'd never seen a revolutionary. What did they look like? She was sure they didn't have horns or a pointed tail, but could you tell that's what they were from looking at one?

Silently, Olga slipped from tree to tree to the back of the yard. She had rarely ventured back here. It was way beyond the servants' quarters, and even more deeply shaded than the front of the yard. Quiet. Very quiet.

She looked over the few stones that seemed to mark the boundary. There was a sagging wooden fence, too, and then beyond it: it wasn't a yard at all! It was a jungle! Well, maybe not a real jungle, but a yard that had gone completely wild. She could just make out, through the tangled green, a pinkish back wall of what must be a house. She couldn't see the roof, though. She walked along the fence, trying to peer through the tangle to see if she could make out any more of the house.

"He a Syrian," Blaine said, suddenly near her, startling her. "Went away years ago. Shame what happen to a garden when that happen."

When Olga caught her breath, she asked. "Who was the man who was there just a while ago?"

Now, Blaine looked startled. "You see him!"

Olga shook her head. "I heard him. And heard you tell him to go away."

Blaine shook his head, his face looking even darker in the shadow. "I don' know, but he can't be up to no good. Know he not the Syrian. Syrian man ain't a comin' back. Bankrupt, they say. Who this one is, I don' know. I was thinking about those gangsters. Heard some was getting liquor down here for smuggling. It prohibition up there, you know, in Chicago, New York...."

"Oh!"

"Or," Blaine's face went all twisted as if he had just realized another possibility, "could be someone..." he startled as if he saw her before him for the first time: he shook his head. "No, no, I don' know." He looked scared.

His fear was reassuring.

"Someone else?" Revolutionaries? Like the ones her mother had told her about? Her uncle, as Venezuela's Consul General, was here to "protect the people of Venezuela," her mother also told her. Were they the enemies he was protecting them from? Were those people going to fight back!?

She realized she'd sort of lied to Magdalena. Her uncle may have been protecting Venezuelans, as her mother said, but he was just protecting some Venezuelans, not all of them. He was here to protect people like her mother and her.

"Someone? Well, Miss Olga, I jus' don' know." Blaine looked puzzled.

There! She'd gotten him to doubt what really happened. She bet he had sort of known. She knew what almost nobody else did. Had she just gotten Blaine to not know it?

Olga was proud of herself. She had done the same thing with Magdalena; she had deceived them both—all by herself.

She watched Blaine begin to fashion little crosses with sticks, and she knew: in his own way, he thought he was protecting them, even though he didn't know what it was all about.

Olga smiled to herself as she made her way back down the garden to the lounge chair with the book on it.

That's when she worried, for just an instant: had either of her brothers seen the book? They could get her in trouble with Mama—

It was still there, just where she'd left it, and she could see Henry in the breezeway; he was playing with his truck, so, everything was all right—unless there really were bad people out there. Would they grab her?

Blaine had made her realize; there could be. He'd almost put into words what she hadn't wanted to; there might be people out there who would want to hurt them, because of what Uncle Benjamin had done to their people—if he really had done those things—if his people had done them, she amended to herself, thinking of how elegant her uncle always appeared. But how—

She shook her head. The police said they were both suicides. The police wouldn't be wrong, would they? Uncle Benjamin had just said that was "the story" and Mama shouldn't ask any more questions.

Olga frowned. She hated it when Mama said that to her! "Basta! Mas preguntas no!"

At least Uncle Benjamin was smiling when he said it; she had heard it in his voice. She'd even glimpsed it.

Olga shook her head. That made even less sense!

Would Blaine's secret fence protect them?

7

Olga felt terminally tired, wearied by the years. She opened her eyes and was reassured to find herself in her chair, in the common room. The old people were sleeping in their chairs, except for Doris, who always stayed at the table; she was reading, as usual.

It was tiring. Olga wasn't sure what 'it' was, just knew that it was. All those years? How many? Had something happened, a long time ago? She had been a girl in Trinidad, and then?

It felt as if something had happened. And then she was in New York. How did that happen? Was it luck; did it just happen?

It was tiring thinking about this, so she closed her eyes, drifted away from the common room, heard the cockatoo screech, but it turned into....

Sister Chalfont! The old nun was calling roll.

It took a few moments for Olga to register: this was when she could find out something. Oh, yes! Who was that girl who had snarled at her, when they saw that man hanging from the tree?

At first, Olga was just curious. The first thing she noticed, as she looked back at the rank of upper-form girls in the back of the chapel, was that Amalia wasn't there. Had she and her family gone "home," wherever that was? Back to whatever family had been left on the mainland? Maybe not. Maybe they'd gone somewhere else; they wouldn't go back to Venezuela; it wouldn't be safe for them. Maybe, New York! Lucky her, if she did!

There was Top-Heavy. She nudged Magdalena in the ribs and cocked her head towards the girl with the big chest. Magdalena smirked.

"Elena Gutierrez?" rasped the old nun.

A girl near Top-Heavy held up her hand. She said, "Présent." Olga recognized the snarl on her lips! It was her! She had never really looked at her before. Elena. She had a shape. Olga scowled. She was pretty, as pretty as the Rodriguez sisters.

Was she a revolutionary? Her family, were they rebels? She dressed well. Amalia had been well dressed, too.

She hadn't been very nice that day; probably she'd been the one who spread the rumor Olga had something to do with hanging Amalia's father. She didn't look very nice; she looked like one of those silly older girls who were always talking about boys.

At first, she wanted to tell Mama, to get back at Elena for her meanness, for spreading the rumor, and she imagined her mother again telling her she had done it "for the good of the country." She had felt good when Mama told her that. But telling Mama Amalia's family name—and what happened to her father—had made her friends scared of her; her friends might be scared of her again—if she told Mama.

Besides, maybe it wasn't Elena who spread the rumor, and maybe her parents weren't revolutionaries, either. Maybe, she had been having her period—she'd heard older girls talking about that. Or maybe she was just mean. Maybe her uncle would just have to find out the *subversivos* himself. The more she thought about it, the less she was sure that Elena, who at that moment was piously kneeling and praying, was any kind of revolutionary.

Olga was kneeling, too, but she only went through the motions. The whole Mass was just a lot of mumbo-jumbo and nice smells, as far as she was concerned. The priest had on a pretty surplice, but she couldn't see why the nuns thought he was so wonderful.

She shook her head. She wasn't going to tell Mama.

She wished there was something she could do herself, something to get even; Elena was just mean, she decided. So, she wanted to do something, but not something that would make Magdalena and Antoinetta scared of her again. She looked over at Magdalena and grinned, then at Antoinetta; she looked bored. Well, Mass was a bore. It was in Latin, after all, not any of the three languages Olga knew.

How could she get even? Elena saw her and frowned; Olga pretended she didn't know her.

Uncle Benjamin came to dinner with Mama, after Olga and Henry had their supper, and had been sent off to their rooms.

Olga didn't care. She hadn't told Mama, and wasn't going to, at least unless she found out something else. And, since they'd had supper early, and her brothers were in their rooms, Olga felt free to go out into the garden—and eavesdrop.

She had tried reading *Love Your Enemy*, but it didn't live up to the promise on the cover; it was all sighs and heaving bosoms, silk stockings and manly chests. She'd rather find out what was happening between her uncle and her mother; that was more interesting.

She had located the stump in the daytime, the one where she'd sat at night, where she could see and hear everything in the sitting room, or Mama's bedroom. And she'd mapped her safest route to it, too. Now, she could have gotten there with her eyes closed—well, almost.

When she sat down on the stump, her mother was saying, "...don't think I should have any more for a little, um, time, Benjamin. I already feel a little dizzy. I just want you to hold me."

Her uncle laughed softly. "Then, it had the desired effect—except that I need to tell you something, first."

Their heads, almost together the moment before, were now separated by a space, part of the bookcase seemingly between them.

"Remember," his voice softened further, his Spanish softer, too, "you told me about that Gutierrez lady, whose daughter is in the same school as yours?"

Elena's mother!

"Yes, yes. I told you I saw her making such a face; I was telling Nadia how El Presidente helped us. That woman looked as if she was about to plunge a knife into me!"

El Presidente helped us?

"She didn't think I could see her, but her face was reflected in the glass."

"Well, you were right, your instincts were just so. She was a regular Mata Hari in the European war."

What's a Mata Hari, Olga wondered.

"She was working for the Russian revolutionaries! A Spanish-speaking go-between. That's where she met el Señor! He's a Communist! He looks just like any other lawyer, doesn't he? But under that middle class exterior, we're pretty sure about his inside: he threw bombs in a street riot in Madrid. We think he's high up in the Venezuelan politburo!"

"Oh dear. There is such a thing? Can't you get them away from here before you...you know? It would be very upsetting to Olga, I think, if another girl's father is, is...."

Uncle Benjamin's laugh was muted. "And mother. Yes. Well, Ana, this is war, you know. I would certainly like to take care of them elsewhere, but in a war, one has to take advantage of opportunities when they come along. You can't expect them to be there, just when you want them. Hmm...

"It does bear thinking about, however. We might be able to spirit them off in a fishing boat."

Elena's father and mother!

Uncle Benjamin started to chuckle, low in his throat. "Actually, I like that idea. They could go out deep sea fishing, and just not come back."

"But why would they go deep sea fishing?" Mama's voice was shrill with anxiety. "Why would a woman, a woman like her, especially, want to go out deep sea fishing?"

"Ana, Ana! Some things just happen, don't they?" His voice was rich: deep and calming. "One never knows about a person like that, but it's better not to ask too many questions, correct?"

Mama sighed. "You know what you're doing; I don't really want to know. I just want to know I did the right thing, by telling you."

"Of course you did, Ana! That's what I was trying to tell you. Your instincts are what the English call 'spot on,' meaning absolutely true. You can trust them—and so can I."

"So, my dear Ana..."

Olga could see that he'd moved closer; there was no space between them now.

"Oh, Benjamin!" Mama's voice was a comforted sigh.

"Is this what you really wanted?"

"Mmm."

Carefully, silently, Olga slipped back to her room, but not before looking up at the black sky, the sharp white points of the stars. She thought, they stay the same, but everything else changes. She didn't know what she meant by that.

Elena's parents actually were Communists!

Uncle Benjamin was going to 'take care of them?'

Elena wasn't very nice.

Olga shrugged. She wasn't scared of them, so she didn't care if they were Communists. But she also didn't care much about what happened to them; she didn't know them, and the only thing she knew about Elena, was that she had snarled at her, once.

Besides, she'd read about Communists in the school library. What stuck in her head was something Marx had written: "From each according to his ability, to each according to his needs." She'd almost laughed when she read it. That could never work! It just seemed silly.

She knew now and had known for ages, without admitting it, even to herself, that her uncle was a patriot fighting a war—or a murderer. Well, he arranged for people to be 'taken care of,' but he said it was to protect Venezuela.

Both were more interesting than just being Consul General.

Olga lay back on her bed, looking out at the garden—and closed her eyes.

When she opened them, she was in her room in that northern place. There was no door to the garden, but it wasn't night-time, and she could see trees outside, barely green at the very tips; when she pushed herself up and looked out the window, she could see the shimmer of rushing water; there was a creek out there. She wondered if it was time to get up for breakfast. Then she heard the care person rousing someone down the hall.

She was hungry. She silently said goodbye to the night-time scene—it didn't make sense where she awoke, but then nothing did, really, and it didn't matter. She shrugged her shoulders at the world and braced herself for getting up. "Tengo hambre," she said to herself, and then grinned. That was Spanish. She had spoken it to her mother. Could she still speak it? It didn't matter. Nothing did.

Except food—and sleep. She could "go to bed" in her chair after breakfast.

For the next few minutes, she pushed forward, with her walker; she was minimally aware of someone next to her: the caregiver. Arriving at the dining room she looked about her. Was it breakfast time?

Glancing out the glass door to the patio, she could see: the sun was high; it also felt like, like breakfast. Then she saw the food waiting for her at her place: she angled her walker towards it. Breakfast..

And then she'd go to bed.

Olga closed her eyes even before she'd finished; she was too tired to eat any more. But sleeping in her dining table chair wasn't that comfortable. She drifted in and out of dream, could hear someone talking nearby, but the words made no sense. She'd have to wait until—ah, someone was helping her to get up. With supreme effort, she rose from her chair, and maneuvered her walker towards her morning chair. She sat down in it; she leaned back with a sigh that expressed relief and satisfaction: relief that she didn't have to be present any longer, and satisfaction that they let her sleep in the morning. To bed; to bed. Was she a 'sleepy-head?'

Olga glanced around her. The first thing she'd been aware of was girls' voices, all around her. She was waiting with her friends, Magdalena and Antoinetta, for school to begin.

"But I don't see why we have to read *The Confessions of Saint Augustine*," Magdalena was complaining.

"Hah!" Olga retorted, "just be glad you don't have to read it in Latin!"

What was that she heard behind them?

"...she hasn't come back! It's been days!"

"I heard they just disappeared, her parents, too!"

Olga hoped it was Elena, and then she hoped it wasn't, but she wouldn't ask.

"Elena didn't tell her friends she was going anywhere," said a third voice.

So. It had happened. Her uncle's idea must have been carried out. They had been 'taken care of.'

Olga wasn't sure why she felt a stone in the pit of her stomach. She tried to ignore it. So, the Reds got what was coming to them. Why did that bother her? It served them right.

"I think *Confessions* is interesting," Antoinetta was saying. "He tells about life in a city long ago, and what he did wrong, before he..." Antoinetta put her hand to her chest and pretended to look 'religious,' "...was saved by The Holy Catholic Church."

Olga and Magdalena laughed.

The older girls behind them were suddenly confronting all three of them. "How can you laugh," one of them grimaced at them, "when Elena, our classmate—and her whole family has completely disappeared? Don't you care?"

Olga pretended surprise. "Disappeared? I didn't hear anything about this. Did you, Mags? Tony?"

Both shook their heads: as surprised as Olga pretended to be.

"Has it been long?" asked Magdalena.

"Three days," said the first girl.

"Maybe they just went to the beach and didn't come back in time," Olga suggested.

The girl shook her head dismissively. "You're so dumb, Little Girl!"

"She's the one probably knows about it," said another girl, the one Olga recognized as 'Top-Heavy.' "She got a ride from the Venezuelan Consul. I saw her."

"My name is Olga," she said, proudly, to the first girl. Then she turned to Top-Heavy and answered, "He's my uncle, but what's he got to do with this classmate of yours and her family disappearing? My uncle, the Consul, is here to protect us. Maybe they got picked up by pirates, at sea—there are some, I've heard. Or maybe they just left, who knows why? People do."

The older girls glared at her as if they'd like to bite her, or spit at her, but that's all they did: they stood there, their eyes smoking. Then, as the Sister started to ring the bell, they turned away, without saying a word.

"Wow, Olga!" exclaimed Magdalena. "They didn't know what to say!"

"It looked like they wanted to kill you, and you knew they couldn't. You didn't let them scare you!" Antoinetta was impressed.

"Of course," agreed Olga, as they came to the room for their first class. "I told you," she paused for dramatic effect, "I am Princess Olga."

They all laughed.

It wasn't until she was walking home, alone with the silent Shem, after Magdalena had turned off towards her house, that she had time to think about this. She realized: maybe they wouldn't kill her in the schoolyard, but anywhere else their parents could, or people working for them could. They'd want to kill her mother, or her uncle, too, of course.

That's why Uncle Benjamin had Martin, a coachman as big as a bear; he wasn't just her uncle's coachman; she understood that now. Maybe that's why she wasn't scared. Besides, she knew she was right. It wasn't right to take things from other people.

As she turned into the drive at her house, she saw a little cross, made of twigs, hiding beneath a bush, just by the entryway. Then she spotted another, along the walkway, tucked almost out of sight behind a wooden screen. Had Blaine put them all along the boundary?

Olga thanked Shem; he nodded, saying, "Welcome, Miss," and went off to the kitchen. She dropped her books by the door of her room and kept on going right to the back of the yard; she saw the little crosses all along the boundary line, but you wouldn't notice them unless you knew what you were looking for.

Would they work?

That's when Olga had a feeling, a sort of trembling, up and down her spine. She was glad Blaine had put them there, but what if they didn't work?

There were bad people out there!

"Bad people...." Somewhere? Olga shrugged at the thought. She felt safe here.

She looked around her; she was in the common room, but her son was in front of her. What did he say?

"Como estas tu?"

She answered, without thinking, "Muy bien."

She couldn't understand why he smiled. But soon he was talking, talking, talking and she closed her eyes.

"Aaahh, c'n beat you, I know I can!" boasted Henry, as they wheeled out their bicycles. Hers was a Raleigh, a genuine English bicycle; his was still a little boy's bike—he was a year younger, after all, and he looked a lot younger; most boys did.

"Yeah," said Olga, "bet I c'n beat you to Grandma's house, without even trying."

"Cannot," shouted Henry, pedaling off as fast as he could.

Olga waited what seemed like a decent interval, to give him at least a little chance, and then she jumped on her bike in hot pursuit, standing on her pedals, pumping, pushing. Before they were at the end of the next block, she passed him in a blur, and he wailed behind her, "Hey, that's not fair!"

"Hah!" she shouted back. "I even waited before I started after you."

"Did not!"

Olga slowed down. "C'mon, little boy! Bet you can't catch me!"

"Ooh, you make me so mad!" Henry peddled furiously,

Olga almost rested on her pedals, waiting for him to catch up. When he was just abreast of her, winded, getting red in the face, she jumped on her pedals; in one huge heave she was ten feet ahead of him, the gap widening; another giant pump and he was falling fast behind.

Henry whined: "That's not fair!"

Olga kept going. She wanted to see her grandmother Braulia, and she wanted to see the old house on Dere street. She wished she didn't have to wait for her annoying little brother at each turn; but luckily, there were only two turns. It was her mother's rule: neither of them could go beyond The Savannah, unless they were going together. Mama had also made it clear to her that she was older and therefore responsible for Henry if they went beyond The Savannah.

They were beyond The Savannah, going down the shady side streets before Dere. She looked back; Henry was way back, so she stopped to wait for him. She didn't start going again until he was fairly close, and pumping with all his might to catch up and pass her. She stood up on the pedals and pulled way ahead of him, and then coasted right up to Grandma Braulia's walk.

She was just about to turn down it, when a mean-looking, Venezuelan-looking man suddenly lurched away into the shadows of her grandmother's gardens. She peered along the side of the house, but there was no one there; he'd disappeared!

It had been a cruel face, more Indio than her mother's family, but something brutal about it. And the eyes; suddenly, she could see those eyes again; they were like a tiger's eyes, a hunter's eyes. Now she knew how a rabbit would feel if a dog saw it.

Henry swooped up with a crash, and dropped his bike on the sidewalk. He was huffing and puffing, and saying, "Not fair!" But not with much conviction.

Olga set her bike on its stand—Henry left his splayed across the walk—and together they went to their grandmother's door.

It had been their front door, thought Olga, before they moved to Belmont Circle.

As she knocked on it, she remembered with a smile that the door had seemed so huge to her, and she couldn't push it open. It was just an ordinary front door now, in dark mahogany, with old-fashioned brass studs on it; they were polished, and they gleamed even in the partial shade.

The yard boy, who could have been Shem's brother—he probably was—, opened the door. She could tell he was the yard boy, because his shorts were off-white and stained and his shirt was, too.

As she stepped through the doorway, Olga looked sideways towards the corner of the house—she barely glimpsed a brown man's skin masked by the shrubbery. But a malevolent eye —she had just learned that word—peered through the greenery at her. Being eyed like prey, that's what it made her feel!

A shiver trickled down her spine. But before she had time to worry further about the man lurking there, Henry started chortling: "Candy! Yes, yes, I love you Grandma!"

It was the first thing he always thought of: treats.

Olga frowned at him and shook her head. "We're just going to say hello and goodbye, Henry! And you'll only get candy if you don't ask for it." Her brother was so stupid!

"If I don't ask for it?" Henry looked puzzled.

Olga shrugged. "Asking is bad manners." She put on her best know-it all expression, and stared him down.

"Humph." Henry turned away, pretending to ignore her.

Their grandmother's room was dark, not just because the one window was partially shrouded in a heavy velvet curtain; all the furniture was dark, almost black, all old, elaborately carved mahogany, and the one lamp was dim, after the outside sunlight. On the wall there was one painting, also dark, of the Christ, bleeding from his crown of thorns, looking down at her with tired, tortured eyes.

Their grandmother, their abuela, looked up at both of them and smiled. She put down the ornate white cloth she had been working on—she was always making lace—and held up her hands to them. "Come, my children! You are getting so big!"

Her Spanish was less pure even than Mama's; it had an 'island' twang to it that was even stronger. She was tiny, and pale, from living in the dark, her hair was long, silver with just a few black streaks in it, tightly tied in back. She was dressed in black, but then, she was a widow.

Henry still looked puzzled. He could hardly speak a word of Spanish and he didn't understand it a lot of the time. They only spoke English at his school, even the boys, so he only heard his mother speak it, since the servants didn't. Julio spoke Spanish, but mostly just insults to his little brother.

"I know what you like," she grinned at Henry, and then at Olga, the gaps in her teeth were like deep wells in her mouth. She reached behind her chair and took out a metal tin. Henry was all eyes as she opened it. He reminded Olga of a dog, saliva dripping from his jaws, as he impatiently waited for his treat.

How could she tell her abuela about the man outside, about what was happening, and why he could be dangerous, with Henry there?

She watched, as Henry took out a piece of turrón, beautifully wrapped in edible foil. He was about to take another, when Olga said, "That's enough, Henry!"

He glared at her, but turned away from the tin, and from her.

"Would you like one, too, my beautiful granddaughter?"

"Gracias, mi abuela."

Henry edged off to a corner of the dark room, and Olga came closer to her grandmother to pick out her piece of turrón: it was very pretty. She decided that Henry wouldn't understand enough Spanish, anyway—he resisted speaking it and understanding it—and he obviously was fixated on his candy.

"Mi abuela, there is a man outside, and he looks dangerous," she told her, close enough to her that she didn't have to raise her voice. "There have been some of our paisanos here who were killed—and some people are angry at our family: they think, because of our connections with El Presidente—"

"No, no, my dear, " soothed the old woman, "I'm sure it is only my gardener. He isn't as mean as he looks. Besides, you shouldn't worry about such things! You are my beautiful granddaughter! Let the men concern themselves about such silly things. That man won't hurt you."

Olga wasn't so sure, but she knew better than to argue. At least her grandmother now knew about the deaths—and Henry, she could see, was exploring down the corridor towards the other rooms in the house, so he couldn't have heard or understood. He probably didn't remember the house as well as she did; they'd lived there until a few years ago, but he was younger when they moved.

The turrón melted and crunched in her mouth; it was so good!

Her abuela asked her if they were all well, and if their mother liked her new house—to her it was new, Olga realized.

"Oh, yes, mi abuela, everyone is fine. Mama likes the house. She is seeing—no, never mind." It suddenly occurred to her that other people might see her mother's being with their uncle as not quite right. And her grandmother hadn't taken in what she'd just told her about those people getting killed. But maybe there was no point in telling her again.

"And your father? Do you hear from him?"

"Yes, mi abuela." He always sent a bag of gold coins, every month—or almost. With her uncle around more, Olga wasn't sure that it was such a good thing to have a man in the house. She had never seen her mother scared before.

Magdalena had asked her once, "Don't you feel as if your father abandoned you?" She didn't. He sent money. Maybe that's what her father was good for. She didn't remember what it was like when he lived with them. She did remember, a little, of the time when he came to visit: her mother hadn't been at all happy most of the time. She hadn't realized that until later, after he'd left. At the time, she'd been so focused on him, her father, whom she hadn't remembered at all.

He'd said she was pretty, that he was glad he had a Princess Olga for a daughter.

No, she didn't feel abandoned.

Henry came back down the corridor; he'd finished his treat, and looked as if he was about to ask for more, so Olga began saying their goodbyes and thank yous.

Olga peered out the door, both ways, before she came out to retrieve her bike. The man wasn't there, but she could hear someone raking behind the house. Maybe her abuela was right, maybe he was the gardener.

Henry pushed past her and grabbed up his bike from the walk.

Olga considered, as they cycled back towards home: there really could be bad people out there, and they could be after either of them, because of Uncle Benjamin.

She wasn't going to tell Mama, though. She wanted to be able to go out on her bicycle and Mama might not let them if she told her. This was their Saturday bicycle outing, and they'd always been allowed to go at least as far as Abuela Braulia's.

Olga gritted her teeth. With her uncle spending more time with her mother and with his pursuit of *subversivos*, or whatever they were, they might not be allowed out on their own much longer!

She wouldn't like that!

Olga opened her eyes. She still glimpsed riding down a leafy street—on a bicycle? The next instant, she saw the sun shining on a chair beyond the glass door facing her. She could go out; it looked warm out there. She reached for her walker, and rose stiffly from her chair. The sun was shining outside, and vaguely she remembered hearing someone say something about its being warm outside. She pushed open the sliding glass door and rolled her walker out onto the plain boards of the patio. There was a chair there, so she sat down on it. It was warm, so she began to take off her shirt.

"No, no!" said someone from inside, who was then beside her, outside in almost no time. The care person. "It's not appropriate for Ladies to take off their shirts in public," she was saying, fitting her shirt back on and buttoning the buttons.

Olga wondered why. She had a vision of herself flying out on sand, somewhere, with nothing on at all. Was it a long time ago? Oh well. A phrase drifted past: "among the natives...." She wasn't sure what that meant. But the sun was warm. She closed her eyes.

She was following Julian, who had curly red hair, and was deeply freckled; he was carrying most of their beach things, but she had the hamper with sandwiches and some RC Colas.

There were a few people here and there on the beach. The waves were crashing not very far out, and rolling in and up the beach. The sky was a wonderful blue, so much bluer out here than in the city.

"We could stop here and swim," she suggested, but Julian, that stubborn look in his eye she had begun to recognize, shook his head. They had been married just over a year.

"We've got to keep on going! Around the point we'll have it all to ourselves."

All to ourselves. Well, she didn't like swimming in a bathing suit, either, and she had her diaphragm, KY and the other stuff in the hamper, so she was ready. She smiled to think of it.

Soon, they were spread out on the sand, on top of a large blanket. There was no one else in sight; they had walked almost a mile beyond the last person on the beach. She rubbed cocoa butter on Julian's back and his behind. He rubbed some on her back, too, although she hardly needed it—she was already so brown. But then he fondled her breasts, so she turned over.

He looked down at her, his eyes shining. She nodded up at him. She had gotten ready as soon as she took off her bathing suit; she wanted him inside her.

Oh, yes!

Afterwards, she went swimming; her thighs were slippery, and she needed to wash them off before they dried. The cold water hit them with the incoming wave. She thought about having his baby someday, but not yet, not yet; they couldn't afford it yet.

Julian was already further out, waiting for a wave to break. He could ride the waves for hours.

"You better come in now, Olga. Don't want you to get burned!" The care person. Olga wondered why she had to, but then, struggling to get out of the chair, she remembered: she wasn't young anymore; her skin was very thin.

It had happened.

It was Saturday, again. They had been about to go on their bike ride. If she had been younger, she would have stamped her feet and yelled, but she knew Mama was right. She just wished she wasn't.

"You must not go beyond The Savannah," she had told both of them in Spanish, and then, seeing Henry's confusion had added in English, "No go, uh..."

"Beyond," Olga suggested.

"Yes, no go beyond Savannah. Entiende?"

Henry nodded solemnly, and didn't object. He also didn't ask why. Olga knew why: she didn't have to ask.

Instead, she asked, "But how will I go to school? That's beyond The Savannah."

"With Shem. That's a weekday, when your classmates will also be on the road. "

Olga could feel herself frowning.

Her Mother asked, "Do you want to know why?"

"I already know," said Olga, scornfully. "It's because of the people who died, and the people who think Uncle Benjamin did it."

Mama looked startled. Then her brows knit in anger. "Who's telling you things like this?"

"Huh?" Henry looked confused. "Did what?"

They both ignored him.

Olga shrugged. "I just know." Then she added, "I know a lot

more than you think I know, Mama—after all, I helped—with Amalia Suarez."

"Oh." Mama's face closed, then it hardened, as she looked Olga in the eye. "You will not say anything about this to anyone! Understood?"

"Of course, Mama."

Her mother sighed. "All right. Go! But only as far as The Savannah!"

"C'mon, Henry!" Olga jumped on her bike; Henry jumped on his. He was far behind her in only a few pumps, but she didn't care. He was wailing, "Wait for me, wait—" but she didn't care. She'd go as far as the other end of The Savannah, and she'd go around it, and, and then what?

Anger made her go faster, and faster, Henry lagging further and further behind. She could see Miriam and Henry's nurse, Rebecca, rushing out of the yard to catch up—they were supposed to keep an eye on them. Even worse.

She just didn't care, didn't care, didn't care!

What good was it just going around The Savannah? After the third time around, puffing a little, she stopped and did what she had wanted to do all along: she threw her bike on the ground and stamped her feet. She was going to yell and carry on, but then she knew it would be no use. Her mother was right.

She just growled, instead.

What she was angry about was...Uncle Benjamin. He was ruining her life.

"What'd you do that for?" Henry was looking at her as if she'd gone crazy. He didn't understand: he didn't know what was happening; didn't even know what to ask.

"Oh, never mind!" He was such a little boy, even though he was only a year younger. Well, all boys were stupid; it took them longer to grow up.

Then she grinned at him. "Bet I can beat you home!"

75

"Can not!" yelled Henry, peddling away furiously.

She grabbed up her bike, jumped on and in four or five thrusts she was abreast of him. She poured on the speed, leaving him far behind.

Miriam was shouting for her to come back, and Henry was wailing, "Not fair!" but she kept right on going.

When she stopped in the drive next to their house, she was aware of the sudden quiet.

The wind makes noise, she thought. No, it's the air when it rushes past me. It's so quiet without it.

She didn't feel like riding her bike anymore, so she put it in its place, next to the kitchen, and went out into the garden.

But even here, she thought, we might not be safe!

She wished Uncle Benjamin hadn't messed up her life, had left those people alone. She bet they couldn't start a real revolution, anyway.

Olga could vaguely hear a voice; it was Norm. She opened her eyes just long enough to take in the common room, with Doris sitting at the table, reading from her stack of books, and Norm just getting up from it. She didn't know, or care what he was saying.

She sighed and closed her eyes.

She was in a crowd of people! They were all chanting something; she was too! She recognized one of her fellow teachers at Little Red. They were shouting: "Up with the workers! Down with Nazis! Stop the Fascists!"

Tall buildings surrounded them: it was New York's downtown, that much she knew. Then she remembered: she'd come to this demonstration with a group of her fellow teachers after school. She didn't really remember what they were demonstrating about, but it didn't really matter. The forces of Repression were taking over, especially in Germany, and they were standing against them, in Solidarity with the revolutionary Soviets. It made her happy to think of the Socialist Man standing firm against the Italian Fascisti and the newly emerging Nazis in Germany.

Julian had shaken his head, when she'd asked if he'd come. "The firm would object—the old man" (he meant the head of the firm) "is an America Firster, after all—so, as long as I'm the one bringing home the bacon, I have to be careful. But you go ahead." He had smirked at her: "If you get arrested, I'll bail you out. Too bad we don't have the money from the guano your father sent."

She was an intern teacher; The Little Red Schoolhouse just paid her carfare.

They, all of them, including her, called out their chants, sang Solidarity Forever, but had still attracted only a few passersby to stop and watch for a minute or two, before they went on their way.

Their leader, whoever he was—good-looking, dressed like a worker, jeans, work shirt; Olga could see they were new; she grinned at that—finally shrugged and said, "Guess that's enough for today; can't even get the cops interested."

A tall woman, a teacher at Little Red, called out, "Maybe next time, you should tell them we'll be here—without a permit."

"Good idea—except it was supposed to be spontaneous." He shrugged again. "Well, maybe we should all march on down to Bleecker, you know, the tavern."

Olga laughed. "That's the kind of demonstration I like!"

Someone else laughed, and then, they all straggled down the street. It was warm, summery, the street holding the heat, even in October.

Well, at least Julian wouldn't have to come bail her out.

As she was toying with her second Manhattan, the tall, good-looking man who had been leading the demonstration sidled up to her. "Hey, Beautiful! You look like you must be from one of our Spanish affiliates. I'm Bob."

"She's from Venzuela," said Marilyn, one of her fellow teachers.

Olga laughed. "Hello, Bob. I'm Venezuelan," she pronounced in her best Lana Turner voice, "but I've only been there once—as a visitor."

"Oh!" Bob's eyebrows raised in interest. "Organizing there against the Dictator?"

Olga considered saying yes, but she shook her head, instead. "Just visiting my father, but that was years ago." She didn't add, but thought: my whole family is working for the Dictator! Except my mother.

"Got family there, eh?" He came close, and whispered, "We can help get them out if they're in danger, you know."

"Why thank you!" she effused.

"Um, we've got a little party going down at my place, when we leave here. Like to come?"

She liked it when men came on to her. "Well...thank you, but I'm afraid I've got other plans." She smirked at herself to think of what they were: to help her mother and Aunt make dinner for the four of them. But she liked the idea that an "adventure" might be possible some other time. "You can always get ahold of me at Little Red, though."

She was aware of herself, leaving the bar, aware of her tight-fitting suit, of how it showed off her hips and breasts; she could feel his eyes on her perfect body as she made her way out the door and down the street—

And then she opened her eyes: she was in the common room. Norm was sleeping in the chair nearest to her. Somehow, it didn't feel real. Where had she just come from?

She shook her head and closed her eyes. She was so tired!

Commotion. Miriam, Rebecca, Dominic, Blaine, the cook, Shem, they were all busy carrying things to and fro; Miriam was packing clothes for her; Cook was packing "supplies;" Blaine and

Shem were carrying things to the carriage. Shem and Dominic carried Mama's huge steamer trunk to it.

Olga had offered to help, but her mother had told her, "Just don't get in the way. And maybe make sure Miriam packs what you want to take."

She had. She grinned as she remembered taking out the stockings and sun veils and hiding them at the bottom of the wardrobe when Miriam was out of the room. They were things she didn't want to take.

A vacation was a vacation. She didn't remember the last time they'd gone to "the beach." During school vacations, they had mostly stayed at home. Mama hadn't wanted to go anywhere, and besides, their uncle Benjamin had to stay in Port of Spain.

Fighting "the rebels."

Olga grimaced.

Ever since the first Venezuelan here had died a "strange, unexplained" death—the one who had drowned in his carriage—things had gotten worse and worse. Mama had even gotten a new carriage boy: Max, they called him, and he was big: almost as big as Uncle Benjamin's Martin.

Max was fixing the carriage, or tending to the horses—or something. He'd walked her to school the last few weeks; Olga didn't much like him. He was very quiet, like Shem, but he didn't smile at all. He was constantly looking this way and that, as if he was afraid of someone jumping out of the shrubbery and attacking them. He was unfriendly, or just grim, when her friends joined her on the way to school. They all found it hard to ignore him, to talk about boys, or silly things, and especially to laugh together, something they had loved to do.

So, Olga was glad they'd be going away, even though she wouldn't see Magdalena or Antoinetta until they came back.

She'd heard Julio complaining that he didn't want to go to some "nasty old beach cottage in the middle of nowhere," but she knew what he really hated about it: he couldn't just hang out with his friends. He didn't know anything, so he didn't know there was something to be afraid of. To her, "a beach cottage in the middle of nowhere" sounded wonderful. They wouldn't have to worry about the *subversivos y trastornadores* (her uncle's phrase) while they were away. Uncle Benjamin had embarked on one of his travels, so he wasn't there to "protect" them. Her mother had said that, not realizing that Olga understood what she really meant.

Julio was off somewhere with his nasty friends. She wished her mother would let him stay with a friend, but no, she insisted he come with them. She didn't explain why. That made Olga feel superior: she knew why.

She wondered, momentarily why she allowed Julio to go out whenever he wanted, while she and Henry were pretty much kept within The Savannah and Belmont Circle. Maybe because he was so nasty? Julio did get away with stuff, and it wasn't just because he was older.

She realized, suddenly. That creep looked like Benjamin and probably like their father. He was the first born, and the eldest son. He was tall, light-skinned, dirty blond and with blue eyes. So was Benjamin; so was their father, although she didn't remember him very well.

That wasn't why she hated Julio. He was nasty: he called Henry "Negrito." He was never friendly, always overbearing. And so stupid!

Henry was stupid, too. Boys were stupid.

Henry had complained when Mama told him he couldn't take his bike. You couldn't ride on the beach with a bike! She could have told him that. And she knew Mama wouldn't want him biking up into the jungle, along the one road.

Mama was scared enough already.

She wished Uncle Benjamin didn't have to "stop" *subversivos*. Before this, Olga had admired her mother; she was strong, on her own, buying up property, important, and sending them all to school.

But then along came Uncle Benjamin, and—she had a vision again of his bare buttocks and Mama's bare midriff—and then glimpsed the bodies of those dead men. Antoinetta, Magdalena, afraid, the other girls, even more so; she could see their faces: closed when they looked at her. Afraid of her! Afraid like that, they could hurt her, too. She didn't feel safe. Anyone in her family could be a target.

She wished she could stop them; stop Uncle Benjamin, stop it all: but she was still just a girl. She sure wasn't going to help Uncle anymore!

"You go early, first of the morning," Miriam was telling her. "It a long ride."

Olga looked up at her: she had been sitting on the bench in the garden, staring out at Belmont Circle. "I'll get breakfast first. Right?"

Miriam grinned. "You do always think about food! And you eat everything! Course you have breakfast first. You Mama, too."

Olga was eating breakfast at the community table, with Doris, Norm and that blob-faced man. She wasn't hungry for much. A piece of toast, some oatmeal, a glass of milk. She picked at the fruit.

Then, she closed her eyes.

It was unprecedented. That was a word she'd just learned from the dictionary. She liked its sound. She rolled it around her lips and tongue as she and her mother and her two brothers all had an early breakfast together.

Max was getting the horses ready.

She couldn't remember ever having breakfast with all of them. She grinned to see them all: they didn't grin back; didn't even look at her, but she didn't care. Her hot chocolate was hot, and the bun was crispy. It was going to be a good day.

She looked over at her mother. She looked tired, her eyes still bleary from sleep. She was never up when Olga went to school. Olga felt superior; she wasn't tired! She was excited.

But seeing her two brothers and her mother, she kept quiet. Julio looked cross, sour. He picked at his breakfast. Henry just looked blank. He was completely focused on his bun and his chocolate, but then he almost always was at breakfast. He was the only one she ever had breakfast with. She wondered when Julio had breakfast, usually. She never saw him in the morning, but he did go to school. Maybe he didn't have breakfast. He sure didn't look much interested in it.

That was something Olga couldn't fathom: not eat breakfast?

Max came in. He stood there until Olga gestured towards him for Mama to see.

"Oh. We ready?" her mother asked him.

"Yes'm. Horse ready; wagon ready."

"It's a carriage," said Olga, "not a wagon."

Max shrugged. Then he smiled at her. There was something about his smile that she liked, but she didn't know what it was.

Mama nodded, drank down her coffee—it was coffee, not hot chocolate—and told them all to finish up: "We go, vamos, ahora."

Julio said, "I can't yet, Mother. I'm not finished." His glance at her was really mean!

Now, he wanted to eat!

Mama sighed. "Well, mas rapido, por favor!"

So, everybody had to wait for Julio, just because he had refused to eat when everyone else was having their breakfast.

Olga had finished, and she didn't want to just sit there. "Mama, I'll go wait out in the garden."

Mama shook her head, and said in Spanish. "Then I would have to send someone to find you. If you want to wait somewhere else, go out to the carriage, or to the entrance, but not out onto the road."

"I know, Mama!"

Mama never explained. Even though Olga knew why, it made her mad, but she didn't say anything. She just wanted to get away from everybody, if only for the few minutes that Julio chewed his bun and drank his coffee. That's right, he drank coffee. Mama had told him that he was just like his father: "He'd put cube after cube of sugar into it, just like you."

So, Olga nodded to Mama, and went down the driveway to the carriage, and then to the horse, patiently munching at something even with his bridle on.

Olga looked out at the road. It was before sunrise, and everything was still dark, although you could see a little. Then, as she watched, the road ahead of her turned from dark in the darkness into gray; the rest of the world was gray for a long moment. Then the sun turned everything golden and the birds started singing as if they'd never sung before.

She had never seen the sunrise!

Not long after, here came Mama, a glum Julio, a now sullen Henry—Mama must have stopped him from eating more—and all the servants behind them. Mama looked proud, instead of asleep.

It still took much too long for them all to get into the carriage. Then, after another long moment, Cook, puffing as she climbed, pulled herself up beside Max.

And then, with a lurch of the wheels, and a creak of the horse's harness, they were on their way!

9

Olga didn't realize Port of Spain was so big. It took them almost an hour before they were out of it; then they were headed down a jungle road, with almost nothing on either side but green jungle that looked as if it never stopped, just kept on going and going: vines, trees, a tangle of bushes and flowers beneath the silent trees.

Olga tried to peer through the jungle, to see beyond, but there didn't seem to be any beyond, except more jungle. The horse's feet made a steady beat, there was creaking and squeaking of the harness and the low voice of Max up front, talking to the horse; there was the bumping and creaking of the carriage, and the whir and bumping of the wheels on the dirt road.

Occasionally, she could hear Cook say something in her low, round voice. Max's voice was higher, which was funny when she thought about it. She couldn't hear what they said.

Beyond their talk, and the sounds of horse and carriage, she could hear wild jungle noises, too. Squawks, cries, birdsong: what was out there?

"Mama? What are those noises, in the jungle, do you know?"

Her mother shrugged. In Spanish she mumbled, "Birds, monkeys, maybe, other things: No se." Olga could see she didn't like the jungle.

"Are there lions and tigers?" asked Henry, wild-eyed.

"No, no, Henry! El tigre, no, el león, no."

Henry looked disappointed. Olga had to grin at that. Of course, there weren't any tigers and lions! Probably big snakes, though.

"Snakes, Mama?" She asked.

Her mother looked unsettled. "I hope not!"

"Probably," sneered Julio, "snakes big enough to eat both of you, you're both so small. Then, all gone brother and sister."

Henry looked scared.

"Julio. Basta!" Her mother looked angry. Then she turned to Henry. "No. Is not true. No es verdad. "

They were passing by a clearing in the jungle. A small hut was in the middle of it, built of faded boards, with a tin roof. Two children stood staring at them as they passed. Neither of them wore any pants. The boy's penis was tiny and brown, the girl covered herself with a hand. Both looked like East Indians.

It was their eyes that Olga remembered for long afterward: they were wide open, amazed, as they watched the carriage pass. Olga waved at them. The girl raised one hand, tentatively, and shyly waved back. The boy smiled at her.

What would it be like living in a place like that? It was only a small clearing. The jungle spread out from it on all sides. What did you do there? Where were their parents? Was their father away, working in the jungle? Was their mother in the hut?

Olga kept on looking back, even after they'd passed. Such a small place. Then she saw a small, stooped woman peer out from the hut. She didn't seem to have any color but shadow.

Then, they were in the jungle again, just green, and dark trunks, and occasional tiny flakes of golden sun even in the darkness of the trees.

"Mama! We gotta stop!" cried Henry, in anguish.

Mama's face softened. "Tan bello!" She was suddenly the mother Olga remembered when she was little, her voice so warm and sweet. Then, raising her voice, she called forward; "Max, stop. Basta!"

"You have to, uh..."

"Go?" suggested Olga, who realized at that moment that she did, too.

Henry nodded his head, almost violently. Julio looked on with a disgusted sneer.

"Bueno. Girls a la izquierda..." she pointed past Olga.

"Left," Olga prompted, "and boys to the right? A la derecha?"

"Correcto!"

"Correct, Mama."

Her mother waved her hands. "Si, Olga, es verdad."

The carriage stopped. Henry, after an instant's confusion, going left, scuttled out the door to the right. Julio sneered at both of them, and slowly climbed down to the right, as well.

Mama turned to her. "We go down here." She pointed to the left. "Into jungle."

"Yes, Mama." Olga stepped down to the step, and then down to the ground. It was soft to walk on, not hard like the paved road, or even like the sand road. Ahead of them was green in almost every shape and shade: bushes rising over their heads with huge leaves, vines growing over them spangled with flowers, mosses growing on the nearby trunks, a fine, soft spongy grass, or was it moss, underfoot.

"You go that way," Mama pointed right, "I go this way," she pointed left. "But not far."

"Yes, Mama." Olga pushed some vines aside and stepped through what felt like a doorway—and she was in a green room. It was magical, even if all she was there for was to pee.

She could hear her mother very close, but couldn't see her; she heard her *whoosh* just before her *phisss*. She wiped herself, carefully, with some paper Mama had pressed into her hand, but then dug a little hole with the heel of her shoe, and put the paper in it; she covered it up. Her room was too beautiful for her to leave paper where anyone could see.

When she and Mama climbed back into the carriage, Henry was gloating. "What took you so long!" It wasn't a question.

Julio smirked at him. "Hey, little boy, girls take longer 'cause they don't have what we have."

Henry looked confused and Olga was tempted to whisper, "penises," just to shock them both, but she decided not to. She hated Julio, but it was better her little brother stayed confused.

"That is enough!" said Mama, in crisp Spanish. Julio looked sullen, then looked away.

Max clucked at the horse, and the carriage began to roll, faster and faster; the horse picked up speed. He was in a full trot now.

They rode on in silence, which suited Olga just fine. She was too interested in the green jungle they were passing through to mind that her stupid brothers didn't talk to her. It was all so much the same, and yet everywhere she looked, she saw new things. She knew, somehow, that her mother was concerned about something—well, she knew about one part, anyway. But she didn't want to talk, either. Mama wanted to doze off.

Sometimes, Blaine said, people told things in their sleep that they would never admit to in public. Olga wondered if that was true. She'd never really listened. She hadn't been in the same room when her mother was sleeping since she was a baby, or when she'd rushed in after a bad dream. She must have been a very little girl when she last did that!

Olga watched their eyes close; first Henry's, then her mother's, then Julio's, a smirk on his face. Olga turned her face to the window, looking out at the endless sea of green, the richness of it, the movement of birds and monkeys, but nothing else for miles—and then they passed by another hut, an older boy in rags looking out at them from behind a tree.

Behind her, they were all sleeping. Olga felt so superior.

Mama was snoring softly; then she gave a soft sigh and mumbled, as if she were a little girl: "Don't! Don't make me!"

Olga looked back at her, but as she did, her mother began to snore loudly, so loudly that Olga was afraid Mama would wake Julio or Henry, but she didn't, and after another moment, her snores subsided. Olga looked back into the jungle. She saw what looked like a small lake, hidden by jungle downhill. It sparkled—

"No!" Her mother's whisper cut like a razor.

It cut through Olga, a sudden fear. Was Mama afraid of something? Of those people who—

"...No...please, Benjamin...."

Mama's voice pleaded.

Olga frowned: was her uncle threatening? Threatening Mama?

Olga looked back at her mother, who was now hunched in upon herself in sleep. No answers there, only questions.

Well, at least they were leaving all that behind—for a little while.

Olga looked out at the green wall of jungle. Then she peered ahead, out the window, the soft breeze almost wet on her cheeks and forehead. She could see sunlight far ahead, shining on what looked like a low white wall.

Olga frowned. What was a wall doing out there? Then she realized: that was sand; it was the beach!

"Mama! We're almost there!"

It was beautiful. Sand beach stretching from north to south, palm trees casting long shadows from the late afternoon sun, the shadows reaching out almost to the water....

Olga opened her eyes and saw the common room. Doris was squinting at a book, a pile of other books next to her on the dining room table. The blunt-faced man was snoring in his chair at the other end of the room. Two little girls were whispering to a young woman—oh, their mother, one of the care persons—and weren't there more people here?

Olga shook her head and closed her eyes. She'd rather see....

It was the prettiest little cottage: thatched roof, weathered wooden walls, all by itself along this whole stretch of beach. Only the ocean in front of them, the waves asserting that, yes, this was the ocean, not the gentle sea that was on Trinidad's west coast. Olga brought in her bag and left it in the room she was going to share with her mother, but then she went back out. Into the sun and wind.

She stood, her face into the rush of air coming from the sea; it smelled of fish and seaweed, and salt. You couldn't see anything but water, as if it stretched on forever. Olga had read about the difference between a sea—their Caribbean Sea, the Mediterranean Sea—and the ocean. This was the Atlantic Ocean; it had a different feel looking out at it.

Olga had peered out from the harbor at Port of Spain, but this just felt different—she was looking across at Africa, not at Venezuela, even though for both the land was invisible, way beyond the horizon. Someone, maybe Uncle Benjamin, had reminded her about the curve of the Earth; those lands were beyond it.

"C'mon! Let's run up the beach," Henry yelled at her.

Olga looked back at the cottage. Mama was just coming outside. "We're going to run up the beach, Mama."

"Just stay I can see, please. And don't go in water!"

As soon as Mama said it, Olga wanted to go into the water, but, "All right, Mama." She turned to Henry. "Beat you to the point."

"Cannot," shouted Henry, launching into a run. His legs were even shorter than hers.

Olga grinned, and took chase, overtaking him easily, halfway up the beach, and kept on running—until she looked back and her mother was only a tiny speck, the cottage a little doll house. Her mother was gesturing: it looked like she wanted them to stop. Olga stopped.

Henry ran up and collapsed beside her, breathing hard. "Why'd you stop?"

Olga pointed back towards the cottage. "Mama said."

"Oh."

Olga walked closer to the waves, surging up the sand, conscious that Henry was following close behind her, still panting. "She said not to go into the water," said Olga, as she took off her shoes. "I'm only going in a little bit—and you're not going to tell!"

"Can't I go in?"

"No. You'll get your pants wet. I'm just going to hold up my dress."

Olga scanned the view between her and her mother, far down the beach. Probably, she could only see their heads; they were mostly behind the curve of sand. Safe.

She walked slowly towards the roiling water, marking its high point in the waves before her. The wave rushed away; another rushed up, towards her. She stood still. Water, cool around her feet and ankles, then as she took another couple of steps towards it, it rushed up towards her knees. She held up her dress and inhaled from the shock. It wasn't cool; it was cold!

The Atlantic Ocean.

"It's not fair!" Henry was yelling behind her.

She turned back. "Is too. I'm older than you. And see, I only got my legs wet. My feet will dry in the sand, but I'm not going to put my shoes back on." In a charitable gesture, she added, "You can take your shoes off, too, if you want. The sand feels nice! But you better not walk in the water. Mama would see if you got your pants wet."

"But then I gotta carry them." He meant the shoes.

Olga shrugged. "So? You can carry them both in one hand, if you want. That's what I'm going to do."

So, Olga walked back barefoot, reveling in the feeling of the sand, moving down to the damp sand when it became too hot in the sun. Henry walked back in his shoes, complaining when they sank in soft sand, running when he found sand that was packed hard.

Olga was behind Henry, still far away from Mama and their cabin, when she heard, behind her, the 'creak creak' sound of something rhythmic, coming towards her, out in the water!

They've found us, already! I can't get away! She felt rooted, frozen, unable to move. Then she looked back and heaved a sigh of relief. It was two black men in a rowboat. One was bent over something at the stern, the other was rowing along the coast, just beyond the breaking waves; he wasn't looking at her. He glanced forward, and then back at the other man. The man said something without turning around, but Olga couldn't hear words, only that he'd spoken.

They weren't in the least interested in her! Olga felt a flush of anger. She wanted to stamp her feet and shout: "Hey, look at me! My Uncle's the Consul...."

But they wouldn't even know what she was talking about.

At least, Max was here!

Suddenly they turned and rowed straight out to sea; they were far out when they actually passed by, as if they were avoiding the beach near the cabin.

Maybe people thought her family was dangerous! That was exhilarating for an instant, but then she shrugged. She was hungry; she smelled fish cooking.

It was cooking over the fire by the cottage; Max had caught it. Cook was cooking it, along with breadfruit, which never tasted or smelled like much of anything—at least to her. She didn't care what they were having; she was hungry. She had been chewing her hair; she hated that.

It wasn't until after dinner that she wondered what all four of them would do, in that small cabin in the evening.

Mama got up from the table, clearing the dishes herself. "I'm going to read," she announced, "I hope you've all brought something to read, or play with." Mama was speaking in what Olga realized was the way she spoke when she was relaxed; she usually sounded more formal, her speech more educated. But she had grown up in the Caribbean, not the Andes, and her Spanish was slurred and hurried at the same time.

Olga was surprised to see Julio bring out a small paperback book from his room. All she could see were the bright colors on the cover, before he saw her looking at it and held it close to his chest. He turned away and pulled a chair up to a corner, put down the book face down, and fussed with a lantern. He actually read books! She bet it was even worse than the one she'd found in the Sister's room.

She was going to read *Anne of Green Gables*. Did you pronounce that 'e' at the end, she wondered. Mama's name was Ana. Of course that wasn't how you said Anne.

Mama was still reading, or pretending to, when the boys went to bed, first Henry, who tired of playing with his truck in the low lantern light, and then Julio, still guarding his book from her sight. Mama was snoring softly now, so Olga turned off the lanterns and tiptoed to her room.

She wasn't tired and she wasn't sleepy. With the lanterns off, the dark inside the house contrasted with the starlight outside. The little cabin shook a little in the shore wind; palm trees clattered nearby; the surf boomed and receded. Olga tiptoed back into the main room to peer out the front window. From there she could see the moon, high up, more than half full. It was a luminous ship, with wisps of cloud just beneath it; it looked as if it was riding moonlit surf.

She had to go outside.

To do that, to get to the door, she'd have to pass close by Mama, snoring on the couch. The door had a latch that clanked, and hinges that squeaked. Well, she hoped she could keep them quiet enough. In any case, she'd have to have an alibi—where had she heard that word?

She planned her route by eye, and then began to tiptoe past her sleeping mother. Halfway there, she had rehearsed what she would say—her alibi—if Mama awakened: I'm just going to the outhouse.

Mama jerked, mumbled, stretched with her eyes closed—Olga froze—then Mama settled back down on the couch, breathing loud and steady.

Silently, Olga opened the door. The sea wind felt like a gale whipping into the little cabin, so she quickly stepped outside and closed the door as quietly as she could.

She looked back. Good. Mama was still sleeping. She looked up and gasped. The sky was black, thickly spattered with tiny bright sparkles: stars, like our sun, a Nun had told her. The sound of the sea was huge, so clearly a living thing, inhaling with each incoming wave, breathing out with each receding one, slowly gathering power, rising to a peak and then subsiding.

Olga set off down the beach in the opposite direction from her run up it with Henry in the afternoon.

She was barefoot, the sand feeling warm under her feet. Mysterious sounds came from both the jungle behind her and the sea in front of her.

Olga sat down in the dry sand and felt the sea breeze riffling through her hair. She threw open her nightdress, unbuttoning all the buttons, and felt the cool, moist wind blow all over her. She thought about lying down, right there on the warm sand. She wouldn't tell anyone; she'd be like Sleeping Beauty.

She lay down, but instantly she felt things biting her, and whining all about her. So, she got up.

Prince Charming would have to find her some other time.

She understood, after she trudged along for a few minutes, that if she just kept moving the bugs would leave her pretty much alone, so she kept on going. Also, if she stayed on the damp down-slope of the sandy beach, the sea breeze kept the bugs away.

Here, the palms came closer to the water, almost hanging over the incoming surf as it boomed and surged up the sand. Something long and black loomed in front of her, and she stopped, wondering what it was. Then she saw; it was the broken off trunk of a palm tree; it reached nearly to the water. She stepped over it, and found herself in what felt like a little beachside room. The palm trunk must have held the sand here, because the sand curved up more steeply, and behind it was a soft, dry space that felt protected from the wind and surf.

Again she sat down; no bugs buzzed about her, even though she was surrounded by the blackness of the overhanging trees, almost blocking out the sky, and the wind was only a susurrus eddying about her; it was a wild clatter in the palm leaves above.

She lay down on her stomach, her head and neck just over the lip of the swale of sand rising from the surf. The waves were a constant, roiling thunder; she wasn't tempted to go swimming: the waves looked so much bigger in the starlight, black, menacing.

That's when she heard 'creak, creak, creak' out somewhere on the water. It sounded as if it was coming towards her, heading towards their cottage behind her!

Olga remembered the two black fishermen she'd seen in the day, but this wasn't daytime! Was someone sneaking up to attack them at night?

Where was Max? He hadn't been there when she'd snuck out of the cottage!

He had taken the carriage up the sand road, she reminded herself, and was sleeping in it. So, no one could sneak down the road to hurt them? And now, instead, they were coming by sea!

Oh, why had Uncle Benjamin done those things! He was off in New York, or someplace, too far away to help.

The creaking came closer, ominously close. Olga peered over the lip of sand, and saw—it looked like the same two men, doing the same thing: one was rowing, the other was holding something over the stern. Probably a fishing line.

That's when Olga realized: her nightgown was completely

unbuttoned; they could see all of her if she stood up. Hurriedly, she buttoned up, then stood up. She'd better start back. She had no idea how long she'd been outside.

She stepped over the log and began walking back. The wind was almost at her back, and it was a lot easier to make her way over the sand. Looking out at the sea, she was amused to see that the men in the boat were already a long way behind. Maybe the waves, or current, or something, was running the other way.

Anyway, they weren't a threat, and the waves weren't a threat as long as she stayed on land, and the sky was now wide above her, the stars so bright they felt like molten holes far above. Again, she was alone, as she approached the cottage, which she could make out from a distance as a square block of darkness, the only sharp, straight lines in sight.

When she was opposite the cottage, she decided to wait for the fishermen, just to be sure that was all they were. She'd run to warn Max if they started to beach their boat.

Slowly, so slowly, inch by excruciating inch, the rower passed by, the man in the stern pulled up what looked like a fish, glistening in the starlight, threw it flapping into the boat, and returned to tending the line, or lines, at the stern.

Olga waited until it was clear they were just going to keep on rowing north, then she got up and went inside, carefully unlatching the door as soundlessly as possible, bursting inside with the breeze, then re-latching it, again as soundlessly as possible.

When she turned around, her mother was looking at her!

"Where were you!"

Olga shrugged. "Just to the outhouse."

Mama just looked at her—and Olga sensed she was trying to stare her down, make her tell the truth. Well, she didn't want to. It was her secret.

"Just to the outhouse, but the sky is beautiful, Mama."

"You were gone when I went in to go to bed! You've been gone for, um, a long time."

They didn't have a clock. Mama had noticed that when they brought in their things. It made Olga smile inside to realize her mother really didn't know how long she'd been gone.

"Oh, Mama," she smiled, careful not to look pleased with herself, "it just seemed so long, because it was me you were missing. But I'm all right; it just took awhile. Good night."

Mama was about to say something, but stopped as Olga closed the door. She didn't follow after. Olga didn't care if her mother slept on the couch, but she was going to go sleep in her own bed.

She was almost too excited to sleep. Her mother knew she was lying, but didn't dare call her on it! And Mama was scared, still, the way Olga had been, but now she could tell herself: there were only those fishermen, and they didn't know who her family was—and didn't care.

A few moments later, her mother came in, and sat on the other bed. "Please, Olga. I know you went out on the beach; I don't know how far you went, but you have to tell me if you go out again." Her Spanish was even more Caribbean than usual.

Olga considered telling her mother the truth then, but she decided not to. It was her secret, and she was even more protective of it now, given her mother's prying.

Her shrug was world-weary. "Mama, there's beach right up to the outhouse, so of course I was on the beach when I was there. Sometimes, um," she pretended embarrassment about 'going,' "it just takes a long time—and it's not fun."

Henry sometimes looked as if he would explode when he ran to the toilet, and the stink was so strong it stank up her room two doors away: Julio's was pretty bad, too. Her own didn't stink, but that was natural.

Her mother looked embarrassed. Good. It worked. Olga was pleased with herself. She didn't let it show.

10

It was wonderful, spending all day on the beach. Mama kept within the shade of a tree, or inside, reading most of the time. She went swimming with Olga in the early morning before breakfast and told her the first day: "I see you can swim," she grinned, "like the fishes. But you must not go out far. The waves are big. And you must not go in the water when I can't see you."

"Okay, Mama."

Olga was especially gratified, because Henry couldn't swim, even though Mama tried to teach him in the early mornings, and Julio seemed to have no interest in doing anything but lying on the sand by the cottage. He was so unfriendly! To all of them. She wished her mother had let him stay in town.

After a couple of days, her mother shook her head when she saw her: "You are almost as brown as an Indio! It's not right!"

Olga shrugged. "It's all right, Mama. It's what you're supposed to do at the beach. Even the English do it."

Her mother muttered in Spanish, "They don't have to worry; they're so white, anyway!"

Olga looked around her. Doris, sitting at the table, was very white. And so was the blunt-faced man snoring in his chair at the other end of the room, although maybe not quite so pale. Was she white? Why was she asking? She had a fading vision of her mother looking anxiously at her wrist, worrying that her skin was too dark.

She got up and made her way, a little shakily, to the screen door opening out onto the patio. She could see it was sunny out there. There, she'd be by herself. And in the sun.

She sat down in the patio chair next to the wall, and felt the sun warming her skin. Yes, that's what she wanted! She closed her eyes.

"You're like a cat, Olga!"

Her eyes opened with a snap. It was her son standing in front of her, arms akimbo. He was grinning at her. His hair glistened in the sun, gold for a moment, and she glimpsed her beautiful little boy with blond ringlets—then the instant passed: his hair was gray.

She had already forgotten his comment. "How's everything?" she asked. She didn't really listen to his answer.

The carriage was rumbling along a jungle road, dwarfed by the trees; it was dark, almost like night at first, after the sunlight on the beach. Henry was sitting next to Mama; Olga was sitting facing them both, but she was more interested in what she could see outside; so was Henry, although he occasionally ran his truck along the seat. Julio, of course, had insisted on staying at the cottage.

"Do you know where we are going?" Mama asked them both.

Henry shook his head.

Olga asked, "Where are we going, Mama, and why?"

"To see a cacao plantation. And I wanted you with me, Olga, because I may need your English speaking."

"Oh!" Olga felt important.

"I speak English!" objected Henry.

"Si," agreed Mama, "but you don't understand Spanish very well. And you don't read as well, you know?" She smiled protectively at him. "But you have something important to do, too."

"Importante?"

"Si. The people there have children; you must play with them."

Henry looked to Olga to be sure he understood right. She asked, "What people, Mama?"

"The East Indian family. They run the plantation; they have children."

Henry nodded. He understood.

"How do you grow cacao, Mama?"

"There! You see, we are almost in cacao country. You see?"

Olga looked out the window. At first, it just looked the same, although maybe even greener, but then she saw. The big trees were regularly spaced apart, and beneath them were many of the same bushy trees, with shiny deep green leaves and occasional white blossoms—and then she saw her first cacao fruits; they looked like American footballs, but some were light yellow, others a little orange.

"It's the next plantation, I think," said Mama, as they trotted by a poor looking hut, with only a little girl staring out at them as they passed, frozen with fright; at least that's what it looked like. She was East Indian.

Olga could see the line dividing the two plantations. The one they were driving into had smaller cacao bushes and younger trees shading them, but it was very neat between the rows, unlike the other plantation, where the spaces between the rows just looked like more young forest.

Mama pointed. She looked excited; "The older trees we saw back there, they are too old. They produce for a few more years, but not for long. These younger trees will last longer, and they'll out-produce the older ones very soon, maybe next year. That's why I want to buy this plantation."

"Buy a plantation?" Olga stared at her as if she were crazy.

Her mother shrugged. It was a disarming gesture. "Your father sends gold coins, verdad? But sometimes they don't come, you see. There have been months.... It would be good to have an income, money that comes in even if the gold coins do not. The plantation, if the price is right, would be a good *inversión*. Do you know what an *inversión* is, Olga?"

She did know. "The English word is investment, Mama. It means something you put money into and later more money comes out; you earn money from it." She had read about investments in *Le Rouge et le Noir*.

"*Correcto!* More money if it is a good..." she searched for the English word, "investment?"

Olga nodded.

"A friend told me: this Englishman who owns it, he needs money—a gambling debt, she said. With her brother." Mama grinned. "You must say nothing of this!"

"Your friend's brother is a gambler?" Wasn't gambling a crime?

Mama half smiled, half shrugged. "It's only horse racing. They, they all gamble on horses. All," she sniffed, "the gentlemen. Not on whey whey, though. That's what the poor people play; that's illegal."

Olga was amazed. This was a whole side of Trinidad she knew nothing about: they had horse racing? Men gambled on racehorses? Poor people gambled on something else?

She was about to ask if her Uncle Benjamin gambled on the horses, when they pulled into a little compound: a hut, or small wooden house without glass in the windows, beaten earth around the house, a few chickens scratching at the ground, and an East Indian boy staring at them with eyes wide as saucers. All he wore were dirty shorts that might have been white once.

Out of the little house strolled a tall, thin Englishman with a pinched face and a sunburned nose. He wore khaki shorts and shirt, both with many pockets. Behind him was a short, dark East Indian man in dirty white Indian pants and no shirt. Behind them, Olga could see the Indian man's wife, peering out the door at them. She wore something faded and draped, probably what they called a sari.

The Englishman introduced himself as "Mister Edward Cook." Mama said "encantada. I am called Señora Heriberto Quintero."

"You can just say 'I am,'" explained Olga.

The tall, red-nosed man looked from her mother to her, and smiled. It was an unpleasant smile. Olga instantly disliked him.

When he asked, "What's your address, Señora?" and Mama told him: "Belmont Circle," his expression suddenly changed. Now, it wasn't, 'how do I deal with this woman who's not white and not British, but may have some money,' to, 'she has some money.'

It was funny, awful, and so obvious to Olga, although she was only ten, and she kept on telling herself that: I know this, and I'm only ten.

"I suppose you would like a tour of the place before we dicker?"

Mama looked to Olga to explain. Olga explained. His English was very British, clipped, but one of the nuns talked like this, so it wasn't hard to understand him. Out of the corner of her eye, she saw Henry talking to the little boy, and then they both ran off around the house after some chickens. Good.

After hearing Olga's explanation, her mother agreed, but said as well, "I already read su libros."

"Oh." Mister Cook didn't look entirely pleased at this. "Well, c'mon then. Batoo!"

Mama looked mystified by the word 'batoo,' until the East Indian stepped forward, and gestured for her to follow.

Mister Cook stayed behind, while Batoo showed Olga and her mother the extensive plantings of cacao bushes, and Batoo explained, in panyol, that these nearest bushes had been planted only last year, that the ones further on had been planted five years ago and the ones beyond them were ten years old, "Before I," he explained.

Olga was surprised to realize that her mother understood panyol as well as she did.

Batoo was about as dark as any East Indian Olga had seen. He seemed nice, soft-spoken and eager to please—unlike Mister Cook, who sneered, no matter what he was saying.

The brief tour over, they found Mister Cook sitting back on a wooden chair in the shade of the hut; he was smoking. Seeing her, he stood up, and threw the burning cigarette on the ground and stepped on it.

"D'ya like it? Meet y'r expectations?"

Olga translated and her mother said in Spanish, "Tell him it looks like good land, and his asking price is almost reasonable. Tell him I'll buy it for one thousand pounds."

"Mama!" Olga didn't know anybody who had that much money.

"Don't worry, Little One. I know what I'm doing. You just tell him." She grinned slyly, and added, "It's more than his gambling debt." She looked very certain of herself, and Olga remembered her mother talking about how her family was all business people: they owned pearl fisheries in Coché, and stores in Margarita.

Mr. Cook nodded when Olga told him what her mother had told her to say. "Well, that'll take care of the mortgage, and the lien," he said, ruminatively, "and, hmmm." He stroked his chin and looked her mother in the eye. He must have seen her confidence, and her determination, because his sneer disappeared. "Well, of course I'll have to check your bona fides, and I'll want half of it down."

"Tell him we must together sign an agreement and I have the money with me."

"Five hundred pounds, Mama?"

"Si. I told you. I know what I'm doing."

Olga was amazed, but she told Mr. Cook what her mother told her to say.

"An agreement? Yes, I have a preliminary agreement right here," he produced a sheaf of papers with stamps on them, seemingly from nowhere. "She has the money?"

Mama held up a bag of coins and shook it; it jingled. Olga knew they were gold coins.

Despite himself, Mr. Cook grinned broadly as he saw and heard the money. "Well, well! We shall sign, then. Would you like to read the agreement, first?"

"Si. Voy estudiar lo ahora." She turned to Olga. "You will help me? I can read a little English, business English, but...."

Together they read the document. Olga didn't understand a lot of the terms, but she knew the Spanish words for them, somehow. Her mother scrutinized it, thought about it for a moment, then nodded to Mr. Cook.

"Is good. I sign. And give? dinero to you?"

Olga looked at Mister Cook to see if he understood. He was nodding.

"Bi-yen," said Mister Cook, attempting Spanish. He called to Batoo. "Here, Batoo, you ought to sign as witness, all right?"

Batoo came over from the house and stood there, looking a little worried. "Yes, Mister Cook, I sign, but in devanagari only."

Mister Cook shrugged. "Courts accept it, I've heard." He looked at Mama. "It's all right with you?"

Olga explained.

Her mother nodded. "Is okay." She commented to Olga, "I've seen Hindu writing in some of the land documents, already."

Mama handed the bag of gold coins to Mister Cook to examine, saying: "Is fi' hunderd."

He opened the bag, poured out the coins on a little table, scrutinized them, counting them with his forefinger, then smiled broadly. He nodded. "Looks like it to me. All right."

So, finally, they signed, all three of them. Then Mr. Cook shook Mama's hand, and turned to Olga. He was smiling now, without the sneer.

"Well, young lady, you'll go far. Translating for your mother like that. And you said you live on Belmont Circle? Nice place, that. Seen any of the new automobiles there, yet?"

Olga shook her head. "I've read about them."

Mr. Cook looked over at her mother, who was talking with Batoo, and said, "Well, I wouldn't be surprised if she gets one of the first. Anyway, I'm going back to P of S day after tomorrow. Anything you'd like me to take there?"

Olga had a stroke of genius. "I think so. My older brother wants to get back there. Do you think you could take him?"

Julio had been like a hot damp rag to all of them, the way he moped around all day. Olga didn't know if her mother would let him go, but she hoped so. She knew that's where Julio wanted to be: with his friends.

"I'd be delighted. How long did it take you to get here?"

"Maybe two hours." It had seemed forever—so much same greenness and heat—but it must have been less than two hours, because the Englishman's watch had said eight when they arrived, and they had left shortly after sunrise, which was always at six.

"Well, if he could get here by eight or so, that would be fine. I'll wait until a bit after eight, but no later. It gets beastly hot in the interior, and the earlier we start, the less of it we'll have to endure." He looked at her then, noticing again, as he probably had when they arrived, before he'd learned where they lived, that they weren't exactly white, like him. "I don't suppose it bothers you as much, the heat, I mean. It doesn't bother Batoo, at all, but then Indians, you know...."

Olga had never thought about the heat, but she was not going to admit it, not to this white man. "It does get hot up there. If he comes, Mama will make sure he's here on time."

"Excellent. Well, glad to do business with you—and your mother—young lady!"

At that moment, Henry and the Indian boy came running around the house, and Mama called to him.

In a few minutes more, they were climbing into the carriage. Mama clutched a carbon copy of the Agreement, and Henry dusted himself off. Mama thanked him for playing so nicely with the little boy, and then turned to Olga.

"Well, Olga, you really helped! As translator. And now your

mother is a businesswoman. You will see. This," she held up the carbon copy, "will be a good investment. Investment in land always is."

Olga woke up; it was the common room. There were the usual people there. The care person was bringing in some food to the table. She knew something would happen after that, but she didn't remember and figured she'd just find out.

Then she heard her mother's voice, 'investment in land always is.' Always is what, she wondered. Oh!

A vision of Olga's lake came to her then. It had been her idea, and it looked as if it had always been there. And so peaceful.

"It's so beautiful here!"

People, (many) had even said, "it has such a wonderful feeling."

She made that.

For just an instant, she remembered, remembered the school she had run, the children in the classroom, the women working in the kitchen, and above all the early morning meetings. She smiled to see the children in front of her, looking up to her, shiny in the morning, looking up, even though she was so small; her teachers, they followed her lead, the day began....

Then, the memory faded. The care person was putting their plates on the table. It was time to get up. Time to eat; she liked to eat. She was hungry.

Mama hadn't liked the idea, not at first. But when they pulled into the sandy clearing by their beach house and she saw Julio's unfriendly grimace, she turned to Olga and said, "Maybe is good idea."

Faced with a chance to go back to "P of S," Julio was even willing to get up before sunup, eager, in fact. He and Max set off long before sunrise, just to be sure.

Oh, it was so wonderful not having him there! She lost track of the days. One wonderful day on the beach, and wandering up and down it, even for miles, merged into another and another. And she went out at night, too, just telling her mother that she probably would, but she wouldn't go into the water.

One day they took the little boat that Max used for fishing, and went "to see a friend," her mother explained. He rowed them up the coast towards a small island Olga had seen in the distance when she had gone her farthest up the beach.

"Her family owns it, you see," explained her mother as they approached.

"Does she have any children I can play with?" Henry asked.

Mama shook her head. "But you can play in sand, and in water. Hay no ondas..." She looked to Olga for help.

"Waves, Mama."

"Si. No waves."

Olga could see palm trees fringing a sunny beach in calm water. No waves. The island on this side was sheltered from the ocean, but the offshore breeze ruffled the palms. She could see the roof of a small house beneath the trees. Pretty. As they came within the lee of the island, the wind dropped, and the quiet, you could feel it.

At their cottage, the breeze and waves were always loud. Olga hadn't realized it until that moment.

A tall, light-haired woman was standing on the beach waving to them.

"Se llama Gloria," Mama told them.

Mama and Gloria sat on chaises; they drank from funny-looking glasses, with rims of crystals, "Salt," her mother explained. Olga wasn't thirsty, at first: she had been swimming, so much easier than in the waves.

When she got out, she could see the change in her mother, and in Gloria. Before, they had been sitting, backs almost straight, feet on the ground. Now, they lay back, their legs askew, no, apart, the way she and Miriam and the nuns all said no Lady should sit, the way Mama had told her over and over when she was little: "Don't sit like that! Keep your legs together! That's how Ladies sit."

She knew they'd had two drinks, because they dropped the used ones on the sand, and they were almost finished with the ones in their hands.

"She's so cute, Ana!"

She thought she was whispering, Olga realized, so she just smiled as if she hadn't heard. She wondered what they were drinking, and if it would feel even better than the wine they had had that time at dinner.

"Please. Is there something for me to drink, Gloria? After the salt water, I'm really thirsty."

Gloria grinned, as if she had just thought of something funny, then she pointed up into the palms. "I'm told the coconut milk here is some of the best in Trinidad. Would you like to try it? We do have other things: the mix for these drinks—my cook made it—and, I think I even have some Trinidad Cola—"

Olga looked. There was a green cluster of coconuts, up, just under the leafy crown of the tree; it was twice as tall as the cottage. "But how do you get one?"

"Didn't you say his name was Max?" Gloria asked her mother. Mama nodded, "Si," looking a little confused.

"Oh, Max!" called Gloria, simpering at her mother, and then at her.

"Yes, Señora?" Max came lumbering up.

"Olga wants a coconut from that tree, do you think you could get it for her?"

Olga had never seen someone do this before, but she'd read about it, how Gloria used her mouth and eyes, face, shoulders— yes, Olga noted the artful movement of Gloria's shoulders—to get a man to do what she wanted.

Max's grin was as wide as the beach. "'Course I can, Señora!" He flashed the wide grin at her, too, but with a difference; he'd walked her to school. Now, it was as if he saw her, but she didn't know what he saw. Then, he ran for the tree, and started almost running up it!

Gloria and Mama were both watching him, Gloria with a strange little grin, Mama, well, Mama caught Gloria's eye, and Gloria said, "Don't you ever think about getting a little of that? I mean look at his," she realized Olga was close enough to hear her, hesitated, and whispered, "uh, adorable little...how it shakes as he goes up that tree! I mean, black is good, believe—"

Mama giggled, and then gasped as she caught sight of Olga standing there, right next to them. "Don't talk about things like that, Gloria! Not, not with," she indicated Olga's direction with just her eyes and eyebrows.

Olga turned away. Max was at the top of the tree. He was breaking off a coconut; he threw it down, and then another. And almost flew down the trunk.

They were being like that because of what they were drinking? She didn't care. When she was older, she'd drink it, too. But Max had climbed for her. He sliced off the top of the first coconut with a machete, sniffed at it, then handed it to her with the widest grin she'd ever seen. "Here y'ar, Señorita!"

It was cool, only slightly sweet; just right. She smiled up at Max, and said "Thank you!"

He looked even taller; it wasn't just his grin.

Olga drank a little more, thanked him again, and asked—anyone—"will it stay cool if I leave it in the shade until I come back from swimming?"

Max glanced at Gloria, and then nodded. "You c'n leave it under de table. Is cool there."

He was nice.

Olga wandered back to the beach, then waded way out—it was very shallow. Henry was in the water; it was safe enough even for him, but he wasn't swimming; he was staring down into the water, watching a school of tiny fish. They darted away when she came near, and he looked up, with a strange grin.

"Gonna catch some."

Olga shrugged, trying to mimic the voluptuous gesture, she'd seen Gloria make before. "Go ahead." She didn't ask what he would do with them; they'd die even in a jar of water before they got back; it had happened before. Things he caught were always dying on their way to the house, or later, in his room.

She didn't much care. "I'm going swimming."

The water was warm and calm; it rolled in with little lines of foam, but with hardly any waves. Olga watched it for a while, then looked back at her mother, and began to swim farther out.

"No, Olga!" Her mother was standing, shouting; she looked alarmed.

Olga treaded water, and thought about calling back that it wasn't dangerous, when she heard Gloria saying, "It's all right, Ana. She's a good swimmer, but it's also very shallow, and very calm. Look at it!"

Her mother asked Gloria something, and then waved to her, "Is all right. Just be careful."

Olga waved back, and turned to swim further out. She wanted to swim out far enough to see beyond the curve of the little island, but before she got that far, she heard a regular clicking in the water every time she put her head into it. That's strange, she thought: what could that be? Then, looking off to the north, she saw it: the boat with the two black men; the clicking must be the oars; one of them was rowing. They were coming down the coast towards the island.

Then she remembered seeing the line with hundreds of hooks, following behind the little boat. She didn't want to be caught by one of those hooks!

She started swimming in as fast as she could. The boat came nearer. As she raised her head out of the water before the next stroke, she saw her mother rising from her chaise. She raised her hand; she was alarmed. No, she looked terrified!

"It's okay, Mama!" Olga shouted, "They—"

"NO!" Mama was shouting at the rowboat, not at her. "Basta!"

Olga kept on swimming towards the beach. When she looked again, Mama's friend, Gloria, had a restraining hand on Mama's shoulder, and was saying something, but it was too far away to hear.

Olga looked back at the rowboat: it was headed away from the island now. She glimpsed the face of the black man rowing; he looked scared!

When Olga came out of the water, and went up to get her coconut near her mother and Gloria, Gloria was saying, "It's okay, Ana! They are just fishermen. I see them almost every day. And they know not to come in too close when people are swimming."

Mama was collapsed on the chaise; she looked terrible. "Are you sure, Gloria?"

"Of course I'm sure. They know not to hurt people with their hooks. Sometimes, they sell us fish, too."

Gloria didn't know what Mama was afraid of. Olga did, but she didn't say anything. She was pretty sure, now; they were safe out here.

As she sipped on her coconut, she thought, but we won't know if we'll be safe when we get back in town. She hated feeling scared of every shadow, of every strange man's face. Then she looked over at Max. He was standing, his huge arms akimbo, staring after the fishermen. It was hard to tell what his expression meant. Was he confused? He looked puzzled as he surveyed Mama. He, too, knew the fishermen weren't dangerous. But he'd protect them if someone threatened.

He glanced at Olga: bright white teeth and smiling eyes, dark face. Olga nodded, smiling back. He looked pleased.

He thought she was pretty. Miriam had told her Mama was pretty; no one had ever told her she was.

She wasn't sure what to do about it, but she couldn't help smiling, and thinking, I'm pretty. Maybe someday I'll be beautiful.

Olga smiled as she awoke from—wherever she had been. Of course, she was beautiful. Had she ever thought she wasn't? She didn't remember. She looked around the room: the other residents were sleeping in their armchairs. The blunt-faced man—what was his name?—looked as if he'd poured himself into his chair, his mouth open—her mouth was very dry.

It was sunny outside, so Olga got up from her chair—not easy, but she could do it herself: she grabbed hold of her walker and headed towards the glass panel door leading out onto the patio. She slid it open, maneuvered her walker over the door track and then stepped outside. It was nice and warm in the sun. She reached a chair on the sunny side and sat down. The warmth of the sun seeped through her chilled bones and she closed her eyes with pleasure. Now, she was warm.

Henry was building a sandcastle at the high water mark, and Mama was lying on a chaise under some palm tree. Max was lumbering down the beach to her mother. Something was up, but Olga decided she wanted to go swimming, anyway. The waves were small today, the water not as cold as usual.

As soon as Olga jumped through a wave and looked back, she could see her mother waving for them to join her. Yes, something was up. Reluctantly she got out of the water. When she told Henry that Mama wanted them, he made a face, and got up from his sandcastle.

Olga pretty much knew what it was: they had to go home. It was about that time, but she wished it wasn't. She wouldn't say anything to Henry.

They stood before Mama, who was now sitting up on the chaise, as if, thought Olga, it was a throne.

"Now, Olgita, Henrito, we have to go home—tomorrow. We start early and—"

"No!" wailed Henry. "I don't wanna! I wanna stay here! I won't, I won't, I won't!" He tried stamping in the sand, but that didn't make any noise, so he began to howl.

Mama looked at Olga.

Olga looked at Mama and shook her head. "I don't want to go home, either, Mama, but I know we have to."

And it wasn't just that she loved the beach, and loved the water and the wind in the palms. It was that they were safe here. Even Mama had finally understood that. Olga didn't say anything about it, but she knew, and knew her mother knew, too: they wouldn't be safe when they went back to Port of Spain. People, Uncle Benjamin and Mama called them "bad people," might know what he was doing to what he called the *subversivos*. Now, Olga could see, from the benefit of distance: it made a horrible sense for them to fight back, and if they couldn't get at their uncle, why not get at him through Mama, or her, or Henry? Why Julio could go everywhere without her mother worrying, she couldn't figure out, unless his friends were connected with one side or the other. Maybe they protected him.

Olga decided it was time to say something, as Henry wound down to sobbing, and collapsing on the sand.

"Mama, it's been wonderful here. It's not only beautiful, it's also safe—from you know who."

"Oh, Olga! Yes!" she sighed, "I know. But we have to go back. I have business and things I have to attend to. You both have school to go to—"

At the mention of school, Henry began to wail again, but he couldn't keep it up for long; he had already worn himself out.

Mama pointed at Max, and whispered to Olga: "He'll keep you safe. Don't worry."

It was the first time her mother had admitted that there was a problem. Maybe, thought Olga, she'd stop doing what Uncle Benjamin told her.

"Now, it's time for lunch," Mama announced.

Henry stopped sniveling, stood up, and actually ran to the cottage.

Olga examined this idea, Mama not doing what Benjamin asked her to do, as they made their way to the cottage for lunch. She shook her head. Mama would do whatever Uncle Benjamin said.

It was up to *her* to change things.

But she was just a girl!

12

This time they started before the sun was up. All three of them had gone down to the water in the semi-darkness; Olga and Henry ran. Mama walked. They all three went swimming—well, Henry got all wet, at least. He could manage a dog paddle for a few feet. Olga was shivering from the cold when she got out, but she didn't mind. She dived through a few waves, swam between the troughs, and actually rode a wave part of the way into the beach.

Mama was waving for her to get out. Well, it was time. And the wave that had borne her inland was a nice goodbye. She was still a little cold, and relishing it, when she climbed into the carriage a few minutes later; they were going to eat arepas Cook had prepared for them once they got underway.

It was hot in Port of Spain, and busy. When they got home, the servants were running about madly uncovering furniture from the dust covers, and scrubbing the floors. They hadn't expected them this early in the day.

Mama was mildly annoyed and she showed it.

"Clean mi camera, my room, immedia'ly! Why casa no lista?"

"Rapido," she snarled as Rebecca slowly pulled Henry's trunk behind her.

The servants' eyes showed their fear, the whites showing; their shrinking shoulders did, too.

Olga hadn't seen Mama like this for a long time. She was glad it wasn't directed at her. Miriam knew not to get in Mama's way.

Olga went to her room; it was nice to be back here, she thought. Her room was dark, and cooler than it was outside. Miriam started putting her things away, but Olga could feel impatience rising in her as she watched. "Not that way, Miriam! Just hang up the two dresses and fold the other things for the drawers." She didn't have that much to put away. She wanted to be alone.

"All right Miss Grown-up!" muttered Miriam. Then she looked at her and exclaimed, "You almost as dark as me!"

Olga shrugged, watched her for a few minutes, but she felt all cooped up in the little dark room, even if it was cool. "I'm going out to the garden," she announced.

She tried sitting on a bench and reading the nun's book with the screaming cover; it didn't interest her after a few minutes, but being inside, after being outside for so much of every day at the beach, had felt too confining.

Up towards the back of the garden, Olga glimpsed Blaine in the shadows; he was doing something, probably digging for treasure. Just for fun, she decided to sneak up on him. She didn't know what she'd do when she got there, but just sneaking up on him was something to do.

She was about halfway there, when a leaf crunched under her foot. Blaine stopped what he was doing and looked around, but Olga had crouched behind a large bush. She'd have to be even more careful.

When Blaine resumed digging—it looked as if he was digging for treasure, all right—Olga tiptoed to the next tree trunk and then to the next, being careful to avoid stepping on dried leaves or twigs.

It took her about half an hour to sneak up, all the way to the back, but then she got careless and stepped on a little twig; it made a loud crack!

Blaine jumped. He whirled to face his attacker, eyes wide, shovel ready to swing!

"Oh, it you, Miss!" He wilted with relief; Olga was about to laugh, when he went on: "Thought it was those people, the ones kep' asking, "Where Missus Quintero? Where she gone? It important!" I don't like the look of 'em, so I don't tell 'em nothing."

"Oh!" It was her turn to be startled. Then, she tried to ask, as if it didn't really matter, "People were asking where Mama was?" Olga felt something familiar and she didn't like it: having to be careful what she said, or what her face said. She had forgotten what this felt like at the beach.

Blaine nodded, ponderously. "Different people, but Blaine don't trust none of 'em."

"Were they...East Indians?" Olga asked: she didn't want to ask directly what she knew he would tell her.

"Oh, no! You people, you know, from 'cross the water." He gestured vaguely towards the south.

Her people. Venezuelans: worse and worse.

"But they didn't come through back here, did they?"

"Oh no, no! They come to street—'cept I see one of 'em back in the jungle there." He gestured towards the abandoned house in back.

"One of the same men?"

Blaine squinted at the patch of pink wall they could see in the distance, through the overgrown foliage. Olga looked, too. It was pretty far. He shook his head. "Don't know."

Olga was about to tell Blaine he should tell Mama about this, but then she stopped herself. She should tell her. Mama could call Blaine if she wanted to, but Olga didn't think it would do any good to get him more worried than he was already.

She hated this!

Olga awoke with her fists clenched and her toes tapping the floor. She could sense the anger fading from her as she opened her eyes. She looked up from her chair. Doris was sitting at the table, reading from a stack of books. The blunt-faced man was sprawled on his chair at the end of the table, his mouth open and his eyes shut.

Here again. It was daylight outside—

Her son, looking straight into her eyes. Gray-haired. He looked so much like...her husband? Julian. Where was Julian—oh. He died a long time ago. Olga remembered, like a cloud floating by, Julian being loaded onto a stretcher.

Once he was settled, an aide asked him, "How do you feel?"

"Dead," he answered. A tight grin barely curved his thin lips. His last joke.

Her son was now smiling at her. "Hel-lo!" she said. She could hear herself, the charm in her voice, still there, from long practice. Had he said something?

"...came to visit. How are you today?"

"So's to be about." She smiled. She liked to say that.

"Do they say that in Trinidad?"

She shrugged. "I don't know." She didn't want to talk about that. "How's everything with you?"

"Oh, I'm fine. And we just heard from Julian..."

For just an instant, Olga was confused. Then, she remembered: the little boy, the beautiful young man, not her Julian. Her grandson?

She didn't close her eyes, but she was no longer there. She was looking into her Julian's eyes, hot, blue, above her, the dark outlines of the log cabin walls behind him. She wanted him so much! She felt his hands on her breasts.... Oh, Julian!

It was so long ago.

What was he saying? Douglas. Her son. Good looking, just like her, and Julian. People had said he looked like both of them. He was gray-haired. "How old are you, now?"

He smiled at her. "Seventy-one."

"Good Lord! How old am I, then? I must be ninety something?"

He nodded, still smiling, "You're ninety-seven."

She was surprised. She still thought of herself as eleven—or was it thirteen?

Yes, she was eleven, thought Olga, as she and Max walked to school. But she'd have to do something.

When she'd told Mama about what Blaine said, Mama had looked as if she was in pain for just an instant. Then her face slackened, quieted; she said, "I'm sorry, Olga," her voice flat. Her eyes were, too. Then, she just turned away.

Olga was stymied. She wasn't used to being stymied.

She'd have to do something. But what?

Magdalena waving at her, waiting for her to catch up! Olga could feel her inner smile, even before she shouted, "Mags!"

A few blocks before school, it was all three of them, and they both wanted to hear about the beach, and Mags wanted to tell her about the party she missed, and Antoinetta told her about a book she'd read and then asked her if she still had that book, "that the Sister...."

They were still laughing about that when they arrived at school, just in time for Sister Chalfont to come out and ring the bell.

As Olga was going from History to English, she heard her voice saying: 'So far, so good.' She looked around, but there was no one near her who could have said that. And it was her voice. But she hadn't said it. Then she understood.

She'd have to do something.

"Time to get ready for bed, Olga."

"I'm not tired." She still had something to do, although she wasn't sure what.

"Well, I'm tired," said the caregiver. "Besides, it's time for bed, so everyone has to go to bed. Would you like me to help you in the bathroom?"

"I don't have to go."

"Ladies," said the caregiver, "go to the bathroom before they retire for the night."

She was the woman, Olga realized, who ran things. And Olga was a Lady. She smiled graciously at the woman: "I guess I should go."

When she lay down in her bed, tucked in, she closed her eyes—what had happened? She knew her memory wasn't what it used to be; it was like a fine lace, with gaping holes.

She glanced about her. She was spread over a bench in the garden, a schoolbook on British history perched precariously on her lap. She was eleven.

"Benjamin is back!"

Mama's face was rosy with excitement; she had kept out of the sun, Olga could see; her face and arms were hardly tanned. They must have been back more than a week.

"We'll have a fine dinner for him, tonight, and he says he has a surprise for me!"

Olga smiled at her mother, and said, "Oh, good!" but that wasn't how she felt. Her uncle was the reason they had to worry about "bad people," like the ones Blaine had told her about. Her uncle's hunt for *subversivos* was the reason she and Henry couldn't just go out riding on their bicycles, anymore. And if there were more people dying, her friends would be afraid of her again.

She had to do something. But what?

Olga was still pondering that question—when she wasn't reading about Henry the Eighth—as the shadows grew long; she knew from her stomach that dinner would be soon. She could smell meat roasting, and could hear the clatter of pots and pans in the kitchen.

Then she heard something else, out on the road. At first, it sounded like someone coughing, but in rhythm. Then it sounded almost like explosions, and it was getting louder. Olga couldn't resist her curiosity any longer. She got up and went to the front of the yard, overlooking the road.

That's when she saw it: a funny-looking thing, like a carriage with a long nose, and without a horse. Then she realized: it was one of those new automobiles. It was rolling down the road, blue smoke coming out the rear. Olga recognized the two people in it: Martin, dwarfing the seat; he was holding what looked like a wheel in front of him; next to him, in a long white coat and goggles, was her uncle. He was waving at her.

She waved back, as the automobile stopped.

In another moment, her mother was standing beside her, then rushing down to the automobile as Uncle Benjamin dismounted.

"Oh, Benjamin! It's very noisy! Does it go very fast?"

Her uncle grinned. "Very fast. They are all over New York City and you should see how fast they go!"

"I'm so glad you're back, I," Mama looked awkward as she glanced from Olga's uncle to her and back again, "um, I'll call you, Olga, when dinner is ready. You should go get dressed. And, oh, there's Henry!" He came running out from the passageway in back, his mouth open as he took in the automobile. "I don't know where Julio is."

Olga understood. Mama wanted to be alone with her uncle.

But her uncle shook his head. "I want to show you—all of you— tu automóvil nuevo."

"Mine?"

"Of course! It's a gift, Ana, for services rendered—to the State, to El Presidente. I have one, too. Larger, with the state insignia, of course."

"But, but, who will drive—"

It was beautiful, shiny, all black, but something about it nagged at Olga. "Services rendered:" She knew what that meant.

"Oh, not a problem!" Her uncle was expansive. "Martin, here, can teach Max in no time. Now, look. Leather seats, fine walnut dashboard, even a large trunk for carrying all your clothes when you go to the beach." He grinned at Henry, who was tentatively approaching it. "You'd probably fit in that trunk, Nephew, but I bet you'd like to drive it, instead!"

"Can I?" Henry's eyes were huge as he looked up at his uncle and then at the automobile.

It was very impressive. Olga had to admit that. But she didn't like what it meant.

Her uncle smiled down at him, pleased. "Well, no, I don't think so, Little Man. Not yet. When you get older, perhaps: only grown-ups can drive it, you see."

Henry looked momentarily deflated. Olga hoped that Julio wasn't a "grown-up." If he could drive it and they couldn't, he'd be insufferable.

Henry got over his disappointment almost instantly. He walked up to the automobile, walked around it, squatted down to peer underneath, and then, finally, very gingerly patted what Olga knew was the hood, although she'd never seen one before. His grin was as broad as his face.

Olga both hoped she'd get to ride in it, and wished Uncle Benjamin hadn't bought it: "for services rendered." It wasn't for what Mama had done with him on the floor of the sitting room. It was for services to El Presidente—and for more of them.

It was just going to get worse. They were going to have to be afraid of everyone, or at least, anyone who wasn't one of theirs! They wouldn't be allowed to go anywhere! Would she even be allowed to go to school?

Olga nodded to herself as she looked at the automobile. They'd want her to spy on her friends, so they'd let her go, but she wouldn't... spy for them.

Were Magdalena and Antoinetta rebels, too?

She didn't know, and she didn't want to know, or care. Maybe, revolutionaries weren't so different, after all—even if they did kill people; so did Uncle Benjamin: she knew about that. Most people didn't know, but she did. That probably meant El Presidente did, too.

She wanted to be free, the way she felt on the beach. The automobile felt like a heavy chain weighing her down.

Olga flicked her toes at the machine, but no one noticed; she was very aware of her canvas shoes. Sand shoes or plimsols. They called them that in England, a man told her. He was the father of one of the younger girls.

Olga turned away. "Excuse me, Uncle," she explained, "but Mama said we have to change for dinner."

Uncle Benjamin almost bowed to her. "Of course, my lovely niece! And you will be even more beautiful, I'm sure."

She couldn't help liking him; he was very nice.

As Olga turned away, she frowned to herself. How could somebody be so nice to her, to her brothers, to her mother—well, she knew about that, of course—and still be hunting down *subversivos*, and making Mama do it, too? His people, people like the huge Martin, they were doing those awful things to them: drowning them, hanging them—maybe the police said those people committed suicide, but she knew better.

Her uncle was so nice to her at dinner, and dinner was so good, and she had un poco wine, and Dominic looked so elegant in a new uniform Mama must have bought for him, that she almost forgot about the *subversivos*, until Uncle Benjamin raised a glass after dinner: "To El Presidente! And may we confound all his enemies."

Olga looked at her wine glass. It was empty. She didn't care about confounding El Presidente's enemies, but it was a good excuse to get more wine. She held up her empty glass and nodded at Dominic. He had just filled her mother's, so he nodded back, and poured some in hers, as well. Julio was already holding up his glass, and Dominic filled it, too.

Henry was unaware of what was happening; his chin glistened with oil from the rich posole, and he must have been playing with the new toy auto their uncle had given him, because his eyes were on his lap, under the table.

Olga glanced at Julio and was surprised. He was nodding enthusiastically. Did Julio actually know what their uncle was talking about? Maybe, he wanted to go out and fight? She wished he would—somewhere else. He had been muttering "negrito, negrito" at Henry since they sat down, and had made a nasty face at her.

Uncle Benjamin drank down his wine with a flourish, and then laughed. Olga drank hers down, too, and felt a warm, fuzzy tingling. She thought, maybe it's not so bad, hunting down *subversivos*. Maybe, it's important. No, maybe it's just silly. No, it's not just silly: her friends would be afraid of her again.

But how could she stop him? Or, at least, stop Mama?

A picture of skyscrapers rose before her, but Olga wasn't sure where she was, only that she knew it was the New York City skyline. When she looked around her at the sunny porch, she thought, Oh, I'm here, am I?

She was on the little porch, in the sun, on the other side of the glass door. She could see her friend, Doris, inside, sitting at the common table, reading, as always. It was nice and warm in the sun. She closed her eyes and soaked in the warmth; she was always so cold.

Still, despite the warmth, there was something bothering her. Was it in that other place, where she went so often? How?

She closed her eyes.

13

She didn't know what to do! She had so wanted to ride in the automobile, and her uncle had insisted he would take her to school in it. He said, "It'll impress all your friends."

She wanted to impress her friends, but she cringed inside, long before she climbed up the step to get into this 'automobile.' She couldn't talk about it with her uncle, or her mother. There wasn't anyone she could talk to! She couldn't very well refuse to go in it, without saying why. What made it harder: she did want to ride in it, but she was afraid her friends and schoolmates would again be afraid of her, if they saw her arrive in the automobile with her uncle, the Consul.

So, of course, here she was, Uncle Benjamin at the wheel, putt-putting down the shady road to school. When she saw Magdalena and then Elizavieta, she waved. How could she not? They looked astonished. Then, tentatively, both of them waved back.

Olga felt proud, but the other thing nagged at her, too. One instant, she wished she could hide, the next she enjoyed being seen, admired. Those eyes on her felt like the sun; they warmed her. She preened.

Olga opened her eyes and again saw the little patio, outside the sliding glass door. The sun was strong in her face; she felt warm all over, so she closed her eyes again.

Now, she was riding in the back seat of a shiny white convertible, people lined the street, waving to her! She waved back. This was wonderful! It was the little town, where everyone knew her, her little town, where everyone loved her—even the silly Republican former Town Supervisor, standing below the podium as her chariot passed by. Even he waved. What was his name?

Olga opened her eyes: the patio. Oh. Now, where was she? She closed her eyes again.

Arriving at the school happened so quickly. The automobile certainly went fast! And everyone, everyone, saw her step down from it, handed down by her ever-courtly uncle. She reveled in the attention, everyone's eyes focused on her, and for just that moment, that's all she felt. She even had an impulse to pose, like the movie stars on the posters, but she resisted it.

Then Magdalena came rushing up to her. "Wow, Olga! That's so swell! Is he the Consul?"

Olga nodded, suddenly back on earth, feeling wary.

Elizavieta and Antoinetta crowded up to her. Antoinetta asked, "Is that his automobile?"

She shook her head. "It's my mother's. He has an even bigger one." Her friends looked suitably impressed. She was about to add that his had an official crest on it, but thought better of it; it could remind them: they had all been afraid of him.

Just then, Olga glimpsed the suspicious glances of some of the upper class girls.

They remembered.

Olga shrugged defiantly at them and turned back to her friends. They were loyal, as well they should be. She was Princess Olga.

Olga turned to the care person, who was telling her to come in from the patio: it was time for lunch. She was Princess Olga. "And what if I don't want to go in?"

The care person shrugged. "I guess you'll miss lunch, but Ladies come in to lunch when asked."

Well, she was a Lady: Princess Olga. She also realized she was thirsty. "All right," she told the care person, heaving herself up from her chair and grabbing her walker, "I'll come in."

Of course, she raised her hand in History, when Sister Marie asked if anyone knew when Queen Victoria was crowned. Antoinetta tentatively raised her hand after Olga, so Sister Marie nodded to Olga, who said proudly, "Queen Victoria was crowned in 1837, when she was just eighteen, and—"

"Thank you, Olga. Yes, and from which King did she succeed? Anyone?"

Again, Olga held up her hand: she knew! Antoinetta shook her head, and the other girls searched their books.

"Yes, Olga."

"William the Fourth. He was the oldest English King to be crowned, and he had ten children with a woman he didn't marry—"

"That's enough, Olga. You may sit down."

Magdalena and the other girls tittered. Sister Marie's face reddened, but the curve of a smile teased at the corner of her mouth. She was younger than the other nuns, and she might have been pretty.

"And," added Olga as she sat down, "two with the woman he did marry, but they didn't live long. That's why Victoria, his niece, became queen." Olga grinned at her classmates.

"Why, yes, Olga, that is precisely why Victoria became queen!" Sister Marie was impressed.

Her next class was English literature; she had just read the whole of Dickens' *Tale of Two Cities* and she wanted to know more about the French Revolution; it sounded so exciting. Not that she'd like the guillotine, at all. But if revolutionaries did things

126

like that—well, she was a princess. She was not one of those nasty Jacques, or Jacquies.

Sister Isobel smiled at her as she arrived a few minutes early for class. "Well, Miss Quintero, you look as if you have read the whole *Tale*."

"Oh, yes, Sister! I couldn't stop reading!"

"I won't ask you about it until—ah, here are your classmates."

Magdalena looked sidewise at her as if to say, 'Buttering up the Sister, Olga?' Then she made a mock funny face at her.

Antoinetta looked a little surprised to see her. "Oh, there you are! Was wondering where you'd got to. Did you get through that Dickens book?" She made a face, and then realized the Sister could see her, so her face closed, she shrugged her shoulders, and her dark eyebrows made those wonderful arches that only Antoinetta could do.

Olga nodded to the question and then grinned, "I liked it."

"I liked Le Rouge et le Noir better," said Antoinetta, playing at being superior. "You didn't like the revolutionaries, did you?"

Olga could do her one better: "Course not! I'm Princess Olga, after all."

"All right, young ladies! Sit and be quiet—or I'll have to thrash the lot of you!" She looked angry, her English skin turning red, but Olga knew the Sister was only acting.

Everyone sat. She smiled attentively at Sister Isobel.

Sister Isobel almost winked at her!

"Now. I heard one of you ladies asking about 'the Dickens book,' so, Miss Hernandez, did you 'get through it?' What did you think of it?"

Antoinetta looked as if she was trapped, her eyes darting to the corners of the room. Then she looked straight into the Sister's eyes and said, "I didn't like it. The revolutionaries were horrible, but the French weren't like that in the Stendhal...."

The Sister smiled, and then turned to Olga. "And you liked it? You liked the revolutionaries?"

"Of course I didn't like the Jacques, or especially Madame Dufarge, but I liked the rest of the people in the story. Especially, Sidney Carton."

"Really!" exclaimed the now excited Sister Isobel. She was flushed. "Tell me, anyone, why is Sidney Carton special?"

"'Cause he looks just like Darnay," said Magdalena, without much interest.

Olga knew by that, that Magdalena hadn't read beyond the second book. Sister Isobel probably did, too. Poor Mags. She raised her hand.

"Yes, Olga." Sister Isobel glowed at her.

"Because he does a beautiful thing, in the end. He goes to the guillotine so Charles Darnay can escape with Lucie. So, all his mistakes are cancelled out at the end, and he dies happy."

The Sister nodded, her eyes almost sparkled. "And, and who else did something like this, class?"

Olga gave Mags a look, and mouthed 'Jesus.'

Magdalena, nodded, and held up her hand. "It was Our Lord, Sister."

Sister Isobel was almost beside herself. "Yes!"

As class was ending, she announced, "Now the rest of you, who haven't read *A Tale of Two Cities*," she stared especially at Antoinetta and the two silent girls in the back, Arabella and Priscila, "there will be a test on it next Monday."

"Boy! I stepped into that one!" remarked Antoinetta as they left.

Mags gave a short laugh. "Thanks, Olga! You saved me. Now, I guess I better read the rest of it!"

Life was good again; even, Olga decided, if those upper-form girls looked cross-eyed at her. She didn't care about them! She certainly wasn't afraid of them. They wanted her to be afraid. Well, she refused. She was Olga. A princess.

She smiled, superior, especially when Uncle Benjamin came to pick her up in the automobile. Everyone watched as he helped her into it, the perfect gentleman.

She knew what those girls would say: her family were murderers—for El Presidente—but then, the rebels murdered people, too. Blew them up or shot them in the streets; took things from people like them just because they had something. They said they weren't just plain old robbers, but two wrongs don't make a right.

Still, she hoped her uncle wouldn't find more *subversivos*. Maybe, he just wanted everyone to know he was there, that he had people watching.

Her uncle seemed to be spending more and more time at their house. That evening was a formal dinner, Dominic serving. Dominic had poured them both some wine, more wine when Mama and Uncle Benjamin were engaged in a heated, whispered conversation. Julio had gulped his down and held out his glass for more, noting to Dominic with a jerk of his head that neither Mama nor Uncle Benjamin was watching. Dominic had grinned conspiratorially and filled his glass.

Julio drank most of it in two more gulps, and grinned over at her as if to say, 'I can hold this stuff and you're too little.' It wasn't long after that, Olga could see: Julio's eyes were half-closed; it didn't look like he could see. She just felt good.

A few moments later, Uncle Benjamin was asking Julio, "What are they saying at your school, Julio? I need to find out what people are thinking about El Presidente."

Slowly, Julio turned to face him. Through eyes like slits, he looked at him as if not understanding. Then his face turned deathly pale; he opened his mouth and his whole dinner erupted onto his plate!

Mama screamed.

Olga and Henry jumped up and stepped back. It was disgusting! It stank.

Their uncle smiled, amused, and said aside to Dominic, "Well, old boy, I guess you better clean that up. Apparently, Young Quintero can't hold his liquor."

Mama was furious: with Julio, with Dominic, with everyone for a moment. Breathing heavily, she glanced at their uncle, who still looked amused, and then at Julio. "I cannot have this!" she exclaimed in quiet outrage. "Ahora mismo, todos niños van!"

All the children go, right now!

Julio staggered after her. Henry kept on asking: "Why'd he do that?"

None of them would get any wine after this. She hated Julio!

She was just as glad, the next night, to have supper with only Henry and Miriam. Julio refused to eat with anyone, so Shem served him in his room.

Mama and their uncle had dinner alone, in the dining room. Olga watched them in the dark of the garden, from her stump, listening in on their conversation.

Most of it was boring, about the meal, about the wine. Olga pricked up her ears when she heard her uncle remark, "New York is such a busy place compared to Trinidad. And you can buy almost anything there—I had almost forgotten! I have some gifts for you and your lovely daughter. I've still not fully unpacked, you see."

"More gifts?" said Mama, wonderingly, "I thought the automobile was more than enough, mi amor."

"No, no! The automobile was not from me. Don't you understand? It was from El Presidente, well, El Generale Velasco, of course, and it wasn't a gift. It was for services rendered—"

Olga could see Mama shaking her head, "But I didn't do very much."

Uncle Benjamin turned to her. His face serious. "You and your daughter did important work. The State values it, so.... Speaking of which, there will be a gala this Saturday, and we both have to go. I want you to keep your ears—and eyes—open. There is something going on, and I have the feeling that it's right under our noses."

"Oh, Benjamin!" Mama sighed. "I don't like doing this, but—"

"You must, you must! Our whole family is neck deep in this. We can't let the rebels get even a tiny foothold, don't you see?"

"I, I know." Mama sounded tired, or as if there was nothing else she could do, as if she wished there was some way out.

Olga did, too. Their whole family? Was her father doing the same kind of thing down in the gold fields? She realized, suddenly, that he wasn't down there digging for gold; he was keeping watch, for El Generale. Others dug for gold. Were her mother's sisters and brother doing the same kind of thing in Margarita? Maybe not: they were business people. Were Benjamin's other brothers doing things like this, too? She knew there were a lot of them; her father was one of the younger ones, Benjamin was the youngest.

All she knew was that one of them was a lawyer in Maracaibo, the one who had an only daughter, Nené. She had no idea why she remembered that. Then she did: there was a picture of her father and another man posing with a doll on a banister. Her mother had told her that it was taken when she and Nené were born, and the silly men hadn't been there, but had been congratulating each other that they both had daughters, one born in Coché—that was her—and one born in Maracaibo; her name was Nené.

'Neck deep,' he'd said. They were talking now about what to do at the gala, but Olga was no longer listening. She had gotten up from her stump seat and was wandering aimlessly back under the swaying palm trees.

She didn't want to keep watch! She didn't want Mama to keep watch, either. Maybe somebody had to, she wasn't sure about that, but she didn't want to do it anymore, and she didn't want Mama to do it, either. She didn't want to be scared all the time. Besides, she wasn't even sure that her uncle and her family were right. Why couldn't people be against the regime; why did you have to kill them?

They didn't do things like that in England; they had elections and parliament, and a Prime Minister. She'd learned about that in school a long time ago: Trinidad was a Crown colony, after all. Why did her country have to be so backward? She didn't ever want to go there! She wanted to go to New York, like Señora Rodriguez and her daughters. They had elections, too. Only gangsters there killed people who were against them, but they were criminals.

She was at the back of the yard, now. It was very dark under the trees back here, but she could still make her way. Glancing back at the lights from the dining room, it seemed very light there, but she knew she should turn away or she'd be blinded in the dark. Besides, she was too far away to see her mother and uncle. Back here, she could think.

She guessed maybe her uncle wasn't a criminal, because he was working for El Presidente, and El Presidente was the government. Maybe her uncle was sort of like a policeman?

The police were supposed to protect people, and stop criminals. But even the Trinidadian police did what her uncle told them. Well, that's what he said he did, wasn't it: protect people from the *subversivos*?

Maybe, he was supposed to—do what he was doing, but she didn't like it; it made people scared of her. And even worse, it made her scared, too. And her mother; she could see it in Mama's eyes.

If somebody else knew, it wouldn't be safe for any of them here. Olga smiled to herself as she thought: it wouldn't be safe in Venezuela, either, but it would be in New York.

But she couldn't just go and tell somebody. Uncle Benjamin and Mama would be angry with her, if they found out. Maybe...

Olga stopped with one foot in the air. She put it down.

Maybe she could get people thinking, so they'd figure it out, but she would have just...made a slip of the tongue.

Mama had told her, "You must not talk about this, Little One!" Her face had been very hard when she said that.

Olga shook her head. How could she say enough, without giving herself away?

Maybe she could trick Julio into saying something. He didn't know anything now, but he was too dumb to know not to say something. He'd want to boast about it. Besides, Mama had told her not to tell other people, but she hadn't told Julio anything.

What could she say? "Did you know how our uncle is protecting us? Those people who supposedly killed themselves? He arranged things; they were *subversivos*. But we don't need to worry. He'll make sure we're protected."

Julio would pretend he knew already. He'd never admit he didn't.

Maybe, she could drop a hint with one of those upper-class girls, too, act superior, and pretend to be dumb enough not to know what she was saying.

She still wasn't sure.

She was back outside her bedroom's garden door. She was sleepy, and she wasn't going to figure it out tonight. She hoped, as she opened the door, that she wouldn't dream about it.

Olga frowned as she opened her eyes. Where was she? Oh, in the room with the old people. Was she old? She looked at her hands. Beautiful, but yes, old hands. She wasn't sure how old. The woman across from her, sleeping on a chair like the one she was in, she was very old, thin, with a sharp nose and straggly white hair. She looked like a witch. Was she old like that? She wasn't eleven anymore.

She had a dim recollection of a dilemma, a problem, something she had puzzled over—was that a dream, or, or had it happened? Long ago? When she was eleven.

But she was eleven! And in—she closed her eyes; the world around her faded. When she opened them, she was in her bedroom, the parrot screaming in the tree just outside; it was morning. Time to get up.

Then she remembered: she had to decide what to do.

She was glad she hadn't dreamed about that. What a strange dream, looking at her ancient hand!

Maybe, Julio. Maybe, Henry.

The more she thought about it, the more she liked the idea of tricking Julio. Henry was a nuisance, but she didn't want to get him into trouble. He was too young and he might go running to Mama—no, he *would* go running to Mama. Besides, she liked it that Julio was already "in the doghouse," because he'd thrown up. Miriam had told her that, and she could see she was right.

So, if he was angry enough, maybe he'd go out and blab.

Perfect.

Olga even agreed to wear stockings; she was so pleased with herself. Her only question was how, and when. She knew she could do it. She just had to lie in wait: like a tigress waiting for her prey.

Olga awoke to see the calico cat, her whole attention focused on a corner of the room, not moving, except for the extreme tip of her tail; it twitched, slightly. Hadn't she just been thinking about a tiger? Where?

She looked around her. She was in her bedroom in the northern place; she could see green trees and a glimpse of water from her window.

Life was confusing. Especially when you'd lived—how many years was it? She shook her head and again closed her eyes.

They were facing each other at the end of the corridor, down near Julio's room. Olga had just come in from the garden; Julio was just going out.

"Aren't you worried about the *subversivos?* As you go to your friends' houses? They might be looking for one of us—to get back at Uncle Benjamin, Mama said."

"*Subversivos?*" Julio looked puzzled. Then he sneered. "Yeah, I know all about that! Hah, suicides, yeah! The high and mighty Consul General takes care of us!" Then he did his older brother know-it-all pose: "You've never met any of our other uncles, have you? Uncle Benjamin is...*no importante*...compared to, um, our father's older brothers; they're generals, and, and governors of whole states!"

Olga shrugged. She didn't care, didn't even care that he didn't know their names, or that he pretended he'd known all about the *subversivos*. She'd hooked him. "But Mama says we shouldn't go out on our own: someone might grab us, or hurt us—to get back at Uncle."

It was Julio's turn to shrug. "I'm not scared of them!" He almost swaggered.

"Well," she wanted to anger him, "I rode to school in the automobile; Uncle Benjamin drove me. Have you ridden in it, yet?" She could hear the apparent innocence in her voice. She knew he hadn't: that she had, would be infuriating.

"Yeah? I'm going to learn to drive it, I'll bet." His snarl had deepened into a grimace.

"Bet you don't! Uncle saw you throw up, too; he's not going to let you drive. Probably thinks you'll get drunk and crash it."

Julio's face turned dark. Olga stepped back, out of his reach; she sensed Julio as a dangerous animal. His teeth gritted; she could hear them grind, and his eyes shone, almost red.

"At least, I don't kill people—*todavía!*" He tried to laugh, to cover his anger, as he wheeled past her, towards the road.

"He'll be here for dinner. Why don't you ask him—about driving?"

"I'm getting out of here! I'm not going into that damned dining room, and I'm not going to speak to your, your damned uncle!" He stamped up the corridor—until, Olga noticed, he came opposite their mother's room; then he walked by quietly. He turned to sneer defiantly at her before he passed into the shadow by the entrance.

Olga felt like dancing round the garden, but she restrained herself. She walked around it and grinned at all the trees, instead. She was looking up at the tall trees in the very back, when she stopped to think. She'd gotten Julio angry with their uncle, but maybe not angry enough, and not angry enough with their mother.

Was there something else she could do? Then, all of a sudden, it came to her.

Olga frowned as she saw the placid scene before her: Doris reading at the dining table, the blunt-faced man and the pointy-faced woman were sleeping on large upholstered chairs across from her—just like, she realized, the one where she was sitting.

Slowly, she shook her head. Had she been here just minutes ago? It didn't feel like it. Maybe she hadn't been here? Where had she been, then? Someplace else? Life, at her age—whatever that was—was very confusing. She looked at her hands, on the armrest; they were pale, liver-spotted and the knuckles were large and misshapen. Those were her hands?

She shook her head again. No. Her hands were beautiful, smooth, perfectly formed; she had never bothered with nail polish, or manicures; they had never been necessary; she was beautiful; always had been.

"Mama, I'm going out bike riding," Olga announced, as she wheeled her prized Raleigh past her mother, who was sitting in the sitting room, reading something, or looking over some papers.

Mama frowned, as Olga knew she would: "Oh, no, Little One! You can't go out alone! You know that. And you can't go out beyond The Savannah, even if Miriam is with you. You know that!"

"Because?"

"It's not safe! There are bad people out there! Benjamin told me—"

Olga didn't want to hear what new danger her uncle had found now. She shrugged. "Well, if it's not safe, then how come you let Julio go wherever he wants? He's not like Max. And if anyone wanted to get at Uncle, he looks more like him than any of us, doesn't he?"

Mama looked worried now, not stern, not angry at her. "Where is he?" Her voice was suddenly shrill.

Olga shrugged. "Who knows? I saw him go out, but he doesn't tell me where he's going—not that I care."

"He went out! How long ago?"

Olga didn't dare smile; it was working. Instead, she shrugged, unconcerned about her nasty older brother. "Oh, maybe half an hour."

For an instant, her mother stared at her as if trying to see inside her, then she sighed. "Put your bicycle back! You're not going anywhere."

Olga shrugged, but didn't protest further.

As she wheeled her bicycle back to its place across from her room, she could hear her mother calling Max, her voice with an edge: she was anxious. Olga nodded to herself and went back to the garden with her favorite book of the moment: W. H. Hudson's *Green Mansions*. She loved the jungles he described—in Guyana, maybe not far from where her father was working in Amazonas.

What was he doing there?

Olga opened her eyes and was momentarily disoriented. Her son was saying, "Hi, Olga! How're you doing?" Her gray-haired son.

She looked around her. She was in the common room, in her usual chair. Doris was at the table, reading, and the sharp-faced woman was sleeping across from her.

The blunt-faced man, further down the row of chairs was saying, "What? What? I can't hear you!"

Her son held up some pictures stuck to thick paper. "Can you to tell me who these are."

The first one, two men in suits, one sitting down with his hat on—"That's my father. The man next to him," he had a mustache, and thick eyebrows, "is one of his brothers, but I don't know his name."

What did her father do in Amazonas? Had she just been wondering about that? 'He's working for el Generale,' people said.

Her son pointed to the next picture, a man in a long black coat and a hat: "That's Benjamin." She knew what he did. He was consul, in Trinidad, but, "He's young in that picture."

Down at the bottom of the large sheet there was a dark picture with several girls in it, all of them relaxing on—was it a beach? There was some jungle in the background. Oh! "That's the beach, in Trinidad. Where we went." What were their names? Was she in the picture?

There was another one, almost the same scene, but waist deep in the water. There she was. "That's on Trinidad, too. The place we went to. I don't remember their names."

There were many other pictures, but after awhile Olga was tired. She closed her eyes. She could hear someone—her son, maybe—say, "Well, I guess you're getting tired, so I guess I should go."

She was jolted by an angry voice.

"It's not fair!" Julio shouted; he was loud. Mama was glaring at him, hands on hips. They were in the corridor, opposite the sitting room. The leaves in the tree overhead seemed to tremble with his outrage.

"You may not go out alone!" Mama asserted, her voice like a sharp knife. "Only with Max."

"With that stupid Bush Negro! I won't!"

"You must. Or you stay here!"

"But why? Because our stupid Uncle—"

"Stop! I will not hear your Uncle Benjamin spoken of with words like that! Go to your room! I will have your dinner sent to you. You are not to go anywhere until school, tomorrow morning. Do you understand?"

"I hate you!" Julio spat, and then ran to his room.

Olga, sitting in the garden, pretending to do her homework, had seen and heard it all. She grinned to herself. To see her horrible older brother in such a state was a pleasure in itself, but that paled against the realization:

It was working! He knew, and he was angry, not just with their uncle, but now at Mama, too.

He'd probably spill it all to his friends tomorrow as soon as he got to school; he was that stupid. And angry.

Olga opened her eyes. Had she been dreaming? Or had she been somewhere else? Where was she now? In her bedroom: outside, the northern trees were turning yellow and orange, that's where. Where had she been?

She heard an echo of a young man's voice raised in anger, but she couldn't remember why; she remembered enjoying his anger, but she had no idea why, or when, either.

Life was confusing. The longer she lived, the more confusing it became, but she didn't mind. She preferred no explanations; she remembered saying that...somewhere? Explanations are for people wriggling to get off the hook—oh, fishing.

She wondered: did her father like to fish? On the Orinoco? Why had Heriberto left them behind? Heriberto, her father. She had seen him two or three times in her life. But he hadn't abandoned her....

Olga shook her head, climbed into bed and closed her eyes. She was too tired to think.

She was waiting for school to begin for the day, with the other girls, outside the gate. Just as the old nun came shuffling out to call them in, she caught Magdalena glance at her out of the corner of her eye, then, pretending not to see her, she quickly turned to Blanquita. She was saying something, hurriedly, something she didn't want Olga to hear.

Olga edged closer as the girls crowded towards the gate.

She heard Blanquita saying, "You mean her uncle?" She looked scared.

"...murders, not suicides..." Magdalena mumbled, then glanced up and saw Olga next to them. Olga stood and smiled, smiled at this girl who had been her friend. It wasn't a real smile.

She pretended she hadn't heard a thing. But she had to speak to them. "Hi Mags, Blanquie! Did you read the assignment for today?"

There was nothing she could say. She couldn't just say, "Mags is right; I know."

Julio must have bragged. What would happen next?

As they made their way to class, pretending they were friends, still, Olga began to think: this was what she'd wanted. Either Julio had boasted to his classmates, or maybe people were just finding out. In any case—

"Eh bien, Mademoiselles!" Sister Josephine had taken over French class since the mid-term break. Her French was better than Sister Marie's, people said. Someone had told her the Sister spoke with a Parisian accent. "Dans la prochaine semaine—" they were going to have final exams! And then, she'd said, if they passed, they would go on to grammar school next year! She added in heavily accented English, "And of course, all of you will pass, now, won't you?"

Olga grinned at Magdalena, and Blanquita. She would, Olga knew; she was the best student in the class, maybe Blanquita was almost as good. But maybe she'd be going to school somewhere else, after this? What kinds of schools did they have in.... She wouldn't even let herself think the name! She looked around her. No one would know about her uncle there.

Olga awoke with a jolt.

"It's time for dinner, Olga. You need to come with me to the dining table now."

Olga frowned. She didn't like being awakened. She had been—where

141

had she been? "I don't want to get up. Why can't I have my dinner in here?"
She knew she was being unreasonable, but she didn't care.

"No, Olga," the care person said, pursing her lips at her, then smiling.
"Ladies come to the dinner table when they're called, you know."

"Oh," exasperated, "all right!" She was a Lady, after all. And a princess.

Olga had already gotten her white dress for the last day of school—at the end of the week—and had shown it off to a photographer Mama had called in. It was long; the first long dress she'd ever worn. She knew she was beautiful: the photographer had said so! After the excitement of wearing it, she had changed into her regular dress, and now, she was sitting on her bench in the garden: reading *Green Mansions*. She wasn't sure she really liked Rima. Rima was, oh, too perfect, and why wasn't her own hair like that? No one ever said her hair changed color in different lights; it was always black. And Rima's skin was just too white. But the jungle sounded so mysterious and beautiful—

Olga turned at the sudden sound behind her: it was an automobile, its tires suddenly screeching on the hardpan road. Then it stopped. She heard a door slam. Footsteps, in a hurry!

Uncle Benjamin came rushing down the corridor. He looked pale, his eyes were black holes: empty. He turned into Mama's sitting room, without even nodding to her—but he'd looked straight at her! Just before he turned; she was sure he'd seen her.

Olga sniffed. Then she glanced out at the garden. She didn't turn back to her book. Well, if he wouldn't even nod to her, something big was happening; something she wanted to know about.

It wasn't dark, but the shade under the trees was almost like night. They wouldn't notice her in the shadows. She liked the tree's shade in the moonlight, too. And, you could find things out when you hid there like a, a tree sloth; she had seen sloths hanging from trees, but only when people pointed them out to her.

She edged off her bench, and into the deep shade beneath the trees; then slowly, from tree to tree, she worked her way towards her favorite stump. She could hear their voices, staccato, alarmed. Until she got to the stump, though, she couldn't hear what they were saying. The stump was in full sun, though, so she sidled backwards and crouched in back of a palm trunk.

"Don't worry, Ana!" Uncle Benjamin's voice was pleading. Olga heard him even better than she did from the stump. "You'll all be well taken care of. Velasco will see to it. But it's not safe here! Not now. I—I'm being recalled to Caracas, but it wouldn't be safe for you there, either—I'll have guards, but Velasco couldn't assign any to you. You wouldn't be safe in Caracas, nor in La Grita, or Margarita—for the same reason.

"It's gotten out. People might know. Some of them might be a little too angry. So, I've arranged things. Señora Rodriguez, remember her? She'll find you an apartment, in New York. We telegrammed her; she's already answered. No one will know about this in New York, so you should all be safe. Heriberto will send money, and, and, we'll just have to wind up affairs—"

"But, Benjamin! How can I live without you?" Mama's voice cracked into a sob.

Olga winced. How could Mama say something like that? It was all Uncle Benjamin's fault! It was what Magdalena had been whispering about. "It's gotten out," he said. Julio must have blabbed. So—Olga glanced around her. They would be leaving this place. She had been so happy here—until Uncle Benjamin had meddled. But, going to New York, it's what she'd always wanted!

"Ana, Ana! I don't even know what Velasco has in mind for me, but I have to do what he tells me. Verdad?"

"And he says I have to go to New York?" Mama sounded in pain.

Uncle Benjamin shrugged. "It's the best place for you. You'll know people there, and it's safe. And, and think: your daughter—you keep telling me she's so brilliant. Well, she can go to better schools there!"

"Verdad?" Mama's voice quickened, just a little.

"Verdad. Even the public schools: much better."

Olga could see her mother nod heavily. She sighed, "Esta bien."

"But I have to leave now! Tonight. A small yacht. You should leave as soon as possible—by week's end: there's a ship leaving for New York, Friday evening. I've booked you."

"But the children! Their schools!"

"Perfect timing! Your children will be finished with school—at the end of the week, correct?"

Thoughtfully, "Es verdad..." Then she sounded alarmed: "But this house, the house on Dere Street, the plantation—"

Uncle Benjamin was shaking his head, as Olga slowly worked her way back to her reading bench. She didn't care if they just left. She peered back at the yard in back of theirs: a solid wall of green. The "Syrian" had abandoned it years ago, Blaine had said. That's what their yard would look like, too. Jungle. She shrugged. It didn't matter. She loved the idea of going to New York!

She had never seen Uncle Benjamin look like that: he was scared!

Well, she wasn't! She was excited! She felt like pirouetting around the garden, but she knew she shouldn't. At the same time, she knew: Mama's whole world was ending.

The big automobile: Max drove Mama, Olga, and her brothers to the dock at sunset. He had picked them up at their last day of school ceremonies, first Henry, then Olga, then Julio; he graduated. Olga was surprised, but it didn't matter; she graduated, too, to grammar school, at the top of her class. He looked proud when they picked him up, with Mama, but then, once in the car, he scowled. No one said anything. In a few minutes, Julio began to look as if steam would come out of his ears. Henry was peering at everything, craning his neck out the window. He was grinning. For him, this was an adventure; he'd never been this far from home—all the way to the end of the Port. She had: silly little brother, silly big brother, too. Mama wore black. Olga looked again; it wasn't just black; Mama was faded, not a blooming flower; not the Mama who dressed up in her cochanos to go on the promenade. She looked old! Max's jaw was set in a determined line: his eyes kept scanning both sides of the road, as if he expected someone to jump out and shoot at them!

Were they all scared?

Olga pursed her lips and shrugged her shoulders. Everything would be all right. They were going to New York!

There it was! The ship was a big liner; it looked crowded: so many heads peered over the deck railings! They pulled up. People saw Max and made way for them; coolies rushed in and heaved their trunks on their backs. The four of them hurried after, up the gangplank. The decks were crowded and Olga began to worry: would they have to sleep on deck? They kept on going. Now, they went up stairs, through doors, down an almost empty corridor; the coolies knew where to take them: to a stateroom, cramped, but better than the deck. Olga grinned as she looked around her: Julio and Henry would have to sleep on the couch; she and Mama would share the bed in the tiny cabin; at least they'd sleep on a mattress. They would even have a porthole. They were going to New York!

Olga thanked the coolies with a smile and a "Thank you!" They grinned back, their white teeth shining in their dark faces.

One of them said, "You a pretty girl! Why you leavin'?"

Olga shook her head. She wasn't sure if she should say something or not. Mama shook her head at them and gave them money. She looked as if she wanted to yell at someone, just anyone. But she didn't.

Mama and Julio looked so grim! Henry was delighted, not with the coolies, but with the room, maybe the steel floor, maybe the whole ship.

Olga glanced at Henry and grinned as she caught his eyes.

"It's so big!" he said, in awe.

Olga opened her eyes long enough to make it down the hall to her bedroom. She lay down gratefully, closed her eyes, and, for the first time in months, she didn't dream.

16

Olga looked about her; she was in her room, the northern one. The one when she was...she looked at her hand, out of the cover: weathered, liver-spotted, crooked. Well, that's where she was, and she was comfortable—but she didn't have to stay there. She could close her eyes and—

She and Henry were looking out from the bow of the ship. Mama had said they could go "wherever you're allowed, but you must stay together."

They were in "Cabin Class," so they were allowed to go almost anywhere. It made her proud to know that everyone else could see she was one of 'the best people.'

The bow was so high, and the water stretched forever. It was sunny, but very windy, and cool. Olga saw American sailors in short-sleeves working on ropes on the deck below. It's probably warm for New York, she thought, just cold for Trinidad. For me.

She took off her own jacket and carried it, so Henry did, too. Olga heard her voice, inside her head: 'I'm going to be just like them; I'm going to be American!' At least she spoke English. She'd have to get used to the cold. She couldn't wait to see the "skyscrapers."

"I'm not cold," Henry insisted through clenched teeth.

"I'm not, either!" said Olga, ignoring him, and the cold breeze. "Oh, look, down below!"

Two men, in down-slanted hats and dark gray suits were strolling across the deck below them. Olga could see: they had bulges in their jackets; they must have guns! Maybe they were gangsters. They sort of looked like gangsters. One of them was reaching for something in his inside breast pocket—she was sure it was a gun! On second thought, they didn't look like gangsters; they looked like Venezuelans! Maybe they were Reds, out to get Mama! The men paused at the hatch leading down to their corridor.

"Don't!" she yelled—and then pulled Henry away from the rail. "C'mon!"

Henry pulled back, whining, "I don't wanna!"

"Hssst! Don't you want to see their guns?" Their cabin was down the corridor where the men were going; she had to stop them!

"Yessss...!" Henry nodded, his face suddenly eager, no longer scared.

Olga glanced at him and heard a voice inside her head: He'd fall for anything I tell him!

They ran down the metal stairs two at a time, ran across the deck, opened the metal door—and the men were nowhere in sight! Had they broken into their cabin? Were they doing something to Mama!

Olga and Henry ran down the corridor, turned left to their cabin, on the outside: the door was closed. Olga opened it with the key Mama had given her, afraid of what she'd see.

The door swung open: Mama looked up from the sofa and smiled at them; she had been reading something; there was no one else there.

"Did you have a nice walk, out on deck?" she asked.

Dully, Olga nodded. Maybe they were safe! Maybe the Reds didn't know they were on this ship; maybe they weren't following them, maybe....

Olga collapsed at the end of the couch. Henry stood, panting.

Mama arched her eyebrows and huffed, "Really, Olga, that's not the way a Lady sits down! Get up and sit down properly! I do hope you two haven't been running all over the ship like hooligans. I don't know what's become of Julio."

"No, Mama. All right, Mama. We didn't see Julio, Mama." Olga sat down the way the nuns had taught her, legs together, bottom gently, gracefully lowered onto the seat.

"Much better."

Olga opened her eyes. Something jiggled in her memory: something about telling children to sit down properly. She smiled and looked about the room. She felt the chair beneath her. Could she sit down properly? The bluff-faced man was splayed over his chair; the sharp-faced woman was curled up on hers, a cat on her lap. Both had their eyes tightly shut. Oh well.

At 90 something—or was it 100—she didn't have to worry about how she sat down, only that she still could. Again, she closed her eyes, and pulled the afghan up around her chin.

She and Henry saw them first: skyscrapers, far off at the edge of the ocean, sticking up before they saw the land. Could those really be buildings, places where people lived? Would they live in one?

Soon, more people gathered on deck. They could see the Statue of Liberty, just as it looked in books, and the skyscrapers seemed to get higher and higher as they came closer. They really did scrape the sky. And yet, now she could make out windows on them: people must live in them!

But it wasn't just one city; there were cities on every shore—or were they all the same city, all New York?

Mama had joined them now. Olga looked from the skyscrapers, getting taller and taller, to Mama: she looked hunched, pinched, as if the huge coast-scape diminished her, faded her.

A man, an American, maybe, in some kind of blue uniform, came up to her. "Ma'am, we're going to Ellis Island, first. Everybody here has to go through the paperwork there. You got yer papers ready?"

He spoke funny, but Olga sort of understood him. She didn't know what Ellis Island was, or where, though.

Mama looked scared, then turned to Olga. "What did he say?" she asked in breathless Spanish.

Olga explained, and asked the man, "What is Ellis Island?"

"Hey? What'd'ya say?"

Olga spoke slowly, this time, wondering: was he speaking English, or did Americans speak something else? American? She'd never heard anyone mention 'American!'

"Oh," said the man. He waved at a low island with long, low buildings: the ship was heading straight for it. "There it is. It's where you people go first. Nobody gets in to America, unless we let'em in—at Ellis."

When Olga explained this to Mama, she nodded, saying, "I know, it's like Customs. Even in Trinidad...." but she looked even more scared than she had before, even smaller, more faded.

Olga had a sudden fear: they'd keep them out; they'd send them back!

She squared her shoulders. No! She was going to go to school in New York!

Long lines, the highest ceiling she'd ever seen, but not a skyscraper. Voices echoed and rebounded, the people huddled below in those long lines; she felt so small! There were people staring down from a balcony, people with worried furrows on their faces. Olga looked up at the front of the line. Not so far; cabin class went first.

She wasn't worried. She knew, somehow, that the high roof was meant to make them feel small. She was sure they weren't, even though most people were taller. Mama had dressed up in her finest. She looked better, but still very small compared to all these people. Julio, well, she had to admit, Julio looked tall and unconcerned. Henry looked small and dark, but his eyes were bright with curiosity. Mama turned to her. "You must tell me what they say. I have papers, but I don't know about all this." She gestured towards the official-looking people at the far front of the lines—doctors, Olga thought. They wore white coats and had stethoscopes round their necks. They peered and pried at each person as they came up to them. And then wrote something in a book. Some were sent into another room—a man in front of them said, "That's if you've maybe got something wrong with you. More medical tests." He rolled his eyes.

At that moment, a man at the head of the line had a big L marked on his back, and as he limped towards the other room she could see he was lame.

Most were sent to another line; it looked like just papers there; the people held up their passports, the officer took them, looked them over, scrutinized the people in front of him, stamped the book, asked some questions, handed them back. The people then were directed out of the building? Only some were directed to somewhere else. Were those the people who had something wrong with them?

She didn't have anything wrong with her. Mama didn't. Julio and Henry didn't. Still, it was nerve-wracking, waiting, seeing these tall people in their white uniforms, peering at people's teeth, their eyes, listening to their hearts, scrutinizing them.

Finally, it was their turn. The man looked at them through squinted eyes. He examined Mama first, Olga explaining to her what he was doing: looking in her eyes, asking her to open her mouth, listening to her chest and heart with his stethoscope, then nodding, asking "How old're you, Ma'am?"

Mama looked to her to translate, then said, in a very small voice, "Treinta-y-ocho."

"Thirty-eight," Olga told the man.

The man looked at her, too, at all of them. She was sure he was charmed, when he looked into her eyes. He smiled a little bit, anyway.

"Twelve," she told him, when he asked her age, but she could see he wrote down '11.'

And then they went on to do "the paperwork," a man explained, as he directed them to another line.

Mama held out their passports: one for each of them, when they came up to the official. He wore a blue uniform with shoulder boards—they had brass buttons on them that looked like a seal. He had a matching cap, but not anywhere near as soaring as the one she'd seen in pictures of El Presidente.

Mama glanced at Olga. "You will translate for me; I am not going to try to speak this English. I am too old to learn. And I don't understand what they say."

"Yes, Mama." Olga smiled at her, determined, and Mama brightened just a little.

The man took the passports, thumbed through them, and scrutinized each of them in turn. He asked Mama, "Where are you from?"

Olga translated, and Mama said, "Coché y Margarita, Venezuela," and then added that she had been living in Trinidad with her children.

Olga was about to translate, when she had a better idea: "She says, we were living on Belmont Circle, in Port of Spain, Sir, on Trinidad, but we come from Venezuela."

The blue cap nodded. He squinted at Mama, and looked thoughtful. "And where is your husband?"

Again, Olga translated, although Mama was nodding: she had understood.

"Tell him: my husband is working in Amazonas State, in Venezuela, in the gold fields and he sends me money."

Olga told the official exactly what she said, and added: "He works for the government."

The official scanned her mother's clothes, her hat, and then he turned back to look her in the face: his was very earnest. "And what is your purpose for coming to America?"

Mama understood this time, and said, smiling at her, "Tell him it is because my daughter has to go to better schools; she is so brilliant."

"Mama! I can't say that—about me—even if it's true!" She grinned and turned to the waiting official. "She says we're coming here so I can get a better education. I was best in my class."

"Is that so?" The official wrote something down and then asked, Mama, almost as an aside, "How much money do you have with you?"

Mama looked at Olga. "Dinero?"

Olga nodded, and asked, a little worried, "Does he want to take it from you, Mama?"

Mama shook her head. "He wants to know we have enough to live on." She turned to the official. "Fi hundert dollares."

Olga was shocked. "You have that much money!" It was a lot of money!

Mama smiled at her. "Of course. Your father sent the money. And he will send it here."

The official smiled at them all: Julio and Henry had hardly said a word. "Welcome to the United States of America! You go down to that line on the right; it's for the ferry; it will take you into New York City."

They had made it! Olga embraced Mama. "It's going to be wonderful, Mama!"

Mama was subdued. She nodded, but she was looking down at the ground, her shoulders hunched.

Henry squealed, "We're going to New York City!"

Julio looked unsettled, as if he was out of place; tried to ignore them. All of them. Olga dismissed him; he'd never be an American.

When they came out of the shed, the big city unfolded before them, just over the water, the skyscrapers looking larger, but still distant. Then, Olga realized: tall buildings as far as she could see, and farther, and there looked like another shore, with huge sheds on them, and buildings beyond them, going out of sight.

Port of Spain was so small!

Here, they wouldn't have to worry about the rebels; the Reds— or whatever they were—would never find them. Olga could feel the smile grow on her face. And, she was going to go to a better school!

School? Oh, she had a school; she ran a school; it was her school. She'd have to remember to tell...would she remember?

Olga opened her eyes. She didn't know where she was! For an instant, she was scared; then she glimpsed the care person beside her.

"It's all right, Olga," the woman was saying. "You've been a little sick, so we took you to the Emergency Room, because it was after hours. You're going to stay here—in the hospital—for a few days, until the infection shows signs that the antibiotic is working; then you'll come home. Okay?"

Olga looked at her, puzzled. Sick? The care person woman smiled at her.

"Not very sick?"

"Not very sick," said the woman, patting her wrist with a reassuring hand. "And I'll be in to see you. Maybe you'll come home tomorrow, but don't worry: already it looks like the antibiotic is helping."

Helping. Olga nodded, and closed her eyes.

*B*ack 'home' the woman said. What home? Olga looked around her. The room looked a little familiar; there were photos on the window shelf and the bureau; a picture of a young man with his shirt half off—oh, that was her son. Douglas.

But it wasn't "home" home. It was that other place, she thought, where the care person was. Where was that?

She looked further. Another picture, of a man and woman: good-looking woman—that was her, of course, and a good-looking man: he gazed down at her, adoringly. That must be...Julian, her husband. There were pictures of a very little boy—her son? And of a very little girl with blonde hair. Wasn't that her granddaughter? She couldn't remember her name; and there was another picture, of a boy and a girl—also her grandchildren? They looked as if they were on their way to school. The little boy was almost a foot taller than the little girl. They were standing outside a front door— not the one at High—wherever it was she had lived—but it looked familiar, too. Oh, and there was a picture of Julian beside a tractor, outside the big barn. She remembered that barn.

Tantalizing: she almost remembered where she lived—used to live, she thought, looking about the room. She guessed she lived here, now.

Comfortable: that's what it was. And she was. She closed her eyes.

The city grew bigger and taller as the ferry came near, and then Olga saw: Mrs. Rodriguez, heavier than ever, and one of her pretty daughters, waiting for them in the crowd at dockside. There were rows and rows of black and yellow automobiles behind them. Were they police?

Olga shrugged: she had nothing to worry about, and neither did Mama. They had so much money! That's why the police were there: to protect them. Besides, her father would send more. Would his man be able to find them?

Where were they going? Looking up along the street between the buildings as they pulled into the dock, Olga couldn't see its end. And it was lined with skyscrapers!

After the abrazos and the congratulations all round—Julio looked so uncomfortable, Olga almost broke out laughing—Mrs. Rodriguez gestured towards one of the black and yellow automobiles.

"A taxi; it's how you get around here, unless you take a bus, or the subway. Gloria," she gestured towards her daughter, "can get all over the place: she understands it, but I don't yet. Besides, with all of us, it's cheaper than all those tickets, to go by taxi. We can all fit, I think, and the luggage will go in the back, or on top."

"A taxi?" Mama's shoulders slumped. She almost looked as if she was about to cry, although Olga had never seen her cry, even when her father, Heriberto, left after his last visit. That was when she was six!

They had one of the first automobiles in Trinidad, and here they were going to their new place all crammed together in a taxi?

Mama looked grim. Then she smiled, or tried to and said, "I'll pay for another taxi; there are too many of us, and too much baggage for just one."

"Of course!" agreed Mrs. Rodriguez almost explosively, "but I will pay for it: you are our guests, after all—and we will help you move into your own apartment—the one just upstairs from us. It's all arranged."

They drove and drove: she and Mama with Mrs. Rodriguez, the two boys with Gloria. They must have been driving for more than an hour, still in the city, when they finally arrived at wherever it was they were going. Mama and Mrs. Rodriguez chattered away about

Trinidad and Margarita and their families. Olga looked out the window at street after street after street. There were some streets with trees overhanging them, the leaves all yellow, or brown—it was autumn here? On most streets, nothing was growing at all: just people and cars, buses and trucks. Some streets were wide and straight, others were narrower, and crowded with cars and trucks, and even handcarts, but almost all were as straight as a ruler, and the houses or other buildings made long straight lines back from the cement curb and the sidewalks: Olga had never seen sidewalks, but she had read about them. The people were all dressed as if it was cold, and it was, even in the crowded taxi. It was cold. Colder than it had been on deck on the ship, but then she hadn't been up on deck the last few days, because it had been raining. She was glad she'd worn a sweater.

They finally stopped. Mrs. Rodriguez knocking on the window to the front seat, and announced, "Here we are!"

Olga and Mama got out one side, Mrs. Rodriguez out the other; the other taxi had stopped behind them, and Gloria was paying the driver. Olga looked about her. In Belmont, everything was green, except for the bright red bougainvillea. Here, everything was gray, or darker; there was not a living thing on the street, except for the people and a dog; she could see the dog way down the street.

After going with Mrs. Rodriguez to her apartment—two floors up; houses in Trinidad didn't have second floors—and having something to eat and drink—arepas and cocoa "Just like home," said Mrs. Rodriguez—then she pointed above her. "Your apartment is just above. I have called some young men to bring in your luggage."

The fourth floor. Olga had never been on the fourth floor of anything, and they were going to live on one!

"It is better than ground floor," Mrs. Rodriguez explained. "Not so noisy, and no problem from people on street."

Some young black men came, Olga didn't know from where,

but Mrs. Rodriguez had arranged for them; they spoke no Spanish, and Gloria told them what to do.

Olga could see that they thought Gloria was pretty, grinning at her in that way she'd seen men do sometimes—the way Max had smiled at her, with his shining white teeth.

The young men carried their luggage up the stairs. Julio tried to carry his own bag, but it was obvious he'd never carried anything that heavy in his life. One of the young men just shook his head and took it from him. Olga had to grin at that.

Their apartment was small, so much smaller than the house in Belmont, but she had her own bedroom, and so did Mama. There was a kitchen, and Olga wondered, who is going to cook? She'd never seen Mama cook in her life!

The boys had a bedroom they were going to share. When they found out, Julio's frown was as dark as a storm cloud, and Henry looked as if he was about to have a tantrum.

Mama's shoulders were hunched, but she ignored her sons and turned to Olga. "We need bread. Go down to the store and buy some. Here. Here is money." She pressed some strange looking coins into Olga's hand.

"But I don't know where—"

"Ask. Ask Gloria, or Mrs. Rodriguez."

"It's down on the next corner," explained Gloria, gesturing and pointing to her left.

Olga went down the stairs. They weren't clean, and the walls were painted in a yellow brown that didn't look clean, either, but Olga shrugged: it was a new place, a new world. She was going to make it hers; she didn't care if Mama didn't like it. They had to live here, anyway, and she was going to go to a better school.

Down on the street, she felt more alone than she ever had—but just for an instant. Then she squared her shoulders: it was a new place, America, and she was going to "prevail"; she'd heard that word and someday she would. This was just the first day.

She looked about her, down the bleak street, and then in the other direction. She didn't see anything that looked like the stores she was used to in Trinidad. It was a little daunting. At the end of the next corner? But she saw no store, no stall stacked with fresh vegetables and fruit outside it. All she could make out was what looked like a large, dingy window, low enough that you could look in; it was at the end of the next corner. Could that be the store?

Reluctantly, she made her way down the block, crossed the empty street and went down the next block. There were a few people about, as gray as the street, even the black people, and they all seemed to be in a hurry, going somewhere else. She stopped in front of the large, dingy window. It had some dusty cans and boxes in rows on a shelf behind the glass in the window: maybe it was the store, after all.

She hoped they had bread, but it didn't look likely. With mounting dread, she climbed the stairs, opened the door; it jingled. Inside, well, it was some kind of store, with rows and rows of cans, bottles, boxes. There was a glass case with bedraggled-looking vegetables, and some very red cuts of meat on a slab of ice.

Olga frowned, and looked up to see a man, high up, looming over the glass counter. He must be very tall. He was very pale, not like the Syrian storekeepers in Trinidad.

"Yemiss?"

Olga was mystified—and a little panicked. What did yemiss mean! Did he speak English? "You got-a-some bread?"

"Whatchyuwant?"

She didn't understand a word! Was he speaking English? Maybe he spoke Spanish, although that wasn't what he had been speaking. "Pane?" she asked. "Tiene pane?"

The man looked confused. "I don' unnerstan."

He did speak English! Sort of.

"Bread," she said, slowly, carefully, and then, "bread?"

"Oh, you want da bread! Gotsome rightchere." He reached below him and held up something in a paper wrapper.

It was about the size of a loaf of bread, and when she took it in her hand, she realized how hungry she was: she could smell it! It was bread.

She held out her hand with the strange coins. The man nodded, and took the larger one, and handed her back two smaller ones, one thin, the other thicker and not quite as large as the coin she had given him. She pointed at the two coins, "What're these?"

"This'ere's a nickel'r fi'cents, an' that'sa dime'r tencents," the man said, pointing to the two coins. "Fifteencents. You gimme quarter: twentyfi'cents."

Olga squinted to understand him. It suddenly occurred to her: he was speaking English, and so was she! Yet, they couldn't understand each other!

She nodded and thanked him. She was going to learn to speak this American English if it killed her! Maybe, it wouldn't be easy, but that wasn't going to stop her: she was Princess Olga.

She mounted the steps to their new apartment, bread under her arm, her teeth clenched.

Oh, Olga didn't like this! She ached all over and she was sooo tired! But she was no longer asleep. She opened her eyes a slit. Doris was sitting at the table, reading. Olga was in her chair. The thin, long-nosed woman with the lank white hair was sprawled across from her, in her lounger; her mouth was open and her eyes were tightly shut. Olga had never learned her name, but now she remembered: the floppy-looking man with the loose mouth sprawled next to her in a chair close to hers was the woman's husband.

Was it time for coffee? Somehow, she remembered vaguely that coffee came and something else, a bun or something, at the time of day it felt like—whatever time that was, wherever she was. Anyway, she was comfortable. She closed her eyes. They'd wake her when it was time for coffee and that was all that mattered—here, anyway—but she yearned to be somewhere else.

She was in a long strange hallway; there were doors along one wall, but they were closed. She could hear voices behind the doors. Oh. Those were classrooms. This was school.

Of course, it was school, she thought. Was I just dreaming before? It was confusing.

Then, she felt, urgently, why she was here, in this hallway with the closed doors. She had to go: badly!

Three girls, older, all three in the same uniform—was she in uniform? Was she in uniform, too? She looked down at herself: she was. They were chattering to each other, ambling down the hall.

"Please! Where's the WC?" she asked the oldest one, with hair so blonde. She'd never seen hair that white, except on old people.

"WC?" The girl looked at her, shrugged, looked superior, and laughed to her friends, "Don't know nothing 'bout a WC! Do you, girls?"

All three giggled and smirked at her. "WC?" "WC?" "Gotta speak English, little girl!" white-haired said, pleased with herself.

"Please!" Olga pleaded, urgent now, her voice rising.

At that moment, the middle door crashed open, and a large, white-faced nun glared down at them all. She was stern, her eyes like hard stones.

"What's all this noise out here? You girls should be in class!"

The three girls hunched their shoulders, and tried to pretend they weren't there. The white-haired girl pointed at Olga. "She's the one making noise."

The nun swung towards her, eyes blazing. "What's the meaning of this? You're new here and already making trouble!"

"I, I just asked...I have to go! I asked where's the WC and they wouldn't tell me!"

The nun's face softened; she smiled thinly. "Here, we say 'the little girls room.' It's over there." She pointed at a door that said, "Girls" on it.

"Oh, thank you!"

As she rushed towards 'the little girl's room,' she could hear the nun scolding the three girls, in a harsh voice: "You girls should be ashamed of yourselves! And...." She didn't hear the rest, because the door swished closed behind her.

Little girl's room. Little girl's room. Little girl's room.

She grinned as she whished, grinned to think of the nun telling those girls off! They deserved it. They'd grinned at her, enjoying her discomfort. She hoped the nun punished them.

Didn't everybody know WC stood for a room like this one?

Water Closet. A strange name for it, but 'little girl's room?' How would anyone know what that was?

And there were no boys at the school, thank goodness, so why wouldn't it just be the WC—or did they say 'little boy's room', too? What did people call it here?

No boys—until after school, on the way home. A whole bunch of boys, from a nearby school, maybe, ran past, and the girls walking with her—it was just a short way home—stood back to let them pass. There were no yard boys walking with them, protecting them, so she caught up with one of the taller girls, taller than most of the boys. She was red-haired; her skin was freckled, like the man who'd sold her mother the cacao plantation—what would happen to that, she wondered? Could her mother sell it from here?

The red-haired girl turned to her and asked, "Where're you from?"

Olga thought of saying 'Trinidad,' but then she thought, No. That's not really where I'm from. "From Venezuela. My father is governor, there." She spoke very carefully, hoping her Trinidadian accent didn't show.

"Didja ever see a movie, in, in Venzu-wela?" The girl was pointing at a movie poster:

Wine, Olga read, in large letters. A pretty young woman was shrinking from the crowd of tiny people beneath her. She was almost life-size, they were small, but they looked threatening. Clara Bow, it read.

"See if your mother'll let you go; it's right around the corner."

"Why t—um," she made herself say the th, "thank you."

The girl looked at her strangely. "What do they say in Venzu-wela?"

Olga shrugged. "Muchas gracias!" She wasn't about to correct her on how she pronounced her homeland.

The girl grinned at her. "You're okay! I'm Clara, too, just like her," she nodded at the poster. "What's your name?"

"Olga. Olga de Quintero." She thought to add, 'I'm named for a Russian princess,' but then knew she shouldn't.

"Olga? Strange name. My family's named O'Flaherty. You got any sisters?"

Olga shook her head. "Only two stupid brothers."

"Me too! Boys are so dumb!"

Clara O'Flaherty. Her first American friend.

Olga woke up smiling, the face of the girl with the red hair was fading, but the face made her smile; she didn't remember why.

The common room. Other sleepers were sprawled on chairs around it, eyes closed—except for Doris. She was reading; she had a stack of books in front of her, on the table where they ate.

She closed her eyes again. Comfortable...so she could just.... Where had she been? She had a wispy sense of a street; walking down it with other girls. Then she was in what must have been an auditorium, or theater—no, she saw basketball hoops hanging above both ends of the room. It was the basketball court, only now it was—

The school assembly.

Olga heard her name called, from the front of the assembly. She smiled graciously at everyone around her, especially the tough boys over at the side. Usually, they towered over her, but now she was standing and they were sitting: looking up at her. Of course, they admired her; she wasn't just smart, she was beautiful.

"Olga, uh, Di Quintero," the silly fat man up front botched her name, again, "for the highest grade average in 11th grade, here at Queens High."

Olga did a curtsey, befitting the princess she knew herself to be, really. The boys in her class gawked at her, and slavered, but their hunger didn't bother her. She had dated a few of them: Dirk,

Ramon, Gugliemo, Nate.... and she had fended them off without any trouble at all. When she began to feel the least uncomfortable with their eager attentions, she had just told them to stop, sharply—and they had.

She smiled to think of the scene she'd had with Nate just to her right; he'd tried to grab her breasts, before she was ready. She'd given him the what for! He'd slunk away like a whipped dog.

The girls, except for her friends, like Clara, looked as if they resented her. Well, let them. Mentally, she tossed her head at them. As far as her audience could see, she was still nodding graciously in all directions. She knew things they didn't know. Nobody else knew why she was here, instead of living the life of the princess she really deserved. No one else could say they'd made their family move here, especially while leaving riches behind. No one else's mother received a sack of gold coins from a series of messengers, the same one for several months, and then another, all dark, all part Indio, all incoherent, even in Spanish.

There were other Venezolanos, here, there; she could see them; mostly sons and daughters of people her mother knew from "home." They knew she was a princess; they knew about her family; they were no longer in any danger.

But they lived in a little house, attached to the ones on each side, on a street that wasn't very special, except that she remembered the other side of the street had been farmland when they first came. Now, it was a row of houses, too, and more rows of houses, on other streets behind them; it had happened so quickly.

But still, she was a princess. She bestowed her beneficent smile on all of them, and they all responded, even those girls who'd looked so resentful the moment before.

Yes. She had always known she could do that. And she was only 15. She would go to college after next year. And then? A whole life was out there, waiting for her.

Olga smiled to herself, and saw the green of riotous spring growth out the window. Oh. She was back here. She could hear the care woman taking someone to the bathroom next door. She knew she'd be next, although she wasn't sure why she knew; her memory wasn't what it had been; she knew she couldn't remember things that other people said had just happened. But, what was it she was remembering?

Was it memory?

Olga didn't mind when the care woman helped her dress. It was hard to get your arm in the sleeve, your leg in the pants leg. Besides, Miriam had dressed her for years, until she was too old to let her. Well, Olga almost smirked to think of it: now she was old enough to let her—or whoever it was. She wondered what had happened to Miriam when they left.

Left?

Trinidad.

She smiled, and closed her eyes.

She was standing in a row, on some kind of dais, in a white graduation gown, next to Clara, and her other classmates, including Nate and Gugliemo.

"Olga de Quintero."

He finally got the name right. She stepped forward, and turned to smile at everyone, but never missed a step up the stairs to the podium where the Principal was standing, holding out an official-looking certificate—or something.

"Olga has shown amazing determination, and dazzled us with her intelligence..." well, maybe he didn't quite say that. He was saying, "Olga is our most accomplished graduate; she has won the first-ever Pan American Scholarship, which will send her to Mount Holyoke, all expenses paid."

Everyone was applauding, and it tasted like wine, like that wine Dominic first served her, back long ago, back in...in Belmont Circle, Port of—she shook the name away.

She didn't have a speech ready! "Thank you," she said into the microphone someone was pointing towards her. Applause felt so good!

But suddenly, it wasn't the same place, at all. Where was she? She didn't know; she wasn't at the high school; she was standing on a platform in the open air, trees overhead, people milling about below her, looking up at her. The street, or road in front of her must have been closed: there were people standing on it, clapping—applauding her! Of course. She didn't know what they were applauding for, but it was her they were celebrating—as well they should. "I want to thank you all very much, especially...." She was about to say 'my teachers,' but then she realized, again, this wasn't the school from before: she did remember that, for an instant. So, she didn't finish the sentence, just nodded in every direction as the crowd applauded her.

"Please, Mrs. Smyth," a good-looking youngish man wheedled in her ear, "tell us your real story."

Her real story? Was she Mrs. Smyth? Apparently, she was. She must be in a very different place and time. Life was confusing.

Then, the vision faded.

She was back in her room, the one overlooking a running creek; the water was in spate. Life was confusing enough. Were her dreams—no they weren't dreams; they were her life, but that was confusing, too. So many things, so many times. She wished, momentarily, she could remember them after they disappeared—on waking? Maybe, at her age—how old was that, actually?

A phrase dangled: a man's voice saying, "the real story."
Whose? Hers?
Someone wanted to know? What story?
Her confusion made her tired; she closed her eyes.

It was early morning. The sun shone on the other side of the street, the newly built attached houses shone in the sunlight, looking nicer than they were. Her mother was leaving the house. She looked old and worn out. She started working, Olga remembered, when her father's bags of gold coins didn't show up for several months.

"Cuando nosotros factory workers van trabajar," her mother explained once; she had to be at the factory at eight o'clock. It was a hat factory, but Olga never understood why her mother kept working. Her father did send gold coins, only not every month. Uncle Benjamin had explained that the couriers were sometimes having a hard time getting there, all the way from wherever it was—Amazonas, or was it that state near Maracaibo? She wondered if some of the couriers just took the money and went their own way, not that she cared much; she wasn't going to stay there forever. She didn't mind living in the little attached house in Queens for a little while longer. Besides, she was going to Mount Holyoke in the fall. She was only sixteen.

Her aunt Berta joined her mother at the door: two old, faded women in black. Why black? Olga loved green. She was wearing a green dress—she looked down at herself and was pleased by what she saw. Then, she glimpsed the boxes stacked in the cramped inner room; her wardrobe for going to college.

Uncle Benjamin had sent most of them. From Paris. He did, occasionally, come to visit, but never to stay. He stayed in expensive hotels in the city. She'd visited him there several times. He was no longer so handsome, though; he'd gone bald: he had a shining forehead that reached all the way to the middle of the top of his head. He tried to comb his black hair over it, but the last time she saw him, he had given up and just combed it across, as if his forehead reached back that far. She was sure he was not doing "nasty things" with her mother anymore. Their expressions when they saw each other were friendly, on his part, stony, on hers.

Oh well. Olga knew she was beautiful—and brilliant. She couldn't worry about her mother. They got out of Trinidad before any of them got hurt—or worse—thanks to her. In the fall she would go to Mount Holyoke, whether her father sent gold coins, or not, whether Uncle Benjamin sent her pretty dresses, or not. She'd have a full scholarship, so nothing else mattered. She was a princess, after all.

Olga glanced at her mother again. She was fussing with her hat and gloves; Berta was helping her. It was warm outside, but her mother always had to wear a veil, had to wear gloves, even though she was going to the hat factory. She always did cover up, even when they went to the beach in Trinidad. Thank God, she forgot about sun veils and stockings for Olga! It was because there was no Miriam Cunningham to make her wear them.

The beach in Trinidad! For an instant, she glimpsed the broad sand beach, the surf, palm trees bending in the constant wind, but then the vision faded.

Her mother, before her, pulled her sun veil over her face. It was sunny outside, but here it didn't matter. Besides, the other women at the factory were so common!

Mama looked sick, Olga realized, not just old. Aunt Berta was old, but she didn't look as worn out, her skin still had some shine to it. Her mother's looked like faded parchment, as if someone had crushed it into a ball and then flattened it out again.

Well, maybe she was just getting old. She had never told Olga her real age. She had dismissed what she'd told the immigration officer not long after they'd landed. So, maybe she was in her forties? She looked much older.

"Bye, Mama, Aunt Berta. Have a good time," she called as they went out the door.

Olga resolved to herself, right then and there: "I will never work in a factory."

Hard to wake up. Why should she? She heard a voice beside her and struggled to open her eyes.

"I was a writer—novels. I hear you operated a school?"

It was Doris, the one who's always reading. She's asking me? Olga thinks for a moment. A school. Yes, she can see the children arrayed around her, waiting for her to tell them, ask them, tease out of them, what they would do that day. The staff is ranged around them, on the periphery.

Operated a school. "Yes, I did. It was a wonderful school."

"Now, that's interesting," she heard herself saying to the children. "Now each of you find out everything you can about him, and then come back to me. Before lunchtime. And anyone who doesn't come back with something about him, won't get any lunch," she ended gaily, not really meaning it.

She watched as the boys and a few girls scattered towards the library, the classrooms, their own rooms. The tall, handsome black boy grinned at her as he passed by a minute later, a book under his arm. She was in the garden, of course.

That voice again. Her eyes wanted to stay closed, but she struggled to open them.

"Did you teach, too?" It's the old woman who—Doris is asking. Her.

"Oh, yes. First of all." She closes her eyes, trying to remember, to summon up the memory.

It only comes when it wants to, she thinks. And then a fragment comes.

"I taught, and then...I ran a school. My school. A wonderful school."

She saw the children around her, younger children, eager eyes, all looking up at her—and Mabel, her co-teacher and best friend. For a moment, she remembered Mabel, the two of them always joking, the way they are now, in front of the children, the children laughing, too.

Olga looks up into the drooping eyes of the old woman who always reads. Doris. The vision fades. Had she asked something? She doesn't joke. Why did she think about jokes?

"I published six novels," Doris is saying.

Olga wonders: how old is she? She looks really old. She, Olga, can't be that old, can she?

"I, I have to go to bed." It doesn't matter to her that it's daylight, maybe even morning. It's bedtime. Besides, she thinks, as she toils down the hall with her walker, it's a long way, and she'll be tired out enough to sleep when she gets there. There. Her bedroom. In this northern place.

She sighs with pleasure as she lies down on the bed. Someone lifts her feet for her—of course they do—whoever they are—and covers them with a blanket.

Her eyes close of their own accord.

19

She made a grand arrival.

She was a little amused to think how much preparation it had taken.

Uncle Benjamin had rented a large town car. One of the Embassy's drivers had driven it, in uniform. Uncle Benjamin had come, instead of her mother—"to present the young Venezuelan woman who has won such an honor for her country, as well as for herself." That was her, of course.

Just having Hernan and Felipe, in uniform, scurrying ahead of her with her bags, and Uncle Benjamin, dressed beautifully, in the most exquisitely tailored suit—he didn't dress this well when he came to visit them in Jackson Heights—that was enough. But she was wearing her favorite new green dress, from Paris, a slinky silk, and she'd just gotten her hair cut radically short in back, in the latest fashion.

She could see her new classmates try not to stare at her, and she could almost hear them thinking: 'princess.' She smiled, graciously, granting them the benediction of her presence. She felt their curious stares as she passed by; almost heard the whispering as she went down the hallway.

As she was moving into her room, her next-door neighbor leaned into the doorway. She was as light as Olga was dark, white hair with only the barest tint of red, freckles, white, white skin, and she sidled up to her and asked, "Um, some of the girls say you're a princess, or marquess, or something like that; is it true?"

Regally, Olga smiled back. "I'm from Venezuela. My uncle is

Venezuelan Consul, my father's a governor and a general in Venezuela." Well, he was, apparently. She'd heard from her mother that he was now governor of Falcon, a state in the west of the country. Governors held the rank of General. Uncle Benjamin had told her that as an aside, when he mentioned her father. "And I am named for a princess," Olga added, "so, whoever's saying that is almost right. I was named for a Russian princess who insisted I be named after her, when I was a babe in arms. Olga. De Quintero."

The almost-white haired girl smiled back, her pale blue eyes sparkled. "I'm Sylvia; people call me Sylvie. Sylvia Smyth. I'm just from Mount Vernon."

Smyth? She wondered about that name. Was it classy, or just a fancy way of saying Smith? Sylvie looked nice enough, though, and her voice sounded cultured. She'd heard of Mount Vernon; it was a suburb, north of the city.

And the campus was so gorgeous, even nicer than Belmont Circle—so much nicer than Jackson Heights. Her room looked out on sweeping lawns and majestic trees. The nearest building, another dorm, probably, was sheathed in shining, dark green ivy.

She was pleased with herself. A princess.

Olga opened her eyes on a familiar scene: at the dining table, an old woman bent over a book—oh, Doris. Another woman, white-haired, long-nosed, sprawled across an armchair across from her. Olga never did remember her name. For a moment, she wasn't sure what was different, and then she realized she was sitting in a different chair, further down the room from the dining table. An old man was sitting, head back, eyes closed, in a chair parallel to hers—the one she remembered using—or did she? She wasn't sure. But she also didn't care. All she wanted was to go back wherever she had been before, before she opened her eyes.

She closed them.

"Why's that old woman in the room next door?" Henry is asking.

He's come up for the weekend. "All those girls!" he exclaimed. He's really too young, still in high school, just fifteen, not skipped ahead as she had been.

She looks at him and shakes her head. "What old woman?" She thinks she knows.

They are standing on the sweeping lawn, outside the dormitory, a red-brick, ivy-covered building, so much prettier than her mother's house in Jackson Heights.

"You know, the one you call Sylvie, the one with that cloud of white hair. Why's there a white-haired woman in college, anyway?"

"You think she looks old?"

"Well, she's got white hair, doesn't she?"

He was still so stupid! He has gotten nicer, though. "She doesn't have white hair, Henry, she's a very blonde strawberry blonde; if you looked, instead of just assumed, you'd see the red in it. Her older brothers are here somewhere, visiting, too. You should see them: they've both got really red hair." And such white skin, she marveled. They all three sounded so cultured, too.

Again, she wondered what kind of family they came from: 'Smyth' didn't tell you much, except it could be a fancy version of 'Smith.' But if someone in the family had changed their name, it must have been generations before. Both brothers, she gathered, had finished college and were working in New York. They were both quite good-looking. And cute.

She didn't want to go out with Sylvie's brothers, though. Silvie was one of her new best friends. She wanted to play the field.

She was no longer wherever she was before; suddenly, without a lurch, she was coming into the common room from outside; she'd heard that male visitors had arrived. Men. After however much time it had been—days, weeks?—she missed men, their aroma, their deep voices, their rough cheeks, their muscled shoulders. She scanned the new arrivals. Not bad. There were several other men besides Sylvie's two brothers—tall and short, good-looking and not so much. As she was passing by, one of the plain ones was holding forth about "Econ," about how the free market would bring us out of the Depression; she didn't understand his reasoning, so, she moved on to another knot of men and girls. Maybe she'd major in Economics.

One of the other men, tall, with slicked-back, light brown hair, nodded to her and smiled. She smiled back, and raised her shoulder seductively; he came over.

"Hi, I'm Dan."

"And I am Olga," she declared, "de Quintero." She smiled up at him as if she was on a throne and he was kneeling below it. She had settled in an armchair a little apart from the others.

He looked a little confused. "Isn't Olga a Russian name?"

"Of course," she purred. "I'm named for a Russian princess, but I'm from Venezuela."

Dan looked only a little less confused. "You sure don't sound like someone foreign!"

Foreign: she didn't feel foreign, but then her very own mother could speak only a few words of English. She was sure she didn't have an accent, at least.

"Thank you!" She was pleased. She didn't want to sound like a Venezuelan, or worse yet, a Trinidadian. "I was born on a tiny island off the coast of Venezuela, and my father is Governor of one of its states, and," she shrugged charmingly, "I speak three languages."

"Venzuela?" he mispronounced. "That where that guy Gomez is President, for life, or something?"

"Why, yes." And after Gomez, el Generale Velasco (her uncle by marriage) was the second-most powerful man in the land.

He looked impressed. "Lot of oil there?"

Olga shrugged, lifting both elegant shoulders. "The only oil I think about is perfumed."

"You are a pretty little thing, aren't you!"

She glared at him. Pretty and little were not in her vocabulary. She was elegant, and beautiful.

"Well!" she said, dismissing him, "it's been lovely to talk with you, but now I must go."

She rose most graciously, and gracefully dismissed him. Little thing!

Olga smiled as she opened her eyes. What a wonderful dream...memory...already fading away. She couldn't remember it at all now, but it made her happy, anyway. Something good had happened, she was sure.

Seeing no one else, seeing that she was still lying down in her room, she pulled the covers back over her, and closed her eyes.

Rafe reached into her undies with his finger, and she liked it, let him probe further. She liked his seaside smell—he came from Gloucester, he said—so she whispered in his ear, "I'll go all the way with you, if we get engaged, but not until."

Rafe stopped abruptly, his finger now hardly even touching her.

Olga chuckled deep in her throat. "Don't worry, I don't want to marry you."

Rafe cocked his head at her; he looked puzzled (men were so stupid). "You want to become engaged, but you don't want to marry me?"

"That's right." It seemed obvious to her.

"Oh!" Rafe laughed. "You're going to trap me, aren't you? You know, get pregnant, then force me to marry you."

"Of course not!" Olga felt an instant outrage." I'm not even 20. I may have children someday—not with you, but now I'm going to Mount Holyoke. I'm going to do something on my own in this world, not just be handmaiden to some man."

"But you want to...."

"Yes."

"Okay!" said Rafe with real enthusiasm. Then, he frowned. "But how do I ask you to become engaged to me without asking you to marry me?"

"Just ask me," she looked up at him through her long, black lashes, "to be your fiancée."

She had found that look always undid them, and it did this time, too.

"Will you be my fiancée?"

"Of course."

He was almost panting!

"There's just one more thing, before we, um, find a time and place." Definitely not on campus. "Get condoms."

He almost recoiled with surprise. She shrugged. "I don't have a diaphragm, yet."

She watched as he left her dorm with a purposeful lift to his gait, and smiled. Women who want something should get it when they want it.

For just an instant, she remembered that her mother's other sister, not Berta—another Braulia, maybe—the one who stayed on in Margarita and Coché, had several children, maybe even four or five, but she never got married.

Nothing wrong with that, but she might marry someday, if she found the right man. Meanwhile, she was young and beautiful: why not take advantage of it? Besides, she was sure she'd enjoy it. Nothing wrong with enjoying yourself.

Olga opened her eyes and for just an instant wondered where she was: then she remembered. She was in that comfortable place and she didn't have to worry about anything. She was lying back in her regular armchair, and opposite her was the old man—she'd heard someone call him Gill, which seemed an odd name, but he smiled at her, and then at the dog in his lap. It was a yappy thing, but it was quiet at the moment, so she smiled back.

Her friend, Doris, the one who read all the time, was reading from a stack of books in front of her at the dining room table. There was another old woman sprawled across from her in another armchair. Her name didn't register.

"Hello, Olga!"

She looked up, slightly startled. Oh. Her son. He looked so like... "Hello. How are you; how are things?"

"Pretty good, actually...." She didn't hear the rest, but that didn't matter. "How are you?"

"So's to be about."

He laughed. "Is that all? Isn't that what...in St Maarten?"

She didn't hear, or understand, but it didn't matter. Something about St Maarten. She shrugged. "How are things?"

"Well, actually, I'm having this problem with...."

She didn't want to hear any more—a problem? No hay problema. She had a hard time keeping her eyes open, so she didn't. Words rumbled on above her, but she didn't pay any attention. She couldn't make out the words, so they didn't matter.

Then, far away, she heard her son say something. It sounded as if he was talking to someone else, so she drifted off....

It was her first time in Venezuela—since she'd been a baby! The guards at the airport were a little scary: sunglasses masking their eyes, high crowned military caps that looked like they were ready to take off, large, visible weapons. Then she realized: these are my people. They work for people like my father, and they all work for El Generale, her uncle by marriage. Then she smiled at them, and they smiled back.

This was going to be interesting: her father was somehow going to introduce her to Caracas society, high society, and she, she preened a little as she promenaded towards the Aduana. She could see her father, in a white suit, with a prominent belly, but recognizably like the last photos she'd seen of him. He smiled and waved from behind the barrier, and then spoke to the officer next to him. The man nodded, and waved her through, she holding out her Venezuelan passport for all to see.

It was like being underwater, and trying to rise to the surface and something holds you down and you struggle—and then—Olga smiled as she opened her eyes: it was that room with the big window and the, the— thing you ate at. She could have sworn she was somewhere else. Oh well.

"Time for lunch, Olga. Let me help you to the table."

Table. That's what it was.

"Thank you." She reached forward to the edge of the chair, pushed up from her hands—it wasn't easy—but she was standing. She gripped the walker in front of her in both hands, and slid one foot forward, then the other.

Lunch. Here. Then, she yawned. To bed? Oh. Lunch.

Such a long time! She keeps on insisting: "Put me to bed!" No one listens! Someone even laughs and says, "You have to eat some lunch, first."

It takes so long! She can hardly stand it, can feel herself shaking with frustration. Why don't they let her, why don't they—finally, she's allowed to get up, grab her walker, voyage off to her room, such a long way, to her bed. Someone helps her into the bed, covers her with, what is that thing? She pulls it up to her chin.

"Thank you," she says, and she means it, as she closes her eyes and drifts off....

They pose for the photographer, a fashion photographer Maria Luisa had called in. He goes on about how beautiful they all are, and Olga knows: she is. And Irma looks like a darker Clara Bow. Her cousin Nené—they've become so close, so quickly—is the only one who doesn't look like some kind of movie star. Ernan and Irma pose together, looking sexy. But Olga steals the show in any picture she's in, leaning back with her legs crossed, or grimacing even better than Julio. Julio likes to play the clown, holding his fingers above Chi-Chi's head as if she had rabbit ears, just as the photographer takes the picture.

Her father is diffident in a white suit. He's only at the edges of the group pictures. He's quite noticeably stout, although tall, and white-haired, and he really doesn't enjoy being in the middle of all the young people. Olga gets the feeling that he likes to look at her from afar, but he's uncomfortable up close.

All her cousins are so well dressed, and Julio, too. She only has a few dresses, and no jewelry, but they keep on insisting she wear theirs. The Velascos must be very rich, and powerful, Olga thinks, but then of course they are; they should be: El Generale is the Governor General of Caracas, the capital city; he's their father. Maria Luisa, their mother, is her father's eldest sister. Only Nené's father, of all her uncles, does not work for Gomez and Velasco, but he's a successful lawyer.

She smiles to think of Sylvia and Bobbie back in Mount Holyoke: what would they make of the huge jewels her cousins and aunts wear as mere accents to their Paris dresses? What would they think of the immense limousine and the uniformed chauffeur who takes them everywhere, and only bows and smiles when they keep him waiting for hours?

She has never felt more at home!

Her father was not very social; he "hated" high society, the high society of the Cariqueños. Nené whispered to her that he was afraid to dance. He watched, awkwardly, from the sidelines the first time she danced, with her cousin Ernan.

But then...is it another time? It's a fancy dress ball: the first dance. She is in her father's arms: they are the first out on the floor, and everyone applauds—of course they do—as an announcer proclaims: "Olga Coello de Quintero, daughter of the Honorable Heriberto Quintero-Noguera."

He is very shy; he holds her at arm's length as if she might break, and keeps on making jokes that she can't quite get: his Spanish is so

181

different from her mother's and her mother never told jokes. Then her cousins, Irma, Chi-Chi and Nené are escorted onto the floor by their fathers. Her father is still making little sense—he's smitten by her, of course. After they tour around the ballroom again, a beautiful young man taps him on the shoulder. Her father hurriedly relinquishes her, saying something like, "a father always loves to dance with his beautiful daughter, but he knows it's time for him to step aside. Thank you my dear Olga."

His face turns quite red as he gives her one last lingering glance.

Olga could see her cousins, Chi-Chi, Nené and Irma—young men were taking their fathers' places, too, almost as beautiful as hers—and other couples were just beginning to drift onto the dance floor.

"Introduced to Caracas Society." Her father had written that she should come, "so that Caracas Society can see you, as befits your station."

She is a princess: she has been announced—as befits her station.

Olga fought to stay where she was, but she surfaced in a small room with a window that let in the late afternoon sunlight. She looked around her. Pictures of people she thought she knew were perched on a dresser, a shelf above her bed, and on the windowsill. One was of a dapper-looking man, in a checked sports jacket and a mustache, looking fondly down at— she was wearing that hat she remembered, a slouch hat that played off her high cheekbones to perfection. That was her husband—and her, of course.

She looked at the picture above her bed: a younger man, his shirt open to the waist. He looked like her husband, but he wasn't. He was…Douglas. Handsome. He should be, after all, if he's her son. He is? Olga shrugged. Did it matter?

But this was tiring, looking at these pictures, having these ideas, thinking of these names. Did names matter?

She doesn't hear anything, so it's not time to get up; it's not time for eating—supper? Breakfast? No, it's light outside, but she doesn't care.

She closes her eyes.

It's a special Sunday; she's going to the Cathedral with her cousins! They're all a flurry of dresses and a tinkle of jewels.

She has only a few dresses, of course: what she could fit in a suitcase. And no jewels, except some small gold earrings. Her favorite dress is green, and her cousin Nené says, "Ooo, Olgita! I have just the emeralds for you!"

The necklace is gold, with a huge emerald pendant, and there are matching earrings!

When Olga objects, Nené says, "No, no, Olgita! I am wearing blue: only diamonds or sapphires. You need the emeralds." She holds up a diamond necklace: it flashes in the light. The diamond at its center is easily the biggest diamond Olga has ever seen. Then Nené holds up what looks like a handful of sapphires as large as pebbles in a brook, all flashing blue light. "Which do you think?" She holds up first the diamonds and then the sapphires next to the dress she's just tried on.

Olga smirks at her. "Oh, the diamonds, really, the diamonds! That pendant reminds me of pictures of the King's coronation—the British King. I lived in a Crown Colony, after all."

"Trinidad." Nené nods. "But you speak Spanish so well, even after all those years in El Norte, and I heard your English: it sounds so American. You are so clever!"

Olga could feel herself preen. "Why, Nené, thank you!" She always liked to hear what she knew was true.

She hung the emeralds round her neck, but she couldn't wear the earrings that matched it; she had always refused to have her ears pierced.

"But, why, Olgita?"

"My mother's family always said it's a sign of slavery."

Nené smirked at her. "I know just what to do."

"Camacho!" Nené called out the door.

"Yes, Miss?" A man's rough voice in the hallway.

"Take these to Umberto, and quick! He must put clips on them! Now!"

"You see, you can wear them anyway. It won't be long."

"But the service at the Cathedral?"

Nené shook her head and pointed her chin at their cousins: they were still changing dresses. Chi-Chi had just pulled off a gorgeous silver lamé dress and was holding out a red one. Irma was shaking her head, and then she slipped out of her own dress, a slinky, skin-colored silk, and held up one that looked just like it, except it was a light pink.

Olga watched as her cousins wriggled into dresses, tried on jewelry to go with them, and then discarded them and tried on something else. All the dresses were exquisite: the jewels were unbelievable.

"Isn't it late?" she asked. "Aren't we going to miss the service?"

Nené and Irma cackled. "Don't worry about it, Olgita!," Irma reassured, "We have plenty of time."

Just as Chi-Chi was putting the last touches on her outfit: white tulle with bright red rubies at her breast and ears, there was a knock at the door.

"It's Camacho," a man's voice announced. "I have the earrings."

"Oh, good!" said Nené marching to the door. "Here. Hand them over. Thank you, Camacho." She turned to Olga. "Now, Olgita, you will wear earrings. It is not proper to be without them." She held them up; they had been converted to clips.

Olga shrugged. "Of course."

And then they were all gossiping, chirping, saying how beautiful everyone looked, out the door, down the stairs to the waiting limousine. The uniformed chauffeur ran round the car opening all the doors. They were a billow of dresses and perfume as they piled into the narrow space.

It wasn't very far. She could see the high spire of the Cathedral from a long way off, or at least it looked like a long way off, but it took them almost no time to get there.

They pulled up in front of the long, high steps, but the steps were empty—except for two guards flanking the huge doors. They were late!

Just as the chauffeur opened the door to the limousine, the great Cathedral doors opened, and people began to stream out.

"Oh," said Chi-Chi, "We are just in time!"

The five of them paraded up the steps, showing off their dresses to the descending crowd, the young men smiling at them.

Olga was just a little disappointed that she didn't get to see the Cardinal.

She heard herself telling someone, "That's how the Quinteros go to church!" She closed her eyes.

"Olga? Time to get up and go to the bathroom."

Olga didn't want to get up. She shut her eyes tight, but it didn't work. She was awake. She opened her eyes: the little room—with a bed in it. The window was aslant with early morning sun. She closed her eyes. Tight. She could feel the woman's presence at her feet, but she didn't open them.

"I don't want to go to the bathroom; I don't want to get out of bed!" Olga kicked her feet on the bed in protest. She knew she was being unreasonable; she was enjoying it. She was a naughty little girl.

"Now, Olga...Ladies go to the bathroom before they go to the table for breakfast."

Breakfast. She was hungry. Ladies... "I'm a Lady," she opened her eyes and smirked at the care woman, "so, I guess I'll get up."

Laboriously, she pushed her way to a sitting position, the care woman pulling the sheets out of the way; she swung her legs down to the floor and glanced out the window: green, sunlight on trees; she smiled sweetly at the

185

woman, as if she were innocent—they both knew she was not—then heaved with all her might, as she leaned forward from the waist. She was rising!

So much work to do now: food, in the morning, but she has to go all the way to—what's that place? Why must things have names?

Things on the—whatever it is. A bowl, a whatever it is, something on it, something in the bowl.

After eating whatever it is, a little mushy—porridge?—and a cylinder of—fruit of some kind—and warm drink, the kind she always drinks—from a neighboring country—Colombia—coffee!

Now, she's going to go to bed!

She sighed as she lay half-upright in an armchair, then closed her eyes.

She had just returned after Christmas in Caracas, she realized. She was unpacking her bags and hanging up all the silk dresses her cousins had given her. She felt like a princess, especially when her friend Sylvie peeked into her room and squealed, "Oh! Those are beautiful, Olga!" She was pointing at the new dresses.

"Thank you," purred Olga. "My father and cousins gave them to me: from Paris. They're very high up in Caracas, you know, Venezuela, the government. You can borrow them, if you'd like."

"You are so generous!" Sylvia exclaimed, and then, mock-solemnly, "You are a princess!"

Her brother heaved into the room with the last of her bags just after Olga mentioned their Cariqueño relatives. He nodded knowingly towards Sylvia. Head down, he muttered, "High up: El Generale, next to El Presidente." Then, actually seeing Sylvia, he looked confused. Henry's thick black eyebrows furrowed like furry inchworms; he was frowning at her.

"Don't mind him," Olga said to her, waving him away as the nuisance he was, had always been. He was looking so confused: he was so dumb! Still.

He'd volunteered to come up with her and Uncle Benjamin, to help carry all the luggage, but he'd confessed to her why he'd really wanted to come: "The idea of all those college girls just makes me dizzy—to be surrounded by so many girls!"

After Sylvia turned back to her own room, promising to sit with Olga at lunch, Henry asked, perplexed, "Why's she got such white hair? Isn't she too old to—"

"Henry! We went through this last time; she's my age. Her hair isn't white, it's strawberry blonde."

"Oh. Really?"

His hair and hers were jet black; their slightly dull older brother, Julio, thankfully back in Caracas, was considered "blond," because his hair was light brown, the way their father's had been. Their father's hair was white when she saw him on Christmas.

"Henry," Olga was scornful, "you've got a lot to learn! Don't you remember? Her hair isn't white; it has just a tiny touch of red. You'd see it if you opened your eyes and looked. She's just a year older than me." She laughed. "You should see her brothers! The younger one has bright red hair; the older one's got light red hair that's almost blond." The cute one: almost the negative to her positive, her darkness to his whiteness, except for the ubiquitous freckles.

No Venezuelan would ever look like him. He was also just a little shy, when he asked her out for the first time; she liked that. All men towered over her; they didn't intimidate her, though she didn't know why, or care to know. But Julian wasn't so tall; in fact, he was small compared to most men; she liked him for that. He wasn't much taller than her brother.

Of course, she had other boyfriends. She was engaged to two of them—what were their names? Olga shrugged. It didn't matter. What mattered was the freedom that gave her.

She glimpsed a suitor's red hair; he was handsome, and he said Tiyousdey and tomahtos. His skin was so white; it was as if it had been bleached, except for the scattering of liver spotted freckles over his face and hands.

"The snow was up to my knees, but the worst thing was the wind—highest wind in the northeast; it's so exposed, you know...." He was telling her about climbing up Mt. Washington in the wintertime. He grinned. "That's when I slipped on some ice! Oh boy, I thought I was done for! I must've fallen six feet! Thank god the snow was deep where I landed."

"Dear me! What did you do?"

He shrugged, "Well, I just got back up, dusted myself off, climbed back to where I'd been and then just kept on going, of course." His smile was self-deprecating, as if to say, 'That's the kind of fool I am.' Then he grinned. "Did you know the Eskimos have 48 words for snow; we only have one. At that point, I'd have liked to curse with all 48 words. Well...." He shrugged.

He was cute. Then she remembered: he was Sylvia's older brother, Julian. Oh well. Maybe she'd go out with him, anyway. He was fun. And, after all, she was only engaged to two men.

Her Mount Holyoke friends had kidded her, "One man isn't enough, Olga?" She had just smirked at them and shrugged; they knew perfectly well why she was engaged. Just because they were so worried about what other people thought, didn't mean she had to be.

She had her own rules.

She'd go out with him if she felt like it; she was inclined to feel like it.

"...pick you up about 5:30, here?"

"Why, thank you for asking. For dinner?"

"And drinks."

"Why, I'd love to!" She had been to speakeasies in the last year. She enjoyed the surreptitious game: the whisper through the little peep window, the hush-hush outside, the raucous abandon within. She liked drinking, too, she realized, just enough to get quite high. She even remembered the first time, when Dominic had served her wine, so long ago.

Julian had said "and drinks," with a little sparkle in his eye, blue, or maybe blue-gray; a twinkle, anyway.

Yes, she liked him. She didn't need to ask him to get condoms, now that she had her diaphragm, something every up and coming Mount Holyoke woman should have, just in case.

She liked it that he was not as tall as most of the men she'd been with. She could see he was small compared to them when he stood next to them, but he didn't feel small. There was something so very solid about him. He was tall enough for her.

She shook her head. She was thinking about him as if she were going to marry him! She hadn't even gone to bed with him; hardly knew anything about him—well, no, she knew quite a bit about his family, come to think of it—all she'd heard from Sylvia—their family. Their mother was the granddaughter of Nathaniel Hawthorne! Their father was the founder of the *New York Times Book Review*!

Did anyone else in her family even know who Nathaniel Hawthorne was? Henry: he'd complained about having to read *The Scarlet Letter* when they were still in high school together. No wonder Julian and Sylvia spoke so well; she wished she could, too, but how could she call her parents Mamah and Papah? For Sylvie and Julian, it sounded natural; for her...she shook her head.

She watched him stroll down the walk, away from the dorm; he looked solid, but he didn't swagger. He was not some effete descendant of such an eminent ancestor. His sister was so delicate; his solidity was reassuring.

And yet, she realized, seeing him from a distance: he was thin, but not like those dangly tall men she'd been with, thin like those runners she'd seen in a race, probably on July 4th.

Most of all, she liked his sparkle.

"For drinks, too."

Time to go to lunch, Olga! You can get up now. We have to go to the table.

She opened her eyes and gazed dolefully up at the caregiver. Why did they always have to interrupt her? Why did she have to "get up?"

Besides, it hurt waking up. She ached—everywhere—but when she slept, she was young again; nothing hurt. Why couldn't she just stay sleeping? It hurt to be old; she couldn't remember how old, but old.

Then she saw the others, sitting around the table. They were old, too; they looked very old. Was she that old?

A plate was at her place, and a cup of coffee steamed just to the right of it. On the plate was some kind of green, some fish fingers—funny name for it—and some carrots.

She heaved herself, with great effort to stand, grabbing the walker the woman was holding steady for her. Then, she pushed forward, the walker sliding over the soft floor.

As she lowered herself onto the chair, she glimpsed him smiling at her. He looked—but he had gray hair and he wasn't—oh, he's her son—Dougle—that's what she used to call him.

"How're you doing?" he asked.

Had she just seen him somewhere else? But with red hair. That was— Julian? Life was getting so confusing! "So's to be about." She remembered seasoned, wrinkled old black men, almost toothless, in St Maarten: they said that.

"Looks like you're going to have a nice lunch."

She contemplated the plate in front of her, reached for the cup of coffee; nice lunch. Nice.

She looked out the big window. It was cold out there; white snow covering the patio floor. Slowly, painfully, she grasped the fork beside her plate; she reached out, her hand shaking slightly, and speared the, the fish 'finger'. And then it was in her mouth. Okay. She took another; it crunched, was salty. She drank some coffee, and then stuck a fork into one of the other things. She felt a moment of triumph as the fork lifted whatever it was, to her mouth. Oh, a cooked carrot. She reached out again....

But this eating was tiring. She closed her eyes as she chewed....

Julian was sitting across from her. They were in a speakeasy in Northampton—better to be a little away from the college, she remembered agreeing. She'd been there before—or to one like it. There was something about speakeasies; they were noisy and furtive at the same time. You had to know someone who knew someone, when you knocked on the door.

It was loud around them, but they had found a table. Julian consulted with the waiter, serious, their heads together, looking at the wine list, and then Julian nodded. "Yes, that one. A German Riesling."

He looked slightly apologetic. "It's a mess over there, but maybe if they can still sell us wine, the Nazis won't take over."

Olga laughed. "Oh, it's probably made in Long Island!"

He grinned. "And they pasted on a German label?"

"Our German department could print up something that looks just right. I know they do some of their own German printing—"

"Fraktur, they call it," said Julian; he grinned. "I don't know why I know." His face went deadpan, his voice went flat: "I didn't study German; I studied a dead language."

"Latin?"

"Worse than that." Julian smirked. "Ancient Greek. My brother, too. He beat me for the Greek prize by a quarter point. I'll never forgive him."

"Poor boy! He's your younger brother, too!"

"Yeah." He made a mock grimace. "We went to college at the same time—same class, same fraternity—at least he had a different major." He grinned. "He's a good man, though."

"His hair is even redder than yours. I saw you both, when Sylvia arrived last semester. And your mother. Me, I studied Latin," she shrugged, saw her bare shoulder rise, so sensuous. "I speak French, as well as Spanish—talking about live languages."

"I figured you spoke Spanish. Sylvie said you're from Venezuela. But you speak perfect English."

191

She noticed: he pronounced Venezuela the way it was supposed to sound, not 'Venzuela.'

"Why, thank you!" It was actually better than her Spanish. Her mother's Spanish was so corrupted with island pidgin, she'd had difficulty at first, following her cousins' chatter in Caracas. They spoke "Andino Spanish" they said. Her father spoke it, too. She hadn't heard it much, since they'd left Trinidad, except during Uncle Benjamin's brief visits—and then the trip to Caracas.

The music was loud. Julian just looked at her, gazed, almost as if he was looking at—a beautiful painting? She liked it when men admired her. She preened.

"Most of my Venezuelan family speaks English—and the best Spanish. They're very high up, you know."

"High up?" Julian looked mystified.

"Oh, you know. Well connected, high up in the regime—my father's a governor, and when I went to visit my cousins in Caracas—you should have seen their limousines, and—"

"What did they drive?" Suddenly, he was all attention. "Hispano-Suizas, Rolls-Royces, Daimlers?"

Olga shrugged. "They were just big and long, that's all I know. The driver had a separate space, a window between him and the passengers. I don't know what kind, sorry."

"Aah, you're a girl. What would you know about cars?" He smirked at her. "Anyway, I'd have liked to see them. You said your family's high up in the regime? That's dictator Gomez, isn't it?" Julian's expression was hard to read.

"Oh, not a dictator: he's El Presidente—" she shrugged, "for life. Oh, it's not a democracy, of course. My uncle Benjamin—he's an ambassador now—says Venezuelans aren't ready for democracy. My uncle—by marriage—is number two in the regime: Governor General of Caracas. We call him El Generale."

"That's pretty high up! Sylvia told me she thought you were a princess when you first arrived. Guess that's pretty close."

"Oh!" she was pleased, "Not a princess, but I was named for one, a Russian princess: Princess Olga. I charmed her—when I was a baby. That was before the revolution, of course."

"And a beautiful baby you must have been! Did Princess Olga survive the Communists?"

"I don't know." Funny. She'd never thought about that! But she wanted to ask him about his family. She'd heard something from Sylvia, "I do know how distinguished your family is."

"You've heard about the Hawthornes?" Julian groaned. "Do you know my mother sent us to Bowdoin by selling Nathaniel's papers to its library? He's my great-grandfather, but the great man died long before I was born. At least, I got a good college education out of it—in Science."

"I've read your great-grandfather's *Scarlet Letter*; even my brother has."

"Well, you see, as a scientist, I don't really care about things like that very much, or people's family background, although yours sounds interesting. But you look like a princess, that's good enough for me. My father even wrote a novel about a girl like you—a fantasy, a princess, too, of the Incas—or something like that. Papah tells stories, still," he grinned and shrugged, as if to say, 'Who knows if they're true or not.' "On the other hand, to me you're a princess, even if Venezuela doesn't have titles, any more than we do. I know that about Venezuela, at least."

Olga reveled in the flattery.

"Why, thank you!"

"No, I mean it, it's something about you."

Olga posed for him. He didn't notice that she wore only simple clip earrings, a silver hair comb and a simple coral necklace; he just noticed her. She liked that even more.

"Um, want to order something to eat? Steak, maybe? I like it bloody!"

"Oh! I do, too." She wasn't sure about the bloody part, though, and when the waiter came and Julian said, "Two steaks, still bloody," she signaled to the waiter and said "not so bloody, for me."

He grinned. "I like that. A woman who has her own opinions."

Olga opened her eyes .She didn't know why, and she didn't want to, but she saw that it was that room; the sharp-nosed woman was sleeping in her chair across from her. The large woman—a friend?—was sitting at the— whatever it was— reading from a stack of books. The little old woman, who had suddenly appeared in the chair to her left, was looking out at the window; she looked scared. Olga had no idea of what, but she turned to look out the window, too. Nothing. Just sunshine through bare trees: pretty.

No need to stay awake. She closed her eyes.

She doesn't know if it's the same speakeasy. None of them have signs. Then she knows it's not the same one when Julian orders Italian spaghetti and meatballs, for both of them, and a "strong red wine." She smells the Italian food as soon as he says that. Funny, how she hadn't noticed it before.

She had savored his maleness. She'd liked his aroma. And his feel when he touched her. She wondered if he'd dare to do more than kiss her tonight. Maybe, she'd have to help things along a little. Her two fiancés both thought that engagement meant they could "take liberties." She hadn't discouraged them. Saying yes did mean that, didn't it? She'd just been careful. But actually, Warren and Rafe—were those their names?—didn't particularly interest her at the moment; Julian did. She had been seeing him for a month; he had come up every weekend. On the other hand, there was something about him, maybe his intensity, that made her hesitate.

They had eaten; she could see that, from the empty, greasy plates. The bottle was half empty when Julian poured her another glass and held up his, not to pretend to admire its color like her uncle—but to toast her!

She raised hers to him, wondering what was coming next.

Julian held up his wine glass and said, to her, "I adore you, Olga! Will you marry me?"

She shrugged, visibly—her shoulders were bare and she knew they were beautiful—she made sure the silver comb bangles tinkled in her hair. She just wasn't sure. She liked him; she liked kissing him; she liked his smell, but…. "Oh, don't be so silly! We've only known each other for a few weeks!"

"Five weeks," Julian gulped. "Excuse me!" He lurched to his feet. His face was almost green. "Be right back." He walked carefully towards the Boys Room and Olga smiled, to see him, keeping himself rigidly under control. Was he sick, or—she looked at the more than half-full bottle of wine and his hardly touched glass. He couldn't be drunk.

He came back a few minutes later. His skin between the freckles was dead white, and his freckles were dull, almost greenish. His eyes were slightly bloodshot. Shakily, he sat down and looked at her.

"I, I threw up. Everything."

Olga reached over and touched his hand; it was cold and a little damp.

She sat back and appraised him; she could feel a smile curving the ends of her lips, without her willing them to. "Oh, all right, yes, if it means so much to you! Yes, I'll marry you!"

"Oh my god!" Julian was transformed, shining, so red, so golden.

Olga almost purred, knowing suddenly why cats did.

She couldn't remember how it happened, but they were dancing, a slow dance. Julian wasn't a masterful dancer, but she didn't care; she just nestled into his chest. He smelled good, felt right and she was god's gift.

She wanted to marry him. He was from such a distinguished family, just like hers.

She knew already, he hated his job; all he did was shuffle papers in an office at WR Grace and Co., but he was just two years out of college. She knew all about the Depression; she studied Economics, after all. He was lucky to have a job at all. But he wouldn't stay at W.R. Grace forever.

He'd talked about camping out in the Adirondacks. Maybe she'd go with him, maybe this summer.

Besides, she wanted to be a coffee trader and WR Grace was a big coffee importer from Latin America. Her economics professor had told her she was a natural, "especially with three languages." At the very least, Julian could find out whom she should talk to. Maybe he could do more.

Marry him. Why not? It would be an adventure!

20

When Olga opened her eyes, again, she could feel her smile, but she wasn't sure why she was smiling. Was it because the care person was bringing the frail old man to the—whatever it was—where they ate? That meant it was time to eat. She didn't know if she was hungry and she didn't want to get up, but somehow she knew they'd come for her, so she waited.

After the man was seated, the care person came for her as she knew she would. "Come on, Olga, time to come to the table."

"I want to eat right here," she could hear herself saying, grinning up at the caregiver.

"No, no," said the caregiver, "you have to go to the table. I'll help you get up. C'mon!"

"Oh, all right!" She hoisted herself out of her chair; could feel a hand steadying her. She grasped the walker, pushing one foot forward and then the other—such effort! She could hear herself grunting with every exertion. She was hearing those grunts inside her: outside, it was very quiet. Was there something wrong with her hearing? She sort of knew there was, but she didn't care.

She was in front of the—whatever it was—near her place. She was happy to see that there was already something there, a whatever it was, with things on it.

She maneuvered the walker around the chair, then grabbed onto the chair arm and pushed herself forward, inches at a time.

"That's right, Olga," said a voice behind her.

With great effort, she carefully sidled in front of the chair, then, holding onto the chair arms, she collapsed downward. She was sitting on the edge of *the chair. She had to lift herself again, and push herself back. Great effort. Finally, she was in place.*

"Don't collapse on that chair!" she insisted to the gangly boy, who had just done that. "Get up, right now, and sit down properly, gracefully!"

The boy glowered, but got up, and sat down slowly. His grimace, directed towards her, was hilarious. She didn't let herself laugh, or even smile. She just nodded approval and passed on into the kitchen, to see if dinner was under control.

Dinner.

Lunch. She contemplated the plate: a sandwich, a vegetable of some kind, a bowl, probably soup, and a cup of coffee next to the plate. Good. She began to nibble, first one thing, then another....

Just as she was about to tell someone to put her to bed, he showed up, his hair heavily streaked in gray, a young woman with him.

"Hello, Olga."

She smiled, as the nuns had taught her, and parried: "How's it going?"

She didn't listen much to his answer; she'd heard, maybe from Doris, that his—wife? Her daughter-in-law—wasn't visiting because—oh, she was sick.

When he kept on talking, she had a moment of frustration. Had she eaten? Then it was time for her to—

"Put me to bed!"

He didn't seem to hear her, or pay attention.

When he kept on talking, grinning at his own joke, she felt her temper rising. Wasn't he going to do something about it? "Put me to bed before I fall apart!"

He stopped whatever he was saying and nodded to her: "Okay, okay, I'll call Pam."

Pam? Was that who took care of her? She didn't remember whether she had eaten, but now she was hobbling to her room—yes, she did hobble; she

knew that. Finally, she arrived at her room, and hauled herself into bed—
was someone helping her? She pulled the covers over her, sighed, glad to be
able to go back to sleep. She must have eaten, but she didn't remember; she
closed her eyes. Ahh, what relief, what pleasure!

The outside office was paneled in dark wood. A lone receptionist, over-made-up, looked up at her in surprise. "Have you come for
a steno job, Miss?"

Olga almost bridled. "Of course not! I've come for the coffee
trading job. Mr. Brown said he'd interview me."

The woman, not much older than Olga, stared at her, her
plucked, painted eyebrows forming exaggerated upside down U's.
"Well! I, I'll just call in to be sure."

"Oh!" she said into the phone. "Well, all right. Oh, you'll come
get her? Yes, of course, Mr. Brown."

She turned to Olga. Her face was carefully noncommittal. "He
said he'd come out to bring you in, in a few moments. He's just
wrapping up a meeting."

"Thank you, so much," said Olga; she was careful not to smile,
but felt like saying, 'You see!'

She knew she looked good. And business-like. She had on her
new tan business suit; her hair was short and stylish, her make-up
was discreet. She had gone over the principles of trading just that
morning, with Julian, and had memorized all the principal trading
venues, like Medellin, Bucaramanga and Porto Velho.

At that moment, a large man, with a large gut straining out of
his business suit, came through the inner door, stared at her, as if
in surprise—what was his problem? And then nodded to her. "Miss
Quintero?"

Olga stood, and held out her hand. "Pleased to meet you. Mr.
Brown?"

"Oh, yes. Er, come with me, please." He tentatively took her
hand. His was large and sweaty.

She followed him down a dark wood-paneled corridor. He ushered her into a large room, also darkly paneled, filled with cigar-smoke, and other men, in business suits, around a long table.

"These are some of our coffee dealers, who work on the floor here, Miss Quintero: Ed Holm, Bill Durham...." The men nodded to her in turn, each one of them looking as if they were hiding grins—well, of course they were: everyone smiled when they saw her.

She nodded back, repeating their names, knew she was smiling.

Introductions over, Mr. Brown ushered Olga to a seat at the middle of the table and then sat down across from her. "So, you want to be a coffee trader."

Was it a statement or a question? "Yes, I do. I can speak three languages—"

She could feel a hand sliding over her knee from the right. She brushed it off. And then, a hand from the left. Really!

"But Miss Quintero," a burly man burst out, "out on the trading floor, a girl like you would be black and blue in half an hour!"

All the men laughed!

"But—" the grasping hands, this ugly man's joke—at her expense—the laughter: for a moment, she was speechless.

"Now, Miss Quintero," hushed Mr. Brown, "don't you think you should try for the steno job?"

Olga stood up, all five feet of her, and glared at him, and then at all of them. The laughter quieted. "I am not a secretary!" She was about to mention Mount Holyoke and her family in Caracas, but then thought better of it, "Good Day!" Certainly, she wasn't going to say 'Good Day, gentlemen.'

She turned on her heel and walked out of the silent room. She felt an instant rush of triumph, as the silence behind her continued, and then a voice inside her moaned 'I worked and hoped for this job.' She withered the moan and tossed her head: she couldn't work with men like that; she wouldn't want to. They were right—in a way. And then she thought, 'But I triumphed. I told them!'

She had glared them down: all of them. She felt powerful. She was actually grinning when she came back out to the receptionist's.

The girl looked up, surprised. Olga sniffed and shrugged her shoulders. "They can have their stupid job! Who would want to work with the likes of them! But I will never be a steno." She smiled a chilly smile. "Goodbye."

Olga was still reliving that flush of power, when she caught the subway home. That's when she saw a small notice in the paper; it said something about a graduate program in teaching, in a new progressive school called Bank Street.

She could still feel her smile, although she didn't remember why she was smiling. Then, she realized: she was emerging into that other world. She didn't want to! She was young, beautiful, powerful in the one she was leaving—even if the, whatever it was—job?—

Her eyes opened. She was in bed, in the room in the other place; the light was low, and looking out at the blackness outside the window, she could see it was night. She didn't know why she had awakened; it wasn't time to get up, and she didn't want to get up, anyway. She could go back to sleep! She smiled, closed her eyes and—

Children look up at her, expectant; they have eager snub-nosed pink faces. That one over there in the dirty pants is Larry, Laurance Rockefeller's son. A Rockefeller. And that snooty little girl over there in the velvet dress is Bobbie Lehman's daughter, Margaret. She insisted on her name; she refused nicknames.

When Henry heard that she was teaching at a school named Little Red Schoolhouse, he was outraged: "Bet they're all Reds! Isn't that what 'Red' means?"

"Oh, no, Henry, don't be silly." She knew perfectly well; it was almost true. A lot of her fellow teachers, and most of the thinking people she knew, went to Communist protests.

Her class at Little Red was wonderful, of course. She knew she was an amazing teacher as soon as she took over a classroom of children that first time, all those five-year olds, cute, yes, but mesmerized by her. What she couldn't believe, though, were the parents: a Rockefeller, and a Lehman in her class, and they both loved her. Of course, their son and daughter did, too. The other parents were very important, too. There were Rolls Royces rolling in with her children every morning.

But this was at Little Red. It was reddish, after all. Julian was amused, but when she told him she was going to go out on a "demonstration" after school, he begged off, remarking: "W.R. and even Peter are America Firsters. I don't think they'd be too happy with me, if I showed up in a Communist protest. But you go ahead. After all, we're not married yet." He smirked at her. "Just don't get arrested."

Somehow, she was on the street, with the others from school, some holding up signs. They read: All Power to the Workers; Revolution; Share the Wealth; Down with Imperialism; and so on. She didn't carry a sign; just her being there was enough. She sashayed alongside the grim parade, and others began a sort of dance, too.

The white-haired man at the front—she forgot his name—frowned, at first. And then even he began to grin and move with less wooden determination.

Yes, it was all because of her.

Olga frowned in her sleep. All because of her?

She could hear her mother and Julio. She was in the garden; they were in the corridor between the rooms and the garden—in Trinidad. Mama was telling him he couldn't go out: it was too dangerous. She could hear his anger. Olga couldn't hear the words now, but she knew he was going to blab. Then it would be all over: they'd have to leave Trinidad. It was all because she'd told Julio about the deaths, and that people blamed it on the Consul, their uncle...it was all because of her.

She had wanted to come to New York. So?

She smiled to herself and looked around her. She wasn't in Trinidad, she was in the street, down on Wall and Broad with her friends, Margo and Bobsey. They were holding up signs; she wasn't. She was dancing. After a few minutes, everyone was smiling. A few onlookers joined them; that had never happened before.

Was she going to lead the revolution? She grinned to think of it: a princess leading the revolution. No. That old gaseous pomposity up front would never step aside. Besides, she hated endless committee meetings. Winnie told her they argued over 'dialectic' and 'vanguardism' for weeks. Marxism didn't appeal to her, except for Lenin's theory of imperialism. Despite her courses in economics, Lenin's explanation of Venezuela, or countries like it, made more sense than economics. Her people were the comprador class. Of course they were. So?

"Police!"

Everyone looked anxiously ahead, then behind. She saw a mass of black, no, blue, coming towards them; she stifled a scream, not because she was scared: no, because at that moment she saw an exit right beside her, an unobtrusive alley. Without thinking about it, Olga ran down the alley and across the next street. Excitement was one thing, but she couldn't get arrested.

She looked around her just in time to see Bobsey emerge from the alley, grin at her and run across the street to join her. Olga wondered, momentarily, what had become of Margo, but—

Bobsey took her hand. "C'mon! We've got to get out of here! You especially, Olga; they could deport you!"

Olga shrugged. How could they send her *back* to Venezuela, when she'd never even been there—except for a visit and...as a baby?

Then, she saw where they were and recognized the street: she'd walked down here, all the way from Harlem, the year they lived up there.

"That way is uptown," she told her friend, pointing, with her elegant, unadorned finger. "I guess you're right. Let's go."

Olga's eyes fluttered open; she saw the sunny porch, a bird perching on the railing, and then she wondered, but where am I?

She listened for a moment, but heard nothing except the bird's chirp. It felt safe, wherever it was. Maybe she was dreaming? Her eyes closed.

They must have just gone through another demonstration: they straggled down the street towards a seedy-looking bar. The police must not have broken up this one, and about ten of them ended up jammed together in a back room; all of them had drinks in their hands—including her, a glass of wine, the same color as the first wine she'd ever had. She remembered Uncle Benjamin examining its color in the glass; had he and her mother slept together for the first time that afternoon?

Uncle Benjamin: every time he visited, he was solicitous of her, not of her mother. He treated her as if he were afraid she would break, but of course, he loved her. Her mother was old now, and she and Benjamin seemed like distant friends. He had a great shining pate, and combed the little hair he had across, to cover as much as he could: about halfway to his forehead.

Julian hit it off with Benjamin, though; he was going to do some photo portraits of him.

Julian was fiddling with his camera, the bamboo Japanese portrait camera. "You can take my picture," she said, almost as an aside.

They were in the little living room, in the house in Jackson Heights. No one else was there: her mother and aunt were working a late shift in the hat factory. Julian had brought something to eat from a deli.

He was still fiddling with his camera, not really paying attention.

She put on what he called her 'Cheshire cat grin' and added, "I can take off my clothes."

"Oh!" Julian stopped what he was doing and smirked at her.

That was the way to get his attention.

He glanced around the dark little room. "A nude?" His eyes shone, then he paused, looked thoughtful: "I could tack up some sheets, get the lamps from the other room—that's the way to do it! Just stay right there, I'll be right back."

He set the camera on its stand, warm polished wood, and then rushed off. In minutes, he was back with an armload of sheets and the two gooseneck lamps. "Do you know where to find some thumb tacks?"

"In the kitchen, in one of the drawers next to the stove," she told him, as she experimented with poses. She knew she shouldn't get undressed yet; he'd get distracted, and she did want him to take some pictures.

Quickly, he moved the couch and end table out of the way, tacked up sheets on three walls, plugged in the lamps, aimed them first this way, then that way, then he grinned at her. "You can get undressed now." His eyes shone with excitement. "Need to see these lights on you, on your skin, and the shadows; have to control the shadows."

She loved getting undressed, slowly, feeling his eyes on her, first her blouse, raising it over her head, then her skirt, reaching back, unbuttoning it, unzipping it, then her bra.... She stood before him, heated by his shine.

"Oh, boy!" He stopped himself. "Um, need to pose you. There." He pointed to a spot in the angle of the walls. "Maybe with your back to me, turning towards me. Can't show you frontally, but anyway, I want your—" he reached out and brushed her behind. "Mmm! Yes!"

She turned her back, raised her shoulder, looked halfway towards the camera, didn't smile. "Like this?"

"Mmm. Oh my god, almost perfect. Just move your shoulders

towards me, just a little, so I can see your breasts. Yes. Now, hold it, while I fix the camera."

He bent to the camera, put the black cloth over his head, fiddled with it one more time, then she heard it click. He took out the film block, looking pleased with himself. He cocked his head at her and then said, "I just want to try a slightly different pose, and a different angle. Here...."

It was the first picture she loved, still. She hadn't dared show it to her mother.

She was back with her fellow demonstrators. Julian was home by now, and she should probably think of going. She could hear the raucous bar voices rising into song in the next room. That's when he turned to her. Tony. He'd led the demonstration. He was dark, like an Italian or Venezuelan, but he spoke like a New York workingman—a bit beneath her, but still...exciting. And of course, he was attracted to her.

"I'm told you're from Venezuela."

"Oh, yes. Most of my family are still there, and—"

"If they're in danger," said Tony, leaning close, speaking in a confidential tone, "we have ways to get them out. That Gomez guy—"

Olga shook her head. "Oh, they're all right."

All right? They were swimming in money!

Her cousins Nené, Chi-Chita and the rest, were getting ready to make their entrance at the Cathedral steps, trying on their different outfits, each with matching jewels almost the size of eggs: diamonds, sapphires, emeralds. Not so long ago. Far away—her only time in Venezuela.

"Thank you, Tony, for thinking of me—and mine." My family; they're the ones in Venezuela that the revolution would be against!

"But Gomez is a terror! Are you sure your family's safe? I've heard stories of torture, especially by some guy in charge of Caracas. Your family in Caracas?"

El Generale Velasco. Tall, thin, white-haired. The few times she'd seen him, he'd been so nice to her. Her father and most of her uncles worked for him. And his children, Cousin Chiquita especially, had been friends of hers. Hard to believe their father—

Olga dismissed the thought. This man didn't know what he was talking about. Torture? "Some of them live there," she shook her head, "but they're just business people." Nené's father was, at least, although he was in Maracaibo. But the last she'd heard, Julio was running a liquor chain in Caracas. "I'm pretty sure they're not in danger."

"Oh. Well, any time that changes, we could get them out," continued Tony, undeterred. "Um, how about coming up to my place—for a nightcap?" He said it so naturally, as if it was a perfectly innocent offer.

Olga knew what he was saying. She glowed, gratified, but shook her head. "Thank you so much," she lied, shamelessly, "but I really have to get home to make dinner for my mother." Luckily, her aunt would do the cooking, not just for her mother and her, but for Julian, as well; he must have gotten home from work by now.

Propositioned by a Communist Party worker! Henry would go apoplectic if he knew. Olga grinned; Henry was still a student down at Vanderbilt.

Maybe she'd even take Tony up on his offer someday; Julian would never know. He was so innocent; she liked that about him.

They had set the wedding date for September 15th.

"Hi, Olga!"

She was startled, didn't want to wake up.

She opened her eyes, confused. In front of her was—her son. Yes. Her son. She put on her smile. He was gray-haired, still handsome—as he should be, a son of hers. "How're y' doin'?" she mumbled. Mouth didn't work right until she woke up a bit more.

"Oh, things are okay...." He looked uncertain.

"Well, I hope they are. If I can help you in any way...," he smiled and shook his head. The gesture seemed familiar somehow, but she knew she didn't remember things.

"Look," he held out a copper-clad block of wood. "I found your wedding invitation. It was in September, 1934."

"Really?" Olga squinted at the block. She could see the letters engraved in the copper, but there was something strange about them; she couldn't read them.

Her son smiled. "You can't read it unless you hold it up to a mirror. It was the print block, so of course it was in mirror writing."

"Oh." She was glad she could still read. For a moment there, she'd wondered if she'd lost the ability; she couldn't write anymore.

"And you graduated the year before, right?"

Yes! She remembered that. 1933. A golden summer. She could feel it pull at her, even as her son told her about something happening at the house— so far, far away. It didn't concern her. She could feel her eyes, so heavy, so heavy.

"I'm going to take a nap, now," she announced.

"Oh." Surprise on his face? She wasn't sure why. "Okay. Well, I've got to go anyway...."

Her eyes were shutting even as he pulled on his jacket. She could hear just inklings of his voice talking to someone else, somewhere else.

Summer, 1934. Jones Beach spread out before them. The sand shimmered in the sun's heat, glistening bodies lay everywhere. People were running in and out of the water, the surf was crashing, children were making sandcastles and Julian had a determined set to his eyes and chin as he shouldered the blanket, sun umbrella and the large bag with their lunch. She carried a smaller bag.

"C'mon." Julian pointed down the beach, beyond the point. "Where there aren't any people."

Olga nodded. "Okay." It was nice to have the beach all to themselves, and now she was used to having to hike to get there.

Around a couple of points, and the crowds had disappeared; there was only sand, surf, sun, and the scrubby dunes stretching inland, but not another person anywhere in sight.

Julian smiled at her; that always made her feel warm inside. "I'm hot," he announced. He dropped the bag, spread the blanket and then stripped off his little bathing suit. His buttocks were so white, except for the freckles, and the red-blond hair. His penis peered out from his red-gold bush. It shook a little as he ran to the water. He dove into the first wave.

Olga had discovered, going to the beach with Julian, how wonderful it was to swim naked, to not have a tight, wet bathing suit clinging to her breasts and thighs, to not be encased in it as it heated and dried in the sun, chafing between her legs, filling with sand there.

She didn't go out as far as Julian. He went out to the "breakers," as he called them, while she stayed close enough to shore that she could touch the sand with her feet when the surf ebbed. She had enough of the water long before he did.

The sun and sand had warmed the blanket, and she lay down, still reveling in her nakedness.

She must have dozed, because his cold hand on her behind was a shock at first, then a pleasant surprise. She turned over. Looking up at him, she almost forgot that he was a small man; he was huge—where it counted. Luckily, she had remembered to put in her diaphragm before she lay down.

He bent down on one knee and kissed her.

"Do you want to?" he asked. She could hear his eagerness—as well as see it.

"Yes!" She wanted him, wanted him inside her, deep inside.

The sky was so blue and clear, and his shoulders smelled of the sea and sun. Ecstasy! Over and over. A lone seagull flew past; it laughed as it saw them. She supposed humans did look funny when they did what they were doing, but she just wanted more.

Olga's eyes fluttered open. Where was the laughing seagull?

She was in the room with the other old people; she was old, although she couldn't remember how old. Old, anyway. The large lumpy woman was ensconced in her usual place, a pile of books surrounding her at the—whatever it was— and the thin, long-nosed one with the cloud of white hair was sleeping in the chair across from her. She hoped food would come soon.

There was no other reason to stay awake. Was there? She closed her eyes.

What a funny little town! It was where Julian had gone to school, at Bowdoin; she had a vision of the campus they had just strolled through, almost as pretty as Mount Holyoke, but all the way up here in Maine. And then these streets with white Victorian houses lining them, beneath stately elms, and a main street that was so wide. "It's like that because of the whalers; it was built then, and they had to haul the boats, or the whales...."

Julian loved to hold forth. Olga enjoyed listening to his voice, not that she listened to the words, actually.

They drove on in the Model A, out onto a peninsula....

"The whole coast of Maine is like this," Julian was explaining, "cut into long complicated inlets, which create long, almost serpentine peninsulas, so you can get to the sea in a lot of places."

Olga loved to hear him talk like this. He knew so much. He could be a teacher, maybe even a professor.

"Anyway," Julian's voice grew more animated, "Meracooneegan Farms is down near the end of the peninsula, and our cottage is right on the shore."

"Oh, lovely!"

As they drove down the long little dirt lane to the huge farmhouse with barn and outbuildings all attached, Olga was impressed, and kept saying, "Lovely, lovely!" The house seemed to sprawl along the peninsula, the sea in back; it was far longer than she'd ever seen a house in the country, but she hadn't seen many. The setting was perfect: sharp pines jutting into the clear blue sky, shining water beyond the house, the darkness of massed pines framing the long silhouette of the jumble of roofs and the sweep of fields embraced it.

Had they stopped? Oh, for vegetables. Now, they turned down a smaller lane off the main driveway, and plunged into the pinewoods. First, she smelled it: hot pine resin mixed with a slightly fishy, salty sea smell, then she could feel the darkness, after the bright sun of the road and fields.

They parked, and Julian took their bags out of the car. Somehow he carried them all, down a winding sandy, stony, root-tangled path between the pines; she followed after with his cameras and the day's groceries.

She looked into the bag. Gentian Violet? Cans of beans, fresh vegetables from the farm's beautiful garden: she wondered what you could do with fresh vegetables. She had never learned to cook; her mother never did, either. It was mostly her aunt who had cooked at home. The farmer had urged them on her before they'd even unpacked the Ford! The vegetables did look beautiful.

She looked up.

The cabin!

They had come around a corner in the root-rutted footpath, and there it was, like a storybook, beneath huge pines, and beyond them was—mud! It glistened in the late afternoon sun, but it wasn't water.

"Is, is that the sea?"

Julian chuckled. "The tide is out. Tides here are huge—30 to 40 feet. This is the time to go collect quahogs—"

Olga made a face; the word sounded ugly.

"You don't understand." Julian's tone was almost professorial again. "Quahogs are like big oysters, only better and fresh from the sea."

"Oh." Olga had eaten oysters in oyster bars. The best people liked them. She liked them with lemon and hot sauce. "How do you catch them?" She couldn't stop thinking of them as 'hogs,' running around on four feet.

Julian turned, looked at her, and then he laughed. She loved the sound of his laughter, especially when it was like that, full-throated and gay.

"You dig for them, when you see their air holes, in the sand. I'll show you, but not until tomorrow. We've got to set up housekeeping first." His eyes twinkled as he said 'housekeeping.'

The little cabin was dark and cool inside, but there was a fireplace with a stuffed white owl over the mantelpiece, a tiny kitchen with a little camp stove, and a hand-crank for water over a kitchen sink. The aroma of pine logs permeated the whole cabin.

There was a little bedroom with birch-bark lamps and picture frames, and most important: it had a comfortable-looking large bed.

She quickly took off her traveling clothes, a suit, and put on a tight polo shirt and the shortest shorts she had been able to find. She was ready for anything.

She opened her eyes. Why did she have to come back to this place? She felt like kicking whatever she was on, the way she had as a little girl, when Miriam insisted she had to go to bed and she didn't want to. Now she did. She was almost lying down in a chair.

She was vaguely aware that something else had been supposed to happen, in that other place, but as she thought about this, she wondered about the 'else.' Had something just happened? She had been somewhere else. Here, the bulky woman—her friend—was sitting at the whatever it was, reading, reading from her stack of books and a long-nosed woman was curled up in her chair, snoring softly across the room from her. She looked vaguely familiar. Maybe the woman lived here. Did she live here, too?

She didn't remember. She momentarily wished she could remember where she had just been. Was it just before she opened her eyes? She shrugged. No hay problema! She would go somewhere again, maybe as soon as she closed her eyes. She didn't have to stay here. She could see where she was: she was comfortable—but she didn't have to stay here if she wanted to go somewhere else. She wanted to go somewhere else. Besides, mealtime was not anywhere in sight, she could see that from a glance across the room and entryway. She closed her eyes.

It was the cabin bedroom; she recognized the birch twig frames on the pictures, a single candle lighting the room. Julian was waiting for her by the door. She pulled off her blouse; Julian knelt before her—she groaned.

Her groan yanked her back to that other world. She was so disappointed, she groaned again. Then, she looked around her; she was in that room. Again. Something, or someone was missing. She knew it—he?—wasn't here in this room. She couldn't remember. She shook her head. She didn't want to be here. She leaned back in her chair; her eyes closed of themselves....

She was in the little bedroom, lying on the bed, admiring her own nakedness. Julian was above her, inside her, kindling heat deep within her. The late afternoon sun streamed through the high window, gilding him, so gold and red; it was what she was feeling, too: golden, red, open, so open—to him.

For the first time in her life, the idea sprang, almost full-blown: I want a baby. I want to have a baby, with him.

When she'd said yes, become engaged, she had hardly considered really getting married, or having children. It was about going to bed with him. Funny, how she suddenly just knew; suddenly, she wanted it all.

She hugged him, first only with her arms, her fingers digging into his buttocks as they thrust, then she embraced him with her whole body.

Falling, ecstasy, all of her; they exploded, together.

21

She resisted, almost as if someone was pushing her out a door, while she was holding on to the doorjamb with all her strength. She was so weak! She hated her helplessness, as she felt herself emerging, unable to hold herself back, like surfacing from a great depth, all golden and red, into this other world, and she so—she opened one eye and glimpsed her wrinkled hand—so old! She sensed someone standing above her. She looked up.

Feeling her welcoming smile, she said: "Hello!" She had switched into automatic gracious mode.

"You told me..." her gray-haired son was saying—

She wondered, idly, if he had been here long. Possible. Had she been awake?

"...that you were engaged to my father—Julian—when you were still in college, right?"

Olga didn't know what he was getting at. She wished he'd just let her sleep, her eyelids felt so heavy.

"Well, what did 'engaged' mean in those days? Didn't you tell me, you were already engaged to two other men?" Her son was grinning. He looked as if he thought he was being clever.

Olga staged one of her trademark seductive shrugs; "We got married, didn't we?" There! That told him off. She had forgotten about those other men, even their names. It didn't matter.

She squinted at him through half-closed eyelids. She didn't want to talk anymore. "I'm tired," she announced with quiet authority; "I'm going to bed."

She was vaguely aware of him saying goodbye, but she was already drifting away, floating....

Julian was looking at her with such longing; it made her want to go to him, but somehow she couldn't, not yet. She didn't wonder about where he was, or where she was. She didn't remember if he had been there before. She didn't bother herself with remembering anymore; it just seemed natural he was there.

Waiting for her?

And there he is, in his business suit, standing to the right of his uncle, the minister, his red hair brighter than any but his brother's, standing beside him. They are in a church—but it's just for the ceremony, to keep his parents happy. Churches just don't have any meaning for her: Julian hates churches.

He looks happy, even so. Of course he does: he admires and adores her—for her brains and her beauty. A good reason to love him—he's so strong, too. They're getting married!

She processes forward, down the aisle, enjoying the admiring glances from familiar faces, and the unfamiliar ones. Her brother, Henry, beside her, standing in for her father, has a solemn expression on his face. Is it because he's trying to keep time to the music and her regal pace? That makes her smile.

She is not anxious; she is excited, and happy, and soaking up all those admiring eyes.

The minister, who is Julian's uncle, says the words, but they pass right over her, even the ones she repeats after him. Someone takes their picture afterwards, a journalist, and somehow her father, in the announcement in the New York Times, has become General Heriberto Quintero.

"Listen," says Henry, taking Olga and Julian aside after the toasts, grim-faced. "Olga, our father sent you a wonderful wedding present, only, uh—it was lost at sea."

"Lost at sea? What was it?" asked Julian, looking mystified.

"Guano. A whole shipload of Guano. Worth thousands. It went down at sea."

"What's guano?" Olga asked.

"It's bird manure, for fertilizer, right, Henry?" asked Julian.

Henry nodded. "It's from the islands, off the coast of Ecuador. The best fertilizer money can buy. A whole shipload."

"And it went down?" asked Olga.

"Yeah," said Henry, not happy to be the bearer of bad news.

"And no insurance?" asked Julian, who knew about things like that.

Henry shook his head. "The old man doesn't believe in insurance!"

So, thought Olga, as the news sank in, her father had sent sacks of gold coins to her mother from Venezuela almost every month, but her wedding present will never get here; it's at the bottom of the sea.

Oh well! They'd managed before, so they'd have enough. Besides, now she was related to Nathaniel Hawthorne.

No! She didn't want to open her eyes! She squeezed them tightly shut. They opened anyway. She was on the patio, outside the room with the old people in it; she could see them in there. She was old, too—she wished she wasn't—but she didn't know how old. Old. Tired. But it was warm here, warmed by the light of, of....

She closed her eyes.

She was sitting on the stoop in Jackson Heights, looking out at the summer world, the 1939 World's Fair just beyond the rooftops. Olga posed for the man walking by. He pretended not to see her, but she could tell he was looking; she knew she was beautiful, even though she'd just given birth a few months before. Her baby was sleeping, and she was getting some fresh air. And fresh eyes. Julian, her husband—she savored that word, still—was due any moment—

Olga sat in the sun, but her eyes were closed. She wasn't here, on the care person's deck, beside a rushing stream.

No, her eyes were open: she was watching the men come home from work; she was relieved for the moment that her precious baby was sleeping. She wasn't above enjoying the men's surreptitious glances. She knew she was good to look at. She even posed slightly, bare shoulder leading her chin.

A young man whistled, pretending it wasn't directed at her. Of course, it was.

Maybe, Julian was bringing home some pot roast or something from the deli. She smirked to think of him when she tried to cook, after her mother died. She had brought whatever she'd cooked to him; he'd tasted it and made a face, and then tried to smile at her. He'd finally said, "A little burnt, isn't it?"

"A little charcoal doesn't hurt anyone," she'd offered. It had happened many times afterwards, and then they'd eat—unless her cooking was beyond "a little burnt." That was why he'd gotten into the habit of bringing something home for them to eat. From a deli on the way, he'd told her.

Olga was beginning to wonder if she'd have to cook something. What?

That's when she saw a familiar face come round the corner, and it wasn't Julian's: it was her brother, Henry!

He was even darker than she remembered him, and his hair was straight, black and coarse; he looked even more like an Indio than he had before.

"Hola, big Sister!"

"Hola, yourself. What brings you back here? I thought you were working in the oil fields."

He leaned in for an abrazo, so she gave him one. He hadn't been that Hispanic when he lived here.

"It's about the trunk. Is, is it here?"

"Oh, that! We didn't know what to do with it, so Julian hauled it in—it's heavy! It's right in the middle of the living room."

Henry looked at her as if she was crazy.

Olga shrugged. "We didn't know what else to do with it; it's big. It's covered with a tablecloth, and we've used it for a coffee table, although it's really too high."

Henry shook his head in disbelief, and glanced around at their neighborhood, shook his head again and then growled, "I better see it, now."

Olga put her finger to her lips and whispered, "The baby's sleeping," as they went up the steps into the cramped kitchen and then the tiny living room. She hoped Douglas wouldn't wake. Not yet.

Triumphantly, she swept the tablecloth off the trunk, a steamer trunk almost four feet high, bound in leather, ribbed in steel.

Henry knelt in front of it, his head bowed and at first Olga wondered, has he gotten religious? He looked up at her, as if trying to remember something.

"What did you send: a ten year's supply of arepa flour? It's heavy enough."

"Ay caramba!"

"Now you swear in Spanish? Can you speak it yet?"

"Of course I can speak it." Henry bristled. Then he shook his head, as if giving up on something. "Quick! When was Bolivar's birthday?"

"July 24th, Henry. It's already past."

"No, no, his birth date, with the—

"Year?" Olga was beginning to catch on. "You want it in numbers?" The trunk, old-fashioned, dark steel and polished wood, reinforced with raised brass corners, stood as high as her chest: it was fastened with a combination lock.

"That's it. C'mon, Olgita, you remember it, don't you?"

"Hah! And you don't. Always depending on your big sister for everything! If it's in Venezuelan order it'd be twenty-four seven, seventeen eighty-three."

"That's it! Eureka—and all that other stuff." He was still the little kid, as he crouched before the lock, and began spinning the dial, looking scared and expectant.

As he spun the last number and pulled the lock open with a satisfying click, Olga could hear him gasp, then hold his breath. He fumbled in his pocket, then in his watch pocket, pulled out a small key, and fitted it into the hole in the trunk latch. She could see his hands tremble; the key turned. He opened the latch, then swung the lid open—and let out his breath.

"Oh my god, Henry!" The trunk was filled with rows and rows of twenty-dollar bills!

Henry pulled out a brick of them, reached down and pulled out another, and another, and another. He looked up at her and grinned. "Solid, right down to the bottom. Ten million."

"Million!"

Out of the corner of her eye, Olga saw Julian's red hair go by the window.

The door opened. Julian stood there for a moment gaping at the open trunk. "Jesus!" Julian almost shouted. "Better close it before the whole neighborhood—"

"Waah! Waah!" The baby, awakened by Julian's outburst, began to cry in the inner room.

In three long strides, Julian was past them. In another instant, he was out again with the baby, her baby, Douglas, in his arms. Julian was so good with him. The baby quieted as Julian rocked him.

Henry looked from Julian to her, and shook his head. "I never will understand Norteamericanos!"

Julian grinned, shrugged, then nodded towards the still open trunk full of cash. "Where did it come from?"

"Velasco. I'm taking it on to Montreal, to his bank up there."

Julian shook his head. He looked amused as he caught Olga's

eye. Together, they earned hardly seven thousand dollars a year. Here, they'd had ten million dollars sitting in the middle of their living room floor for a month!

The lost guano, and now this!

Olga shrugged at Julian, her artful shrug, the shrug of a genuine princess. If Henry hadn't been there, they would both be laughing out loud.

Olga opened her eyes. Afternoon sun streamed through the window. It was a pretty golden light, and dust motes danced in it. She regarded the light for a moment, and then realized: there was someone there!

"Am I dead? Are you an angel?" she asked the person pulling back her blanket.

"No, no, Olga; I'm no angel."

"Then, am I in hell?"

The person laughed. "No, no. You're just in between, like all of us. I just came in, because it's time for you to get up and get ready for dinner."

"Oh." Dinner. In between. "How old are you?"

"I'm just fifty-five, a lot younger than you are."

"How old am I?"

Again, the person laughed. "You're one hundred and one. Today! Congratulations!"

Olga just looked at her, her mouth wide open. Then, she shook her head. "I'm that old? Why am I still alive? I'll be damned!"

She watched the dust motes for a moment, forgetting the other person beside her, and then she closed her eyes.

"No, no, Olga, time to get up."

Her eyes snapped open and she looked at the woman. The woman was smiling at her.

Oh, well, she guessed she'd better get up.

22

Something was happening. She knew her memory had been slipping, but now, for a moment, she realized: I don't know who he is, but he's important to me. He was talking to her, about something, and she didn't really listen. Then, he'd said, "High Valley": she was listening.

High Valley. She lived there? She knew she wasn't there anymore, but he had mentioned it; something about another problem—she didn't want to hear about that—Oh, he's my son!

One minute he was there, the next, he wasn't. Had she fallen asleep? Memory was funny that way.

But something was happening.

There was something about getting up from the...she looked down. She was sitting on a chair; slumped on one. Looking around, she realized: she was in that room, the one with the whatever it was. Her friend sitting at it was reading. Did she always read? Olga no longer knew, but there was still the question.

Her eyes closed.

She could hear his voice, deep, authoritative, then, high-pitched—her smile came naturally. Julian was reading to the older kids: he'd told her *Huckleberry Finn*, when she'd asked. His imitations of older women were always funny, but his best voices were the different men and boys. It was the one time when the kids here really connected with him. Not that they didn't appreciate him in his classes: everyone was always telling her how wonderful he was as the math or science teacher for their child.

She was looking out at 10 or 15 children, ages 6 to 15. They were ranged around her on the sunny terrace beside her flower garden, the one directly below her bedroom picture window. She smiled, but she knew what she was supposed to be doing: running the morning meeting.

She always enjoyed the power she felt, when she looked out at those unformed faces. Dee was beside her, ready to take her cues from her.

She knew every one of these kids, though Dee taught some of them. She smiled at all of them, "Today," she began, "do you know what day it is?" It was the first day of autumn.

"That's right, trees turn colors in the autumn. Does anyone know why?"

"Is it because winter is coming?" Skinny little Ray looks cold.

"Now that's an interesting idea. Any other ideas?"

Larry, tall for his age, stood up and offered: "He means the leaves are scared, turning yellow, but they turn red and orange, too, so I don't think that's it."

"Thank you, Larry. Did you mean that as a joke? I think it's a good one."

He laughs.

She surveys her school: "Well, can anyone name a plant that turns bright red, like a warning, early in the fall?"

Hands wave at her; faces beam with excitement. She's so good at this.

"Why do we call it fall, anyway? Okay, you first, Dorinda." She's always first; she reminds her of herself at that age.

"Um, Virginia Creeper? And, um, because the leaves fall?"

"Very good, Dorinda. Does anyone know why it's called a creeper?"

The children's hands are waving....

She tries to open her eyes. Something's not right. Maybe she's dying?

She can't remember how old she is, but she does remember, saying to some-one, when he told her her age: "That's pretty old!" She doesn't remember how long ago she said that, but she knows she has to be even older now.

What's not right?

She tries to sit up, to see where she is. She can't sit up. And she doesn't know where she is! Unsettling.

Then, he comes in, smiling at her. She knows who he is. She tries to smile back.

"Don't worry, you're being well taken care of," he says.

She tries to raise herself; she can only raise her neck and head a little bit, with great effort!

She has never felt so helpless, but she relaxes as his words play over again in her mind: "...you're being well taken care of."

Oh, well. People will have to move me. She tries raising her arms. Her forearms rise from her chest, but she can't lift either one of her upper arms, and her hands look mute: long, delicate fingers, beautiful thumbs, finely wrinkled, brown. She's unable to move them, too! They're like long, straight feathers—is she becoming a bird?

There's nothing she can do but lie here. No, she can dream. She dreams so well.

Her eyes are barely open. They close, as if of their own will; it's a relief.

"I have a terrible headache!" Julian mumbles, still in bed.

Still in bed, unusual at seven, although that's when she gets up. "Poor Julian!" He's been having more and more health problems. He looks so tired!

She gets out of her side of the bed and stretches, looking out the picture window at the lake: it's frozen.

"I. Can't. Move!" His voice sounds as if it's coming through grit-ted teeth.

She spins around and stares at him! It's still his beautiful face, even though he looks so old. He's only 60; she's only 56. His mouth is in a straight line; his eyes glow with anger.

She doesn't blame him.

"I'm calling the ambulance!"

He lies there as they wait, it seems forever, he hardly moving. She tells him, "I love you, Julian, but you know that."

His eyes soften. They made love last night. She holds his hand; it's still warm, still responds a little to her pressure, but he's so weak; he can't even press hers back! She remembers then, how powerful his grip had been. He had prided himself on the strength of his hands, had even challenged other men to squeeze his harder than he could squeeze theirs. He'd always won, even with his left hand, after the stroke disabled his right.

She hears the clatter of the emergency people and goes down to show them the way to come up for Julian. There are so many twists and turns in this house.

They are young, these rescue people, but she can see they're taken with her—well, why shouldn't they be?

Julian looks up at them as they reach under him to pick him up and put him on the stretcher.

"How do you feel?" one of the ambulance men asks him.

Weakly, he smiles, then with a straight face he answers, "Dead." Then he smiles even wider: it was a joke. A joke he knows is true. How like him. Oh, Julian!

She follows after, to ride with him in the ambulance.

As she comes down to the kitchen, Barclay, one of the beautiful boys who keep coming back—he's visiting from grad school—looks stricken.

She shakes her head at him: "I hope he dies, this time!"

Barclay looks shocked, but he's young. Julian has lost so much, already, from his first stroke four years ago. If he lived, he'd be nearly a vegetable: he'd hate that! He was always so active, so strong.

She sighs, and her eyes open, again, as if of their own volition.

225

She can't move! Oh, she smells food; someone's putting a spoonful of mush up to her mouth. She can still see, at least. And smell, a little.

She always wanted to eat; only now, she doesn't feel hungry for—whatever it is. Or, for anything. She'd like something to drink, though. She wonders whether they'll figure this out. She can't tell them. Even saying a single word is beyond her, but one pops out of her mouth. "No," her mouth says, nothing more. She keeps her mouth shut when the spoon comes near, but when a straw is placed between her lips, she gratefully sips.

"That's pretty old!" she said, so long ago, about herself. Her words echo in her head.

Is it time to go, then?

Will it take long? Will it hurt?

She doesn't know how long it's been.

All she can do is lie here.

Sometimes someone comes and sits with her, someone comforting: a friend? It feels like she's sharing her dreams.

She wants to go, but she doesn't know how.

"There's nothing wrong with her, except she's just extremely old. Her body's giving out; her feet and ankles, already." His voice is above her.

He's explaining to someone, "Yes, she always had good health. Everyone else would get a cold and she wouldn't, so.... She's tough, but that's not much help in a case like this."

A case? She's Princess Olga! Tough: only other people get sick. She did wish she could just get this over with, though.

She remembers her memory, the dream she had: Julian had it so easy: headache in the morning, dead by noon.

The joke's on her; she has to wait, until it happens.

She thinks she sees Julian, standing there, looking at her: is that hope she sees in his eyes? He doesn't look old. Has he really been waiting for her? So many years?

She knows her eyes are hardly open, so she can't really be seeing him. She'll look so old.

Someone is gazing down at her in the bed: she's unable to move, "Even at this stage," his voice wobbles, "she's still beautiful."

Of course, she is; she's Olga.

She's alone now, in the room, wherever it is. Just as well.

"At this stage." The words repeat in her mind, as each breath grows increasingly difficult. Her feet and ankles no longer feel, at all, as if they were no longer part of her. Olga knows what "this stage" means.

Good. She just wishes it was over. Why can't she just decide to go? It's terrible not being able to do anything but wait. No, she'll make it happen. Somehow.

She hopes "the next stage"—whenever she gets there—will be an adventure. It's no fun just lying here!

Now, she knows she's dreaming! Julian is smiling at her. He is such a Prince!

OLGA EUNICE (pronounced Eyuneesay) QUINTERO SMYTH died on December 4th, 2014, at 101 years and almost ten months of age, after a three-months-long fight with mortality. She died of old age, although the official reason given on her death certificate was "congestive heart failure." Her heart stopped at 9:30 in the evening, never to start again.

—

MORE FROM
IMAGINATION FURY ARTS

The Road Home to You by Tim Dillinger

Murder at the Rummage Sale by Elizabeth Cunningham

COMING SOON

Son of Byford by Juba Kalamka

The Return of the Goddess (25th Anniversary Reissue) by
Elizabeth Cunningham

CPSIA information can be obtained
at www.ICGtesting.com
Printed in the USA
FFOW03n1714041117
43256469-41798FF